TRUST TO A DEGREE

BY HORST CHRISTIAN

Loyal To A Degree

Trust To A Degree

TRUST TO A DEGREE

BASED ON A TRUE STORY

HORST CHRISTIAN

This book is a work of fiction based on a true story.

TRUST TO A DEGREE

Copyright © 2013 Horst Christian

www.horstchristian.com

First Printing 2013

ISBN-13: 978-1492761167

ISBN-10: 1492761168

For my parents,

who taught me to bend

without breaking

ACKNOWLEDGEMENTS

I would like to thank my friends, Jerry and Paul, who I consulted during the time I wrote this book. Both of them assured me that I had a story to tell when I wondered if I was on the right track.

Thank you, Jerry and Paul, you know who you are.

I also like to thank again my editor, Wanda Skinner, of deserttranscription.net who found, like always, errors in the flow of my story. Thank you, Wanda; your diligence and your support is very much appreciated.

And then of course, there is Christina Haas of ZenithBusinessSolutions.com. Once again, she did the cover art for the book as well as the formatting for the Kindle version and the formatting for the paperback version for CreateSpace. During the course of my writing, she also became my "virtual assistant" and promoter. Without her untiring help, this manuscript would not be published. Thank you, Chris.

If there are any aspiring writers among my readers, you can't go wrong by availing yourself of the priceless guidance provided by the above named professionals.

And, again, I would like to thank my wonderful wife, Jennifer. While she was holding down our small ranch during a 100 degree summer, I was writing in our air-conditioned office. Thank you, Jenny.

PREFACE

Although this book is based on a true life story, the names of the characters have been changed. However, the people the characters are based on were real, the locations existed, the events actually took place, and the story captures the factual experiences of a young boy living in Soviet-occupied Berlin in the days following the fall of Berlin during World War II.

FOREWORD

This book is based upon the actual experiences of "Karl" during the first few days after the surrender of Berlin to the Soviets, while the Allied forces were standing down at the Elbe River in Germany.

It touches a little on the perception of the outside world Berliner children had when they saw the differences between the decrepit footwear of the Soviets and the shiny trucks of the Americans. (Who always drove and never walked.)

It was also the first time in their life that Berliner children saw people of color; Tatars as well as Americans. At the very best, it was a confusing time with shifting values. At the worst, it was hunger and fear.

Furthermore, this book describes the cooperation between a Soviet political Kommissar and 14-year-old Karl and his friend Harold, also 14 years old.

I fully realize that such cooperation between an intelligence officer and a 14 year old (child) would be unthinkable today. But these were times when 14 year olds were not children. They were "young adults," trained to be soldiers.

While this story is true, it is not about the gory incidents that took place during the first few days after the fall of Berlin. I feel there are already sufficient accounts documented about those atrocities.

Given the different motivations of the participants, as well as their greed and agendas, I hope that this story might provide interesting reading and insight about forgotten times.

Horst Christian, September 2013

ONE

Karl, just a bit above 5'3" tall, sat between two husky, yellow-faced Mongolian guards in the back of a closed Russian troop carrier and kept his head down. Minutes ago he had been rudely arrested while he was sleeping on the kitchen floor in an apartment of a friend in Berlin. It was 6:30 in the morning and he did not know why had been detained. He did know, however, that the date was May 3rd 1945, the first day after the surrender of Berlin. He was 14 years old, and until yesterday, he had been a member of the HJ (Hitler Youth).

Disillusioned with the high command and the tactics of the SS, he had survived the last two days of the war by hiding in a U-Bahn (subway) ventilation shaft with his friend Harold. The boys had learned about the surrender of Berlin by the loudspeakers mounted on trucks that cruised the devastated streets of Berlin, calling for the remaining German fighters to lay down their arms and assemble at certain points within the city.

Karl and Harold had initially considered to follow the call, but then decided to first obtain civilian clothes. Karl dismissed this as a cause for his arrest. He reasoned that he must have been singled out. The commando who had picked him up had not even bothered to ask the name of his friend Harold, who had also been sleeping on the kitchen floor. He could not think of any specific act he might have committed which would warrant being detained.

He opened his eyes and looked out the rear of the truck. At the very least he wanted to know where he was being taken. They were not making much time that was for sure, because the truck moved very slowly to avoid the rubble and debris that filled the streets. Karl could also see that the driver was searching for a specific place, but apparently did not know where it was because they passed through the same areas several times.

He lowered his eyes again and noticed that the boots of the Mongolians next to him were worn down to nothing. They did not even resemble boots. More like incredibly old shoes with some leather patches holding them together. He had seen a few days before that the Mongolian women were robbing the German corpses of anything of value. Mostly their watches and rings, but also their footwear. Now he understood why. His eyes wandered along the floor when he became aware that there was another soldier sitting further away from him, near the front of the vehicle. His boots were also worn but not as bad as the Mongolians and most certainly these boots were SS issue, but more than that, he remembered the hole he saw in the upper leather in one of the boots.

His eyes went up and locked with the eyes of Fritz, the SS Rottenfuehrer whom he knew from the Zoo Flak Tower, and things started to dawn on him. Karl's commanding officer had committed suicide when he was ordered to flood the Berlin subway system. Fritz, who had been in charge of security, had gotten hold of the commander's notebook, which contained annotations regarding Karl's service records, including the address where he could be found if he survived the war. This explained how the arresting commando had known his name and had found him. But why, he still did not know.

"Fritz? How come you are here?" Nobody had ordered Karl not to speak, so he might as well try. The Mongolian guards kept quiet. Their flat faces showed no emotions. They acted very much like a sentry dog would, barely looking at you while still observing.

Great, talking seemed to be allowed.

"Karl, I am sorry for your arrest. It is not what it seems to be. I am not a traitor. I don't even know why I am here in the truck with you."

"Alright then," answered Karl, "but still, how did you get in this truck?"

"I was on door guard at the bunker when the surrender was announced. The bunker commander ordered the doors shut. He did not want to be taken prisoner. I got away."

The guards next to Karl still did not move. They just seemed to follow the conversation without being able to understand a word of it.

"Then what?" Karl prompted.

"The Russians must have seen me coming out of the bunker. I was searched for weapons and they found Sturmbannfuehrer Bernd's notebook on me. They took me to a German-speaking officer who was only interested in the book. There were a lot of notations in the book, which I could not read. They were written in English."

Karl mulled over what he had heard. "Did the officer ask you anything specific?"

"Only if I could identify you. I feared that they would force me to join the prisoners at the assembly places. But, I was kept separated and under guard all night long. Then this morning, they took me along when they arrested you."

"Does not make sense," said Karl. He meant that Fritz's answers did not explain why he was under arrest. He wanted to ask another question when the truck stopped. They were at the Potsdamer Platz, near the center of Berlin. He looked up and saw that the big plaza was one of the assembly places for survivors of the SS.

He could not see any uniforms of the Wehrmacht (German Army) or HJ uniforms.

The place was patrolled by Tatars armed with machine pistols. The rear gate of the truck opened. The officer who had arrested Karl had been riding in the front, and motioned him to stay in his place and then pointed at Fritz to get out. He was just about to release Fritz into the custody of the assembly sentries when one of the guards in the truck made some guttural sounds and began to untie his shoes.

It did not sound like any language Karl had ever heard before.

He was not even sure if it was a language, it sounded so strange.

However, the officer seemed to understand and told Fritz to remove his boots. Karl was surprised at the language skills of the Russian officer. He spoke a perfect German with hardly any accent. It was also the first time that he had the opportunity to observe the officer.

He was heavily built, close to six feet tall, gray haired, and Karl estimated his age at late forty. He had intelligent gray eyes, which changed between gentle to almost intense when he spoke. "Schneller" (faster) he ordered Fritz and waived at the guard to exchange his footwear with Fritz. The guard had taken his shoes off and removed filthy, sweaty rags from his feet. He gazed expectantly at Fritz's gray socks.

"I will not take my socks off," Fritz shouted in horror as he looked at the dirty and bloody bare feet of the Tatar.

"Wie Sie wuenschen," (As you wish) answered the officer, and pulled his handgun out of his holster. He pointed it point blank at Fritz's head. "Now," he said gently as he released the safety lever.

"Fritz, don't be a fool" called Karl, "you can always trade some things later on for better socks."

Fritz realized that he was in a hopeless situation and getting shot for a pair of socks was plain stupid, even for a former SS man.

He pulled off his socks and pushed them together with his boots towards the Mongolian. His face showed his repugnance as he tried to force his feet into the shoes of the guard. They did not fit him. They were at least a size too small. He looked helplessly at the officer, who shrugged his shoulders and pressed the lever on his handgun back to the safety position.

"Good advice, and timely too," he said to Karl, "we will work well together." While Karl wondered about the strange remark, the officer took his seat again in the front of the truck.

As Karl looked back, he could see Fritz walking barefoot towards his comrades on the plaza. One of the sentries was walking behind him. The whole episode had taken no more than maybe ten minutes and after a short ride, the truck stopped again. Karl could see that they had crossed the Mohrenstrasse near the former financial district of Berlin. The truck parked in front of a partially destroyed office building. Apparently, it was being used by the Russians as a temporary inquiry headquarters of some kind. Karl could hear shouting in German and Russian and painful outcries behind closed doors as he followed the officer up to the first floor. One of the Mongolian guards was right behind him while the other one entered a room next to the entrance of the building.

"Sit down," said the officer, and he pointed to a single chair in the middle of the empty room. Karl could see that there were two hooks in the ceiling above the chair with two ropes hanging down. On the end of each rope was a very thin wire or filament attached to it. It looked like a fishing line. Karl had no idea why they were dangling close to the chair and he could not help but get a bad feeling. He had heard about the interrogation techniques of the Soviets and was not about to be fooled by the polite manner of the officer. He was prepared for the worst, even though he did not know why he would be questioned in the first place.

The officer walked next to the window while the guard left the room. "I don't have any time, so I will make this short and easy for both of us," started the Russian. The uniform of the officer looked somewhat different than the ill-fitting uniform of other officers Karl had seen when he entered the building. Not only that the uniform of the officer in front of him resembled a tailor-made cut featuring broad shoulder boards, but it was also void of any decorations except for two braces of small ribbons and several red stars above them.

Karl, who had received interrogative mental training in a special unit of the HJ, figured since he was not bound to the chair, he might be in a somewhat ambivalent position between being needed or entirely disposable, even unworthy of restraints. He also figured that in this situation, any offense was better than a defense. "Excuse me Sir, my upbringing demands that I address an officer by his rank. I just wish to be respectful. Sir."

The officer was visibly taken aback. Whatever he had wanted to say or ask was temporarily on hold. As a long time intelligence officer, he was not used being spoken to by a prisoner, much less being asked a question. He had to admit that it was a perfectly harmless and very polite question, but nevertheless, it was a question. To top it off, it was coming from a boy who should be shaking in his shoes.

He mustered Karl more keenly and somehow liked what he saw.

The boy was exactly what he needed, and therefore he decided on a different and faster approach. Besides, he really could not afford a lengthy discussion. "My name is Bayan Godunov. I am not an officer. I am a Pompolit, a political Kommissar with the equivalent military rank of a Colonel General. Anything else you wish to ask of me?" His smile was almost infectious, but his eyes were the eyes of a deadly determined man.

Now it was Karl's turn to be surprised. He had more expected to be severely put in his place than receive an answer from a high-

5

ranking political Kommissar. "No, sir. But how do you wish me to address you, sir?"

Another question, and now the Pompolit knew what was happening. The boy obviously tried to score points by his politeness; a long-forgotten Russian technique dating back to the times of the Czar. It was a technique, which had become for him, a way of life and of obtaining his present position. "Alright, you can address me with 'Sir' or simply 'Kommissar'; however, I will call you Karlchen." For a second he saw that Karl's facial expression changed.

The bitter look from the boy's eyes became soft and almost child-like, much more the appearance of a child than of a boy soldier.

The last time Karl had heard the kind extension of his name was when his grandmother had talked to him. All the German first names carried the extension 'chen' or 'lein', or for that matter, any extension which made the name sound longer and less harsh. Of course, a father would never call his boy by any such kindness.

The Kommissar had achieved what he wanted. He had put Karl in his place as a little boy. However, Karl also knew that the Russians had very much the same habit, and even called their own grandmother 'grandmotherchen', or their mother 'motherleinchen'.

"Yes sir," Karl's voice was hard and so were his eyes again. Before the Pompolit could continue, Karl got up from the chair and stood erect in front of the officer. "Sir, since you did not slap me around and now decided to call me Karlchen, we both know that you need me, sir. You also said that you are pressed for time, sir. I am ready when you are. Sir."

Godunov was almost happy. Instead of a whining and shitless, scared boy, he now almost had an ally; and God only knew that he needed one. "Then let's begin, Karlchen. How well do you know the layout of the Berlin subway?" The Kommissar pulled a green notebook from his pocket and studied some of the pages.

"Sir, very well, sir." Karl was relieved. The knowledge of the U-Bahn system had been his strong suit during the last few weeks. The subway engineers had all been drafted to the military. Even the SS had relied on his knowledge, which he had gained as a 10 to 12 year-old, when he had played in the tunnels.

"Do you know all the emergency exits and the locations of the service sheds?" The Kommissar still studied the notebook and nicked some of the page's corners.

"Sir, I knew where they were two days ago. In the meantime, there might have been damage inflicted by the last days of fighting. Sir."

"Do you know the extent of the damage caused by the flooding of the system?"

"Sir, there is not much damage. Except there are dead bodies floating around and the power is out. To get the trains running again, it would require pumping the tunnels dry. Sir."

The Pompolit looked up. His skeptical expression had changed to a hopeful one. "Karlchen, are you saying that you are able to enter and navigate the tunnels in spite of the flooding?"

"Sir. It is only the corpses that scare me because they might cause infections. Otherwise yes, I can do that. Sir."

The Kommissar barked a command and the door opened. The guard who had been stationed outside the door entered and received another command, which made him run down the hallway. Kommissar Godunov looked at his watch. It showed a quarter past eight in the morning. He was still on time with the schedule he had set for himself. "Come on Karlchen, we have a few minutes to grab something to eat."

He almost threw his arms around the boy as they left the room.

The walk back to the street was anything but pleasant. The floor of the corridor was stained with fresh blood that had not dried yet and stuck to their shoes. The foul smell of vomit and feces lingered in the air and the sounds of the intense interrogations going on behind the closed doors of the old office building left no doubt what was happening.

Karl was relieved to be able to leave the building. He tried to guess why it was that there had been a guard outside their room while there were no guards on any of the other doors. Most certainly it was not to prevent him from escaping. Maybe the guard had been there to protect the Kommissar. Or, maybe the Pompolit wanted to make sure that they would not be interrupted. Karl had not much time to think about it, but since he had been invited by a top intelligence Kommissar 'to grab something to eat' he hoped that his detainment was short-lived. On the other hand, he had no idea what was expected of him. Apparently it had something to do with the U-Bahn and he remembered that he still had a stash of food and various other items hidden in the exit of a ventilation shaft close to the Uhlandstrasse subway station.

They reached the street and Karl looked around before the Kommissar led the way to the rear of the building. Most of the old office buildings as well as the apartment buildings in this section of Berlin had courtyards in the rear, and this structure was not any different. The Russians had pushed most of the smaller debris to one side of the yard and used the other half to serve food from a field kitchen.

It was some kind of a stew without meat, but plenty of onions and cooked cucumbers. Karl did not care much for the taste, which was very strange to him. He enjoyed however that it was hot. After days of eating dried bread and cold canned food, it was a welcome change.

He sat down on a large piece of rubble and watched the comings and goings of several Mongolians who reported and received orders from the Pompolit. As much as he tried, he could not figure out if they were using an actual language or just grunted and barked at each other. He had heard about the Soviet's using Mongolians or Tatars for their frontline fighting forces. As far as he could determine, he could not differentiate between them.

"Sir!" Karl wanted to test the water, wondering if he had really a friendly relationship with the intelligence officer. "What is the language you are speaking? I know it is not Russian. Sir."

The Pompolit started to enjoy the forward approaches and questions from the small boy. "These Tatars are from the inner regions of Mongolia. Most of them speak Chahar, but some of them speak Buryat."

The answer from the Kommissar seemed friendly enough to invite a follow up. "Sir. I never heard of these languages. Do they also exist in writing? Sir."

The Pompolit waited for a moment before he answered. "Karlchen, your constant 'Sir' is getting to me. Hitler is dead, and so are his teachings. You don't have to address me formally and you don't have to stand in attention. You can relax. I am not out to harm you. The answer to your question is yes, their language exists in writing and consists more of syllables than letters, but none of these Tatars have a command of it. Almost all of them are illiterate."

Karl did not know what to make of the answer. "Thank you...

Sir, but I do not know how to informally address an officer. Sir!"

The Pompolit, who had just about reached the pinnacle of his career had already received his order to return to Moscow and hesitated before he answered. He knew that he had only two days left. He had spent the last night robbing and even killing some of his own officers who had looted a German bank. He had several cases of jewelry, gold coins and other things of value, but no idea how to get them home. It was a race between him and other Mongolian Pompolits and Zampolits to plunder what was available and to secure their new possessions. His biggest adversaries were the military commanders from the Belorussian army under the command of Marshal Zhukov.

Officially, Marshal Zhukov did not tolerate the looting and raping currently going on. However, he also had the good sense not to enforce his orders within the first two days after the surrender. It was not a written consent, but a consent nevertheless to let the hordes of fighting soldiers have the spoils of war. The real irony was that the officers of the Belorussian army were by no means saints. They also wanted their part of the plunder.

Bayan Godunov knew that he needed to hide his loot until he could find a way to bring it home to his small estate on the Crimean peninsula. When he had, by sheer luck, found the notebook of the dead SS officer in charge of the subway defense, he read the notations about Karl, an HJ member with an intimate knowledge of the Berlin subway system. He had also read the notes about Harold, Karl's friend, equally well versed with the U-Bahn. But, he had reasoned that he could only control one boy at a time.

Therefore, he also had, unknown to Karl, arrested Harold.

He kept him under guard in the same building where he had questioned Karl.

TWO

"Karlchen," he began "Call me 'Herr Godunov'. This will be good enough for right now. I would like to build some trust between us and to do this, I am prepared to take the first step."

Karl wondered what this could be and what this might lead up to.

"Thank you Herr Godunov. I don't understand what you mean by trust. Are you asking me to trust you? And why? I am a little confused."

"No, Karlchen. I will first prove to you that I trust you. You are the judge, and then we will take it from there."

Karl wanted to answer with another question but decided to wait.

In the meantime, a huge, almost gigantic-looking Tatar approached them and handed a used Russian gray-green uniform jacket to the Pompolit. As Karl was looking on, they exchanged some garbled grunting and the gargantuan retreated to take a seat on a cement block a few feet away from them.

"Now, take off your uniform jacket, empty your pockets, place all the contents here in this bowl, and try this jacket on for size." The Pompolit was holding the Russian jacket in his hand while Karl took off his HJ jacket and started to empty his pockets.

When he came to one of his inside pockets, he paused and did not know how to continue. His hands were on a small little package he had forgotten about. It had been an object given to him by a German submarine commander. At the time, the commander had told him that in the event that Germany would win the war, he wanted the object back. Otherwise, he had indicated that the content might save Karl's life. For a moment Karl considered leaving the package in the pocket, but it was already too late.

"What do you have there?" The Pompolit's eyes had detected Karl's hesitation.

"I don't know, Herr Godunov, it was a present." Slowly and somewhat carefully, Karl placed the object in the bowl next to his pencil, notebook and some coins.

"Karlchen, you received a present and placed it in your pocket. You don't know what it is, and you carried it around for how long? Come on, you can do better than that." The intelligence officer's eyes were still friendly and his tone of voice was more curious than serious.

"Yes, Herr Godunov, I probably could. But it is the truth."

The Kommissar reached in the bowl and weighed the object in his hand. It was a little package, not bigger than a cigarette pack and just a bit heavier. "Try on the jacket, Karlchen."

It was made of heavy material and void of any emblems or identifications. The sleeves were somewhat long but all in all, it did not fit him any worse than his old HJ jacket. "Stand over there, Karlchen." Godunov pointed to a spot in front of the formidable Tatar.

The Mongol got up and seemed satisfied. He took something like a piece of chalk from his pocket and marked a big white X on the back and on both sleeves. He left the front the way it was and grunted his approval. Karl was appalled when the Tatar walked around him. He emitted some rank odor, which seemed to drift up from his feet.

"Come back, here. Karlchen." The Kommissar handed him the bowl back indicating that Karl should place the items back in his pockets. Karl looked pensively at the small package, which was still in the hands of the Pompolit. "Oh, this? Who gave you this present, Karlchen?"

"A submarine commander, Herr Godunov."

"Really, Karlchen, a submarine commander. Now, let me think. What did you do to deserve a present from a U-Boat Captain?"

"The commander thought that I saved his life, I am not sure, Herr Godunov."

"Well, if he thought that you saved his life, then it is valuable. As a sign of my trust, I will let you keep this item. You don't even have to open it. Put it back in your pocket and carry it around some more. I don't have a mirror Karlchen, but you should see yourself. Now you can easily pass as a Russian foot soldier. The pants will not give you away. They were not uniform pants in the first place. Many of our troops wear pants like these."

In spite of the serious situation, Karl had to laugh as he filled his pockets again. There was no inside compartment in this jacket. He placed the little present in his upper shirt pocket and buttoned it closed. "It's not the pants I am worried about, Herr Godunov. It is my lack of language skills. I neither speak nor understand Russian. I will get shot as an imposter the moment I get questioned. Somehow I have the feeling that I am now more of a prisoner to you than to the Russian army."

"That is correct Karlchen, but think about the alternatives. All the able Wehrmacht and HJ members who have surrendered will be transported to Russian forced labor camps in the Ural Mountains. All the SS members will be transported to Siberia to work on our railroad lines. You, on the other hand, will be my personal prisoner for maybe only two days. And if you help me with my project, I will make sure that you don't have to join the transports."

"I don't think that I like the alternatives, Herr Godunov. What is it you want me to do?"

"I want you to hide for me several boxes, if possible, in the U-Bahn system. And maybe you also have to help me to get them out of Berlin. You think that you are able to do that?" The Pompolit looked expectantly to Karl.

"I can hide them for a while, that is for sure. But to get them out of Berlin? Where to? Through all the Russian troops? I don't know. I would need help, but even with help I am not too sure."

"Consider the alternatives, Karlchen."

"I already did, Herr Godunov."

"And," prompted the Kommissar.

"You said, Herr Godunov, that all the able, meaning healthy, surrendering members of the HJ will be shipped to the labor camps?"

"Yes, Karlchen."

"I have a friend, Herr Godunov who might right now consider to surrender to the Russian Army. And after what you have told me, I fear for him. He could be very helpful to you when you decide to move your boxes out of Berlin. Is there any way you could get him arrested? I am sure that he would be of valuable help to us."

"I already did, Karlchen. But if you don't need him right now, I would rather have you working alone."

"You arrested him?"

"Yes, I did."

"Then I do need him right now. He could do the scouting while I move the boxes. He might have also different ideas than I do. I am sure that we could have your stuff safely hidden in less than two hours."

The Pompolit liked what he heard. "As you wish, Karlchen."

He shouted a command to the Mongol who took off. Karl noticed that the Tatar had an awkward limp. He seemed to be limping with both feet, as if he was walking on a bed of hot coals.

"Now, where are the crates Herr Godunov?"

"They are close by, but they will have to be moved before noon."

"May I see them Herr Godunov? I would just like to know the size and weight, because I have to know if they will fit through the ventilation shafts. If not, you might need to repack them to smaller units."

"I can probably do that, Karlchen. But I would rather not." The Pompolit thought about the danger involved if his soldiers found out what he was doing.

"Then I really have to see the size of the boxes real soon. I have to rule out the places that will not work, and also learn from you in which direction they will have to leave Berlin. Furthermore, I need your help to move them to the intended locations. I fear that the Russian army will stop me."

"Don't worry about the Russian army, Karlchen. I will assign Alex, the big guy who gave you the jacket, to watch out for you. Nobody will dare to question you and believe me, nobody will dare to question Alex and his group either."

The Kommissar started to be concerned; it was getting late. He had the loot packed in the back of a truck and watched over by a special unit of Tatars who only reported to him. But, the truck itself had been 'borrowed' by his group by simply throwing the army driver on the street, and for good measure, they had backed up and rolled over him a few times. The only car under his command was the troop carrier he had used to arrest Karl.

Actually, he had no direct command authority at all. He was, however, a respected political Kommissar of nearly the highest rank, assigned to prevent the very actions he was now engaged in. He also knew why he had been ordered back to Moscow. The high command did not trust him. He doubted that his actions were being watched at this time, but common sense told him that he had to get his burgle off the streets.

"Mensch, Karl, I was so worried about you!" The always-cheerful voice of Harold interrupted Karl who had started to ask more questions of the Kommissar. Karl jumped up and threw his arms around his friend and then held him at arm's length. Harold was completely decked out in a Russian uniform without any rank insignia. His jacket had similar chalk markings as Karl's, and the boys locked eyes.

"Here is your friend, Karlchen. You can chat with each other later. Right now, limit your talk to finding a place for my baggage."

It was the first time that the Kommissar had a chance to see Harold, and mustered him briefly. The boy was a good deal taller and bigger than Karl, but that was not saying much, because Karl was small for his age. He liked the way Harold carried himself. In spite of the situation, there was self-assurance in his walk and in his tone of voice. Godunov was satisfied with what he saw. He knew that he could have done a lot worse.

"Harold, we need to find a place to hide the Kommissar's baggage. I was thinking about the shaft where we got the HJ unit out. Any suggestions?" Karl's eyes did not signal that he wanted a positive response. He was aware that Godunov was watching him. Harold, who had been kept in isolation until the big Tatar had shown up indicating to strip and get into the Russian uniform, understood anyhow. He was so attuned to his friend's voice that he knew what was expected from him.

"Let's see the size of the baggage. If it fits, it might be workable."

"Follow me." The Kommissar walked ahead of the boys and the Mongol shuffled behind them.

"Why that particular shaft? You cannot hide anything in it," whispered Harold.

"I want you to build up your expertise and establish trust. Suggest something better." Karl kept his voice to a low mumble, hoping that Godunov did not overhear their exchange. The truck

14

with the loot was parked around the corner in the Mohrenstrasse. Karl had to admit that the Pompolit had guts. He was 'hiding' the vehicle in full sight. When the Kommissar rapped on the rear gate and Karl saw the Mongolian unit climbing out of it, he slightly adjusted his first impression. This was indeed a formidable bunch. Each one was armed to the teeth and it would have taken a tank with a flame-thrower to dislodge them.

"Get in and take a look. Keep it short. We need to roll."

Karl climbed in and was astonished to only see three medium-sized cardboard cartons. Each one was no bigger than a large machine gun ammunition box. He made room for Harold, who also looked surprised. "That's it?"

"It must be the content," Karl replied, "Think of a tactic to gain his trust." Karl tried to lift one of the boxes. It was not too heavy, between 30 and 40 pounds. "The Kommissar quasselt 'n jutes 'n knorkes deutsch" (speaks a perfect German), Karl said loudly in a heavy Berliner dialect. He wanted to test if the Kommissar could understand him. If Godunov did, he did nothing to indicate it one way or another. He gave Karl a hand as he jumped from the tailgate. His eyes went from one boy to the other.

"What is the verdict?"

"Easy, not even a challenge. I will give the driver directions." Harold wanted to take a seat in the front of the truck. The Kommissar stopped him. "How far?"

"You said you are in a hurry. We can be unloaded and be done in less than 25 minutes."

"Go," Godunov said and shoved Harold next to the driver. He gave his unit an order and Karl could see that they were all going back to the office building, except big stinky Alex, who climbed in the truck and extended his hand to assist Karl.

Karl tried to keep himself as far from the oversized Tatar as he could. He had noticed that none of the other Mongolians, while not exactly sanitary, reeked as bad as the giant. Harold guided the driver to the Kurfuerstendam and had him turn into the Uhlandstrasse. All along the way, they had passed assembly points of the surrendering German soldiers. Armed guards surrounded the gatherings while envying the countless hordes of Mongols who combed the surrounding buildings looking for loot and women. Karl noticed that the assembly points of the SS were especially heavily guarded.

The Pompolit had a deeply worried frown on his face. Mixed within all the Mongolian soldiers were also many officers and now and then he could even spot the uniforms of other Kommissars. He was sure that they were of lower rank than he was, but he did not like what he saw. Not at all.

There was no way that he could unload his goodies without being questioned, or at the very least, being observed. Little did he know about the resourcefulness of Karl, who had given Harold enough hints to accomplish not only their task but also to gain the trust of Godunov.

"Halt," Harold laid his hand on the Tatar's steering wheel. The Kommissar cringed in discomfort. They were momentarily stopped in front of the rubble of a former 5-story apartment building. A bunch of Mongolian soldiers were busy breaking down wood and beams, which barricaded the cellar windows. They had learned how to find the German women. Godunov turned back to say something to Karl. There was no divider between the front and the freight portion of the truck, when he heard Harold.

"Karl, get ready. When I say 'jump' you jump out!" Harold turned to the Kommissar. "When I tell you, order your man to throw the boxes out, but only one at a time." He motioned the driver to make a hard left to cross the street and guided him through the rubble into a courtyard filled with debris. They followed a somewhat wreckage free track. The Kommissar could see that several tanks must have followed each other through the ruins.

Harold directed the driver to stay within the tracks. There was not a single Soviet soldier in the back area of the courtyard. "See anything?"

"What," answered Godunov. He did not know what he was supposed to see.

"Jump," yelled Harold.

Karl dropped out of the truck and vanished from sight. The big Tatar who was supposed to guard him hopped up to look for him, but Karl was gone. The Kommissar heard the grunting from the guard and barked an order back, which caused the giant to reach for one of the boxes. He moved it to the tailgate and waited for the next order.

Harold directed the driver to turn to the right. They had rolled straight through the ruins of the apartment buildings and had reached the Kurfuerstendam again. "We will make three runs. At every run you will drop one box."

Harold looked for a short cut through the ruins to initiate another turn. This time he approached the courtyard from the far side of the Uhlandstrasse. "Get ready to give your order to drop the first box."

His eyes scanned the whole complex of ruins. "See anything?" he asked.

The Kommissar strained his eyes. All he could see was a wide field of utter destruction. He detected about a dozen charred corpses. Some of them were without boots. On others, the boots had melted on their twisted legs. They were obviously the casualties from a flame-thrower attack. The missing boots indicated that they were the remains of SS soldiers, robbed of their valuable footwear by the Mongolian women who followed the combat troops. When they encountered any disabled or wounded, they just slit their throats before they helped themselves to any rings, watches, or, like in this case to the boots. But otherwise, he saw only piles next to piles of wreckage and ruins.

The driver followed the tracks again and Harold slowed him down to a crawl and then raised his hand. "Drop!" The Kommissar barked an order as he was looking to see Karl, but there was no one in sight. The Mongol had dropped the box at the precise moment he had heard the order and almost fell out of the truck looking for it. It had vanished just as Karl had before. Nothing but ruins around them, and the truck gathered speed preparing for the next run.

This time it went faster. The driver knew now what he was supposed to do and everything repeated itself.

"See anything?"

"What?"

"Drop!"

Gone.

After the second box disappeared, the Kommissar stared at Harold.

"How is this possible? I don't see Karl or the boxes."

"You are not supposed to," Harold informed him, "if you know what we are doing, but you don't see what we are doing, then it's a given that nobody else can see anything either."

"But, how is this possible," insisted Godunov.

17

"I thought you wanted a stealth operation," asked Harold in return as he directed the driver to continue following the Uhlandstrasse on the opposite side of the Kurfuerstendam. He wanted to observe from a different location. He also wanted to wait a few minutes before he kicked off the final run and informed the Kommissar accordingly.

"I want to see where the boxes are," demanded Godunov.

"Alright, then here is what we will do. Instead of dropping a box, you will jump out when I tell you. Karl will be expecting a box, but he will receive you instead. If you like what you see, we will drop the third box and Karl will guide you to this corner here, where we will pick you up. If you don't like what you see, just stand up when we approach and wave us off."

Godunov was satisfied. "You want me to jump from this seat or from the rear gate?"

"The rear gate, and stay down when you hit the ground. Also tell your man to drop the box on my command."

As the driver started up again, he received instructions from the Kommissar and grunted back at him. Godunov crawled through the opening and stood up in the rear of the truck. While he awaited Harold's order to jump, he informed Alex what he was supposed to do.

"Jump!"

He heard Harold's voice and dropped from the rear gate to the ground. As soon as he landed, he felt Karl's hands on him pressing him down and pulling him into what seemed to be a short side way trench with an underground entry.

"There is nobody in sight, so I think that you may stand up if you wish to do so." Karl stopped pulling on the Kommissar and disappeared into the entry of a ventilation shaft totally hidden in the rubble. You had to stand exactly in front of it to see it. Godunov was no fool and stayed low to the ground before he entered the shaft.

There was an iron ladder on one side and he had only descended a few feet when he saw his boxes. They were standing next to each other on a sideways ledge. The ledge seemed to extend a good deal sideways into the wall of the shaft. At the far end of it he noticed some blankets and some food supplies.

"This was mine and Harold's hideout during the last two days," Karl explained.

"Is there anyone else besides you two who knows about this place?" The Kommissar liked the lay out. The site was large enough to hide additional loot. It was about three feet high. Not high enough to stand up, but deep enough to sleep in it.

"No Herr Godunov. Harold's parents are missing, my mother is in Wcstphalia, and I don't know where my father is. Harold and I are the only ones that know about this ventilation shaft. There is no more access from the train bed on the bottom. We closed it with debris and rubble."

"Good, this will work, Karlchen. We will discuss the details on our drive back." The Kommissar squeezed to the side when Karl went up to accept the third parcel. Within a few minutes the packages were in safely.

Godunov followed Karl out of the shaft and helped him to carefully move some debris across the ventilation grate, which closed the shaft. There was no visual indication that there was an entry to the subway system. Karl wanted to stay low to the ground, however, after the Kommissar had assured himself that no one was around who could have seen them, he walked upright above the ruins and motioned to Karl to do the same.

They crossed the Kurfuerstendam to the waiting truck. Before they took off, the Kommissar had an idea. "Karlchen, what do you think of leaving Alex behind as a guard?"

"Not necessary," answered Karl, "nobody will detect it from the top and access from the bottom is impossible. You are just depriving yourself of your top man." He wanted to add "or leading a good man into temptation" but did not know how this comment would be taken.

THREE

Harold joined Karl and Alex in the rear of the truck, wondering if and how the Kommissar would direct the driver back to the office building in the Mohrenstrasse. Kommissar Godunov was sitting in the front of the truck. The swift and flawless actions of the former HJ boys were so impressive that he was now seriously considering using the boys to get his loot out of Berlin. All the options he had previously thought of were primitive compared to the efficiency he had just witnessed. The course he had set for himself was not that complicated. All he wanted was to accumulate sufficient material resources to retire in comfort close to the little village Rezervne located on the Crimean peninsula.

Last night, which was the first night after the fighting had stopped, he was busy stealing with the brutal help of his unit, from other robbers. This morning he was only concerned with hiding his newly gained riches. This was now accomplished. His next task was how to bring it home. Initially he had been thinking that he would wait until there would be less rivalry from the incoming Belorussian forces, which were due anytime to replace the Mongolians. But this would now be impossible due to his orders to return to Moscow. They expected him within two days. Not sufficient time to implement a safe transport of his goods.

"You think that the Kommissar will let us go now that we fulfilled his wishes to hide his stuff?" Harold was still using the Berlin dialect.

Karl shook his head, "No way. He cannot afford to let us go. We know where his goodies are. At the very best we will get locked up until he leaves Berlin. At the worst, we will have to join the transports to Russia. He is very polite to us, but he is not stupid."

The truck drove behind the ruins of the Kaiser Wilhelm Gedaechtnis Kirche. Most of the tall church steeple was gone. The big clock was still attached above the entrance, but the inside of the church was completely burned out. Karl and Harold gaped at the scene around them. Wherever they looked, there where Russian tanks. Most of them were lined up around the Zoo Flak Tower, which was located near the church. Their guns where raised and as far as the boys could tell, they were ready for combat.

Kommissar Godunov leaned out of the truck as it came to a stop. While he was talking to a tank commander, Alex motioned to the boys to lay down flat on the truck bed. Shortly thereafter, the truck continued its circle around the church and turned into the Rankestrasse, where it stopped again.

"We will wait for our car to pick us up," said the Kommissar to the boys who were sitting up again.

"Why are there so many tanks around the bunker, Herr Godunov," asked Karl.

"Yes, it is strange. The doors are still locked. No one has left the bunker since the German high command unconditionally surrendered. That was about 20 hours ago." The Kommissar looked at his watch. It was a few minutes past 11:00 AM. "Get ready to board the other vehicle as soon as it arrives."

They did not have to wait very long.

The troop carrier pulled up and the boys, together with the Kommissar, changed vehicles and watched Alex. He was busy directing the driver to roll the truck up the side of a pile of rubble until it reached a tipping point. The driver carefully got out and proceeded to plunk the truck on its side while the engine was still running. The Kommissar watched the performance of his Tatars with a smile, but the boys had a hard time believing what they were seeing. While the truck lay on its side, the transmission somehow engaged and the wheels were racing in the air. Just as the driver and Alex were climbing into the troop carrier, two Russian soldiers came running towards the wreck.

Alex got out again, raised his formidable fist and hit the first soldier square in the face. As the guy staggered from the blow, Alex turned him around and kicked him in the behind, which propelled the hapless body to stumble towards the pile of debris, where he landed face down.

This somehow startled the second soldier enough to slow him down, but Alex was not finished. As he turned on his heel, he was driving his elbow into the kidney of the second guy and then lifted him up and threw him on top of the first one. He was just about to take off his jacket when a barked command from the Kommissar, which sounded like 'kaput', ended his enjoyment. Grunting and disappointed, he boarded the carrier again. The boys could see that he had not even broken a sweat.

"Karlchen," the Kommissar started, "you have just seen how brute force works, but this is not sufficient to get my baggage out of Berlin. I want you to discuss with your friend what you would do if you were in my shoes. And don't bother with your accents; if you want to talk 'knorke' and 'funz' it's fine with me, but don't think that I don't understand you."

"Well, Herr Godunov, I am glad that you don't blame us for trying." Karl was not too surprised. "There you are," he mumbled to Harold, "by now I wonder if he is a mind reader too." The boys could hear snickering from the front and did not know if Godunov had understood Karl's last remark.

A few minutes later they were back at the Mohrenstrasse and in a different room than Karl had been in that morning. The room must have served as a meeting room at one time. It featured a long table in the center and several chairs around it. The Kommissar motioned to the boys to sit down.

He had made up his mind to give the boys some freedom. "You understand, as Karlchen had confirmed before, that I cannot just let you go. Nevertheless, as a sign of goodwill, I will return you to your friend's home until tomorrow morning. Except you will not go alone. I will instruct Alex and one more soldier of my detail to go with you. They will not only guard you, they will also protect you." Godunov looked both boys in the eyes. "You and your friends will need their protection, especially if you have women within your friends. Between yesterday and tomorrow night, all of the Mongolian forces will enjoy their victory and will be roaming the streets and houses looking to plunder and to rape. I could easily keep you here and you would be secure, but you performed very well this morning and I need your continued cooperation. Therefore, I have decided to earn your trust by not only allowing you some freedom, but by also protecting your friends."

"Thank you, Herr Godunov. Are we allowed to change into civilian clothes?" Karl wanted to know.

"Certainly. The uniforms and markings on your jackets only served to identify you as being part of my detail. No Tatar would have dared to question you. I expect you to be in civilian clothes tomorrow. Dress like children with knee stockings and short pants if possible."

"Herr Godunov, may I ask a question about Alex," Karl asked.

"As you wish," answered the Kommissar.

"Is there a word or two with which we are able to communicate with Alex?"

"No, Karlchen, but come to think of it, there might be a word he understands. It is actually a German word. When you say, 'Kaput' he understands that something is broken. Or, that you want someone injured. When you yell, 'Put put' it means you need him to kill someone. But be careful. Once you give him the command, he becomes a Siberian wolf. You cannot call him off."

Karl thought about the actions he had witnessed a short while ago.

"One more thing, Herr Godunov, Alex's feet are smelling terrible, and it is not from sweat. Apparently his skin is flaking off and his feet are fouling away. I think that unless he gets medical attention, he will not be able to walk much longer. Can you tell him to trust me? I have some medical training and also some wound powder at my friend's place. I would like him to wash himself and I will see if I can help him."

Kommissar Godunov looked stunned. He had heard the boy but was apparently unable to understand. "What did you say?"

Even Harold was amazed. He had seen the giant limp and also detected the rank smell. But he had been too busy to put one and one together.

"I am saying that Alex's feet need medical attention." Karl answered the confused eyes from the Kommissionar with a stern look of his own.

"Karlchen, how can you say things like that? We give the Mongolian soldiers medical care when they are wounded. But, if their feet are giving out, that is their business and not mine. If they can't walk anymore, so be it. We leave people behind for less serious conditions. As a soldier, it is their duty to stay healthy."

"So, you don't care for Alex's conditions?" asked Karl to make sure that he understood the Kommissar correctly.

"Well, yes, I care for him, if he would be hit by a bullet or shrapnel. But, if he is unable to walk because he failed to take care of his shoes? If we would have worried about things like that, we would still be deep in Russia and not in Berlin. Surely you understand that it is not the job of a Pompolit to inspect the feet of the soldiers. Besides, Alex can be replaced with four other soldiers or a bulldozer."

Karl took his time to answer. There were many things he wanted to say to the officer, but they would lead to a debate or an argument and the hard answer from the Kommissar did not invite a discussion. "I understand, Herr Godunov, but never-the-less, because Alex will protect us, I feel it is my duty to help him too. I would like you to tell him what I have in mind."

The Kommissar walked to the door and barked an order into the hallway. Shortly thereafter, Alex and two more soldiers entered.

Godunov gave a few short orders and the two soldiers retreated back to the wall and looked at Alex and Karl. While the Kommissar continued talking at Alex, the giant's eyes shifted from him to Karl and back. What seemed to be first a lengthy dialog ended with a few sharp commands.

"I ordered him to wash his feet, and he will allow you to treat him," Godunov looked at Karl and shook his head. "You surprised me, Karlchen, this morning and now again. If you continue this course you might be staying with me for a much longer time than you think."

One of the two other Tatars was the driver who returned them to Karl's friend's apartment in the Berliner Strasse. It was a bewildering ride, because every so often they had to stop when a band of drunken Mongols celebrated in the middle of the street. The most frightening groups were the Mongolian women who shrieked at the top of their lungs when they found some German women hiding in the ruins. First they beat the hapless victims into submission and stripped them bare. Then, as the soldiers proceeded to rape them, the Mongolian women shared the clothes between themselves.

Harold and Karl kept their heads down in the carrier. There was nothing they could do to help. Karl experienced again the painful feeling of being completely and absolutely powerless. He had experienced this feeling before when the SS had executed his buddy beside him because he retreated from the enemy with three bullets left in his pocket. It has been a mistake, as his comrade had not retreated from combat. It did not matter. Under Hitler's order, you were to be shot and hung up on a streetlamp by the SS flying court-martials if you were found to retreat with ammunition. The results of his order were still visible, especially as they drove for a short distance down the Friedrichstrasse. The corpses, old men in their 70's and young 14 year-old kids, swung silently above as the Mongols celebrated their victory below.

The troop carrier came to a stop on the crossing of the Uhland Strasse and the Berliner Strasse. A large bunch of soldiers were beating some old men to death who apparently tried to protect their wives. The whole street crossing was a massive orgy. Harold saw nothing of it as he was crumbled up on the floor of the carrier. He had his eyes shut and was shaking as if in fever. Karl was in no better shape, but he looked up from time to time to direct the driver around detours when the intersections became impossible to cross.

As they turned into the passageway of their final destination, Karl could see that the door to the apartment had been boarded up again. It had been barely nine hours ago that the Russians, who had come to arrest him, had torn it down.

Kete, the friend of Alex, who had been with the arresting detail in the morning, recognized the building and the boarded up entrance.

He looked questionably at Alex as if to ask if they should tear it down again. Alex in turn looked at Karl, who jumped from the car as it rolled to a stop. He swiftly surveyed the surroundings. They were on the rear of the side-wing building, which extended away from the front structure. The top floors had been demolished and burnt out, but the ground floor with its apartments was still intact.

There were no soldiers in sight and Karl banged against the barricaded door.

"This is Karl. Open up. I am with Harold."

There was no answer and Karl could see that Alex moved up behind him, ready to lend a hand.

"Please, answer me. I am with Harold and two friends who are able to protect us."

Again, everything was quiet behind the door. Karl was ready to let Alex have his way when he could hear a woman's voice below the wooden floorboards.

"Karl, Go to the rear yard. There is a garbage bin in front of a cellar window. I will remove the chains so you can move it to the side. Please come in."

It was Frau Becker's voice, which Karl knew well. She had been helping him reuniting school children with their relatives. It had been a daunting task. Most, if not all of the Berlin school children had been evacuated to Poland to protect them from the constant air raids. However, their fathers had been drafted and many of the mothers and relatives had been killed during the bombing attacks. To make it worse, the schools had failed to update their records. When the Soviets broke through the German defense lines in Poland, the evacuation camps had been ordered back to Berlin and when the children arrived, there was no one to welcome them home. Their homes had been bombed out, their relatives were either dead or missing, and the few remaining teachers had to deal with a hopeless situation. They finally just gave up and saved their own skins by leaving Berlin before the Russian onslaught.

Hundreds of children in Berlin waited for days at the railroad stations or schools to be picked up and reunited with their families. All the time being hungry and frightened because the air attacks continued. Bombs kept on falling, the buildings and streets were burning and no one came to help them, because no one knew or cared that they had arrived.

Frau Becker, a teacher in her late fifties was the only one who had been helpful assisting Karl, who had been in charge of bringing a camp of 10 and 12 year-old boys from Poland back to Berlin.

She and her husband, an invalid WWI veteran, were the ones who had given Harold and Karl shelter last night.

Karl attempted some sign language to make Alex understand that he wanted to enter first and alone, in order not to scare the couple.

Alex was a lot brighter than the boys had thought. He understood what Karl was trying to convey. He went to the driver to dismiss him and the carrier.

Kete also took a few steps back and stood next to Harold, who was still trembling. Karl could hear some rattling of chains, but was unable to move the heavy bin. Alex showed up next to him, gave the steel box a push and stayed back again. He pointed to his arm, which was covered with assorted watches robbed in the previous night, and Karl understood that he had about a minute to prepare the Beckers. He squeezed himself between the garbage container and the cellar window, which was large enough to allow access even for a bear like Alex.

The small cellar cubicle he entered was empty, with a door leading into the cellar's hallway. In normal times it was used for the storage of potatoes. This was also the reason to have access to the outside through the delivery window.

"I will tell you in a moment what happened. Right now you have to trust me. I have two Mongols with me to protect us and we have to get off the street."

Frau Becker was nowhere to be seen. Her husband, Herr Becker, a man in his late 60's stood on his useful leg. He had a pitchfork and a coal shovel next to him leaning on the wall. He looked intently at Karl's Russian jacket and then nodded his consent. It did not take long and Alex closed the access window and secured the chain to the trash bin from the inside.

While Harold told Herr Becker about the events of the morning, Karl ventured to see Frau Becker in the nearby coal cellar. The building had no central heating system installed and all the tenants had a private cellar, which was supplied by the landlord to store their potatoes and coal for the wintertime. Frau Becker was warmly dressed. It looked as if she was wearing several layers of old rags with a filthy overcoat for good measure. Normally she looked just about her age. But now, in order to make herself as unattractive as possible, she had put ashes and coal grease in her hair and on her face. With all her unsightly clothing, she could be easily mistaken for a 90 year-old spinster.

Karl doubted that her repellent disguise would work if the Tatars found this cellar. He had seen the Mongols as they raped any woman in sight, regardless of her age.

"We have a chance to make it through the night because of the guards I brought along. But I need access to your bathroom in your apartment to tend to the Mongol's feet." He finished his report to Frau Becker.

"Of course, Karl. Willy, my husband, will let you in. He also has plenty of old civilian clothing for you to choose from, enough for you and Harold. We even have some shorts for both of you. I expect you want to dress as young as possible."

Four

The bathroom was small. Besides the toilet there was a cabinet with a washing bowl on top and a faucet protruding out of the wall with an empty pail on the floor below it. It was a typical toilet room found in an old tenement building in Berlin. The tenants would heat up the water on a wood stove in the kitchen and then fill a wash basin to serve for a sponge bath.

Actually this was one of the more modern buildings. The older structures which were mostly in north Berlin did not feature toilets in the individual apartments. There were no bathrooms. The only toilets in these older tenements were located between the different floors and served the two tenants above or below respectively.

Still, it was completely impressive and modern for Alex who had never seen indoor plumbing, let alone a functioning toilet.

He stared in disbelief when Karl showed him how to use the toilet and how to flush. He could not comprehend that he could do his business within closed walls.

Karl filled the pail with water and pointed to the toilet seat for Alex to sit on and to wash his feet. He left Alex alone and went to find some soap and a candle because it was close to getting dark and the electricity did not work.

When he came back he was nauseated by the rank smell in the small room. Alex had removed his footwear and was in pain from rubbing loose skin from his infected feet. Karl looked at the shoes which were no shoes at all. Alex had been wearing old dirty bloody rags and sheets of newspapers around his feet. All of this was held together with something resembling sandals with a loose leather patchwork on the sides and on top.

He looked at Karl and pointed at his feet. "Kaput"

Indeed, his feet were a blood crusted mess. He must have walked countless miles and probably months in unfitting footwear and was now paying dearly for it.

Karl was appalled. He had expected to see some uncared for blisters on the soles of the feet, but not these kinds of injuries. He could not imagine the pain and discomfort Alex endured by simply walking.

In spite of the awfulness he smiled at Alex "Njiet kaput" Alex seemed to understand that Karl was trying to give him some hope for getting his feet back in shape. He looked sadly at the boy and repeated "Kaput, kaput."

Karl handed him the small piece of soap be had obtained from Herr Becker and conveyed in sign language that Alex should try to get rid of the bloody deposits surrounding the heels.

He went back down into the cellar to confer with the others.

"Where do I find the wound powder I gave you some time ago? I will also need clean rags to bandage his feet and we need a pair of very large shoes."

He looked at the Beckers. "I have some silken rags from an old dress I used to wear. They should be enough to make several bandages" Frau Becker nodded at her husband. "You also have some very old ski socks someplace which you will never wear again. Maybe he could wear them to keep the bandages in place."

The old invalid shook his head, "No, Mutti, I donated the socks to our soldiers last year. You remember, I also gave them our ski gloves".

"Are there any other tenants left in this building" asked Harold, "Maybe one of them has large feet and a shoe size that might fit our pal". He looked expectantly at the couple.

"There is a possibility" said Herr Becker. "I have the keys to the apartment next door. The people left weeks ago to seek refuge with some relatives in the country. I remember that the man had always nice footwear. He was also very tall. I will go and see".

He went to search for the keys.

Frau Becker did not wanted to go upstairs to the apartment and told Karl where he could find the wound powder and the silken rags for Alex, and the civilian clothes for Harold and him.

Kete tagged along with the boys as they went upstairs into the apartment. They could not understand each other but with the help of sign language, they were able to communicate.

Karl was amazed how friendly the two Tatars were to him and to his friends. There was not a hint of dislike and he wondered about the power of alcohol, or in this case of vodka, to turn these simple men into beasts.

The Becker's apartment was small but clean and after the boys changed their cloths, Harold went back into the cellar and Karl gathered the powder and the soft rags. He could see the incomprehension in Kete's eyes as he gaped at the curtains on the windows.

It was obvious that this was the first time in his life that Kete had seen anything like it. He went to finger the fabric and then looked for holes or openings in it. When he found none, he looked to Karl and grunted like a little calf.

Karl was unable to make any sense out of it and opened the door to the bathroom. Alex was done with his scrubbing and painfully stood on his feet when Kete entered. Karl refused to let his imagination get the better of him, but never-the-less, it sounded to him as if the two Tatars just barked and snorted at each other. "You surely got a weird language, my boys," he remarked. The soldiers smiled in return and patted his back.

Alex hit with his flat hand the shoulder of his partner and started to undo his pants. While Karl could not believe his eyes and Kete looked totally bewildered, Alex continued to pull down his pants and urinated all over the toilet lid and the walls.

"Alex!" shouted Karl but the gentle giant pushed him to the side and showed proudly to Kete his newly learned technique of flushing the toilet.

"No, no. no" shouted Karl again as Alex proceeded to wipe down the walls and the toilet cover with the pages of newspaper hanging from a hook on the wall.

He then lifted the seat and wrung out the paper over the toilet. "Holy smoke" moaned Karl, as Alex flushed once more and threw the wad of paper in a corner.

Kete, however, was more than exited. He moved Alex towards the wash basin and turned down the lid to the closed position and pulled down his own pants.

Karl stared engrossed at the Mongol who now proceeded to sit down, his behind slightly above the wooden cover and started to groan.

"Wait!! For heaven's sake, wait you morons!"

Karl did not dare to picture what the toilet room would look like if he would let Kete finish his business. He had to stop him.

He motioned to Alex to help him lifting the Tatar enough off the seat to open the lid. It was a heavy task and Karl almost gave up, but as Alex continued to pull on his partner, something seemed to connect in the brain of Kete. With a low growl he consented to the cover being lifted and then sat down again. A satisfied smile indicated that he was happy in his new found position.

Karl was exhausted and rambled out of the room. The contrast between the multilingual intelligence officer and the primitive mind of the soldiers was nearly beyond his comprehension.

"You should have seen what just happened in the bathroom" he tried to explain to Harold, who thought there was an element of humor in Karl's report and started to grin.

"Never mind" muttered Karl, "I guess you had to be there".

He still had the powder and the rags in his hand. "Is your husband still in the neighbor's apartment" he asked Frau Becker.

"Yes, but he was here for a moment. He told us that he found a brand new pair of large brown leather boots. We think that they are not SS but SA (Sturm Abteilung) issue and wanted your opinion. He went back up to get them".

"What do you make of them", asked Herr Becker entering the cubicle. He had in one hand a large white cardboard box with a brown eagle stenciled on it. In the other hand he was holding an unusually large pair of brand new shiny brown boots. It was a pair of 'Schnuerstiefel' (lace up boots).

"These are SA issue. No question about them. How big of a man was your neighbor?" Karl evaluated if they would fit Alex.

"He was not as big as your Tatar friend. I also think he did not use these because they might have been too large for him," answered Herr Becker.

"Never mind that, you cannot just steal from our neighbor". Frau Becker objected loudly and joined the discussion. Karl turned to his friend. "What do you think, Harold?"

"What do I think? I think the next size up is a small fishing boat. These things are too big for any human. They must have been an advertising gimmick or a door price in some kind of a campaign."

Harold had taken his own shoes off and stuck one of his feet into one of the boots and stood up. The shafts of the boot reached up above his knees. "I almost think that there is enough room to put both of my legs in" he mumbled as he took the ungainly boot off again.

"That still does not allow you to confiscate them. They still belong to the nice gentleman who lived next to us," insisted Frau Becker.

Kete, and Alex, with bare feet, showed up in the door frame. They took one look at Frau Becker and then at the boots. They reached for the boots.

"Halt!!" Yelled Karl at the top of his lungs as Frau Becker scurried back to her cellar unit and locked herself in. Karl grabbed the boots away from Harold and just sat on them.

Kete grunted at Alex and was moving towards Karl but was stopped by a bark from Alex.

"Numb nuts. Sit down!" Karl yelled as if the Mongols would understand him. He knew they were not going to harm him, however, Harold and Herr Becker were not too sure.

"Sit!" Karl got up and pointed to Alex and a bag of coals in the corner.

"You too!" He pointed at Kete and to another bag of coals.

The Mongols quietly barked at each other but sat down. The eyes of Alex stayed on the boots.

Karl gave the boots to Harold to hold and kneeled down to inspect the feet of Alex. They were almost clean; the Tatar had done a pretty good job.

"Get me a pail with clean water, please". Harold was happy to put down the boots and took off to fetch the water.

The arms of Alex were sporting several wrist watches. On one arm Karl counted five watches and on the other arm there were four.

He had an idea and turned to Herr Becker. "Do you know anything about the value of these watches" he asked him.

"No, not much. But I can see that at least two of them are old Swiss watches. They must have belonged to officers."

"Show them to me," said Karl.

"They are both on his right arm. The one on the top and also the one below." Herr Becker described the location of the watches.

He dared not get close to Alex.

"These two?" Karl wanted to be sure. He touched without hesitation the two indicated watches on Alex's arm.

When he fingered the watches, the eyes of the giant moved from the boots to his arm. He caught on much faster than Karl had expected.

With a single stroke he took off all the four watches from his arm, dropped them in front of Karl and reached again for the boots.

"Nice trade,".said Karl to Herr Becker. "Take the four watches and put them in the box and take it back where you found it. We did not steal the boots".

Alex was beside himself in anticipation of his new foot wear.

Karl stopped him from trying them on by holding on to one of Alex's feet. He took the water pail from Harold and wiped with one of his rags the coal dust from the foot. He made sure that the feet were dry before he proceeded to powder and wrap them with the silken rags. Alex grunted in delight as he slipped his feet into his new possessions. Karl thought that there was too much room in the bottom of the boots and fashioned some inlay soles by cutting off the top of the coal bags. After he was satisfied with the fit, he showed Alex how to use the long laces to tie the boots securely to the feet.

"We might get visitors" announced Harold, "There are troops crashing the doors and windows across the street" He came down from the broken staircase leading to the first floor where he had been observing the entry to their building. "Stop your baby sitting. Your new friends should watch what is going on!"

Harold feared that the hordes might spill over to their side of the street. The flimsy barrier on the front door of the apartment was not sufficient to stop anyone, leave alone a horde of drunken Mongols. It was also high time that the entry to the cellar be hidden again.

The piece of carpet which had served to cover the trap door might for a moment fool the intruders but it offered no security.

As Karl was weighing his few possible options he dragged Alex and Kete to Harold's previous surveillance spot. Kete , who had enviously watched the exchange of the footwear, took one look outside and grunted a few syllables to Alex. As he went to the front door he started to remove the inside obstacles.

Karl was aghast when he saw that Alex joined his partner to get rid of the last few barriers. He could not envision that his two guards would ignore their orders from the Kommissar and deliver them to the mob which was now nearing their doors.

But, never-the-less, the fortification was gone and Kete pressed down the lever of the door latch and unlocked it. Karl overcame his shock and darted towards the cellar stairs. He wanted to follow Harold who was already downstairs.

He did not make it. Alex stuck out his leg to trip him and stopped him. He lifted him up and on to the third step of the upward leading staircase. He used sign language to communicate with Karl who gathered that he was supposed to sit and not to move.

The door opened with a bang and the first Tatar stormed into the apartment. He did not get very far. Alex had pushed Kete towards the door where it seemed to Karl that he was stumbling around.

Unfortunately this happened when the next Mongol also tried to enter. The upward flaying arms from Kete knocked the heads of the two soldiers together who retired groaning to the floor.

Still staggering and unable to control where he was stepping, Kete smashed with his feet the nose of the first Tatar.

The groaning became an agonizing cry from the Mongols when Kete finally seemed to get control of himself but by doing so, he had pressed his thumb into one eye of the second Tatar. He used his hand to push himself upwards but his thumb was still in the eye of his unfortunate victim. Kete got up and the eye of the soldier was gone. It had left the eye socket of the flat Mongolian face.

The screaming of these two had stopped for a moment the hordes in front of the door. Alex seemed to enjoy the antics of his friend.

He shrieked in delight, jumped forward and took the improvised fight with his partner outside the front door. Within no time at all, they had four or five other Mongolians on the ground with various injuries. All the while they were yelling and bellowing and bouncing off each other.

Karl watched in amazement the precision fighting techniques of his guards. While he knew what the two were doing, it looked to the drunken intruders as if these two were fighting with each other and all the casualties around them where due to the fact that some of the soldiers had been unfortunate enough to be in their way.

"Stoy," came the sharp command from a Polish officer who was apparently sober. He had entered Berlin with a Polish army unit the previous day and had now joined the drunken Mongolian soldiers to get his share of the loot.

When he became aware of the brawl and that left several Tatars severely injured and unable to move, he had crossed the street.

Neither Alex nor Kete fooled him for a moment. He guessed that these two Mongols had found some German women and wanted them for themselves. He decided to intervene; after all, he was horny too.

The officer had pulled his handgun and pointed it at the chest of Alex. The huge target and the short distance assured him that he could not miss.

He wanted to take the larger of the two Mongols out before he would worry about the smaller one. This was a mistake. The very moment he had called his command to stop, Kete had stayed down close to the soldier he had just enabled. When the gun left the holster he had jumped forward and backward like a cat with a ball.

The Polish officer hesitated a moment too long. He did not know how, but his gun was now in the hand of Kete who turned it around and was about to smash the handle over the officers head when a bark from Alex stopped him.

Obliviously Alex had something different in mind. While he and Kete were fighting the soldiers, he had seen that the hordes around them increased in their numbers. He reached in his pocket and produced a metal badge. It was a red Soviet star with a sword crossing it. The sword pointed downward and on the lower end of the star was the small hammer and sickle emblem.

It was the feared identification of the NKVD, the police branch of the GUGP, the main Directorate of Soviet State Security.

The Polish officer shuddered. It was sheer insanity what he had done; he had pulled a gun on a Mongolian State Police investigator. Or, so he thought.

Alex was fully aware of the power he held in his hand. It was not his identification. He had "borrowed" it some time ago from Kommissar Godunov and had "forgotten" to return it.

The Pompolit had known about it, but he liked Alex. Not only for his unusual abilities, but also for the fact that Alex rejected all kinds of alcohol. He had never seen him drunk and therefore he had let him keep the badge.

Five

Alex resorted to sign language again. He did not speak Polish and the officer did not understand the gurgling sounds of the Mongols. With the badge in his hand, Alex pointed to the officer and then to the mob around him.

It was almost as if everybody who could see the star in his hand became suddenly sober. The ones in front of the mob recognized the emblem and stopped their advancement. The next thing was a brief commotion as the ones in the rear still pressed on, while the ones in front panicked and ran away as fast as their stubby feet would carry them.

In less than maybe five minutes, the mob had vanished. Only the Polish officer stood shaking in front of Alex. He also wanted to flee, but the eyes of the Tatar nailed him to the ground. He stared at Alex's brand new brown lace up boots, the kind he had never seen before, and figured that the Tatar had to be a highly placed official. Alex was temporally satisfied with the impression he had achieved and gestured to Kete to hand the gun back to the officer. He bellowed and barked in a subdued manner to Kete and to the officer as if the Pollack could understand him.

He continued to point to the whimpering casualties on the ground and made some movement with his hands, indicating that he wanted all the stolen wristwatches from their arms.

As the officer complied, Kete stuffed his coat pockets with the watches. Alex looked on and then made some movements with his arms as if he wanted them all to disappear, including the officer, who was beginning to understand.

He said something in return and saluted Alex, then stopped some of the drunken soldiers who kept coming down the street and ordered them to help their hurt comrades. He saw that the soldier with the missing eye needed immediate medical attention and ordered two Soviets to guide him away. He was very persuasive in his effort to please Alex, because within a short time, there was no injured soldier in sight. He looked once more questioningly at Alex, who smiled and waved him on his way.

"Did you see the fear in the Pollack's face?" Karl turned to Harold, who had come up from the cellar and had witnessed the final action from the kitchen doorframe.

"No doubt that everyone in the Soviet army is scared shitless of the political Kommissars," Harold agreed, "maybe even more than we were of the SS," he added, and moved to the side to make room for the two guards who reentered the apartment.

Karl could see in Alex's behavior that the Mongol was not too happy. He walked back and forth in the kitchen and scratched his head repeatedly. Now and then he grunted at Kete, who just stood there quietly and seemed to agree with everything Alex was offering, but had nothing to say.

"Are they gone?" Herr Becker stuck his head out of the trapdoor. He noticed the blood on the floor and grabbed some newspaper pages to wipe it off. It was the blood from the soldier with the crushed nose who was one of the last to leave.

In the meantime the twilight, which in May lasted more than one hour in Berlin, was gone and it had gotten dark. Karl tried his sign language again. He wanted to know if Alex or Kete wanted to sleep in the apartment or join Harold and him in the basement. Alex understood immediately. He made all kind of gestures and pointed to the street, and the sky, and the blood smears on the floor and finally to Karl's wristwatch.

"What is he trying to tell me?" Karl invited Harold and Herr Becker to help him understand what Alex was trying to convey. He looked helplessly at Kete, who picked up some of the broken pieces from the door and the previous barricade. He kind of affixed them to the broken doorframe and then jumped on them, breaking them off again. He also ducked down in the direction of the cellar, shook his head and indicated that he did not like the door, or the cellar, and he used two fingers to indicate that he wanted to run away. Alex watched his partner's gestures and joined in with agitated movements of hiding or running.

"I got it," said Herr Becker, "They expect more violence and don't deem it safe to stay here."

He was right, as Karl found out later. Alex was worried that the mob would return to find out what the two Tatars were so adamantly protecting and/or claiming as their own. The night had not even started and he knew that by the time the morning came, he could not possibly stop the drunken hordes. When he had taken the assignment from the Kommissar, he had hoped that Karl knew of a safe hiding place, like the one the crates had disappeared in. But now it was too late, too many Mongols had seen what had happened. They would be back.

Alex looked once more imploringly at Karl hoping that he would understand and come up with some local knowledge.

"Come on, Harold, think fast. You know the area around here better than I do," Karl knew that the nearest subway shaft was over twenty minutes away. They were in the Wilmersdorf district; and this area was only served by various streetcar lines and buses.

Harold was also at a loss. He knew a little about the nearby street crossings, but he was not up to date on which buildings were still standing and which ones were in ruins. He knew that the former German police station of Wilmersdorf was close by, but this information was also useless.

Karl indicated to Alex that he understood him and that he and his friends were trying to find a solution. "Hilfe, Hilfe" (Help, help). They could hear the panicky stricken wail of a woman and the shrill ear-piercing sounds emitted from some female Tatars.

The cries for help seemed to come from the entrance of the neighboring house, number 27, and they could also clearly hear the additional screaming coming from a girl. The two guards did not understand the words of the German woman, but they did understood the meaning and were momentarily holding Herr Becker back who wanted to limp towards the cries yelling for help.

"Let me go!" shouted Herr Becker. "I have to help. The woman lives alone with her daughter!"

"Stay here or you will get killed. We go!" shouted Harold, following Karl, who was trying to get past Alex. The huge Tatar was not moving an inch. He was holding Herr Becker with one hand and with the other he pushed Harold towards Kete and blocked the exit.

Karl was unable to get through the door and at the same he realized that he was unarmed and unable to render any help anyhow. But the cries for help got more urgent by the second and almost made his blood freeze. "Alex, kaput, kaput!" Karl shouted at Alex and gestured towards the wailing coming from the building next door. He hoped that the giant would understand him and help the women who were pleading for mercy.

Alex tilted his head as if trying to understand what the Tatar women were screaming about and then started to bellow back at them. He apparently was answering to several of their shouts and then he leaped out of the door trailed by Kete, who motioned to Karl and Harold to stay back and out of sight.

Nevertheless, Karl followed them out the door and the darkness allowed him to remain unseen. Some burning debris lighted the hallway to the neighboring house and the scene paralyzed him. There were about 4 or 5 Mongolian women who had found a young German mother and had her stripped naked and holding her spread-eagled on the ground. Two or three other ones were using knives to cut off the underwear from a small girl. It was too dark to tell for sure, but Karl guessed her age to be about eight or nine years old. There were no soldiers in sight, only the Mongolian women with their captives.

When Alex appeared in the hallway, the women were shrieking even louder. They held up the little girl by her arms and forced her to spread her tiny legs, all the while motioning to Alex and Kete to help themselves to their captives. While Alex rushed towards the mother on the ground, Kete sprinted to the trembling kid, and at the same time, he was emptying his pockets. He threw his newly gained watches all over the entryway. The Mongolian women shrieked in delight and while they let go of their victims, they started to fight each other for the plunder. The big Tatar did not waste a second. He hoisted the young mother on his shoulders and ran back to the apartment. Kete, carrying the little girl, was right behind him.

As soon as they reached the apartment they handed the women over to the boys and took defensive positions behind the broken door. They did not need to worry because their action had been so fast that the Mongolian women had not noticed the disappearance of their victims. They were still searching the ground for loot and fighting with each other.

The shouting from Karl had caused Herr Becker to gather a worn-out overcoat and a few shirts. The screaming of the mother and her child stopped on the spot when they recognized Herr Becker who placed the few garments around them.

He looked around for Harold and informed him about a basement breakthrough which led to Berliner Strasse Number 25, the other side of the building.

Harold understood and started to lead the way through the basement connections. He was followed by Frau Becker, who had come out of her potato cellar unit when she heard what was going on. However, the basement of Number 25 was totally unfit for any kind of hiding. An air strike a few days before had leveled a large part of the building and the cellar passageway ended in the open. Harold wanted to turn back when Karl appeared next to him.

He quickly analyzed the situation. He could still hear the faint shouting of the Mongolian women from the building behind them, but the street in front of him seemed to be empty and he was unable to detect any movements. He waited a few seconds for Harold to show up and then sprinted to a nearby rise of rubble.

It looked to him as if the upper part of the apartment house had collapsed towards the street and in doing so, had buried something underneath.

He scrutinized the mound from the street but all he could see were fragments of warped steel and huge broken pieces of cement wreckage piled on top of each other. Glancing back, he could detect in the darkness that Alex and Kete had joined Harold and were waiting for him to conclude his investigation. He waved at them to stay down and continued to circle towards the former inside of the building.

His search was successful when he approached the small portion of the building, which was to some extent still standing upright. He walked close to the former inside wall and over the ruins of the ground floor apartment when he noticed that there was something on the other side of the heavily burnt and distorted window frame leading to the outside.

It looked like a partially crushed large vehicle or bus.

Unable to move the debris out of the way, he retraced his steps back to Harold. "Stay here and wait with the women. We might be in luck."

Harold understood and informed Herr Becker and the women

behind him. Karl took off again followed by Alex and Kete. After the Tatars lifted some of the wreckage away from the window frame, Karl could see that he had been right in his assessment. It was indeed a bus buried on the street under the ruins.

A quick search revealed that the vehicle was only partially crushed, but completely sealed and undetectable from the street. There was sufficient room to serve as a temporary shelter.

"Get the women over to Kete who is waiting," Karl instructed Harold and Herr Becker. "I will take Alex back to the apartment to get food. Do you need anything else," he asked Frau Becker before he motioned to Alex to follow him back through the cellars.

"No. Be careful and come back." She hugged Karl and followed her limping husband. The Mongolian women had stopped their quarrelling and were now loudly singing while moving from cellar window to cellar window further up the street.

Alex motioned impatiently to Karl to hurry up and collect the meager food supplies from the apartment. There were also several blankets on top of the beds. Karl grabbed them, and within a short time they were back at the bus.

Kete had been busy moving some rubble and trash in front of the window frame. The bus offered a much better hideaway than the group could have wished for. The undamaged benches where upholstered and provided soft and almost ideal beds.

The mother had covered her little girl with a blanket and a long dress from Frau Becker, who had shed some of her layered clothing. The girl was still shaking badly and in spite of being told to be as quiet as possible, she was unable to stop whimpering. The mother had also obtained a dress from Frau Becker and now rested warm and comfortable rolled up in the old overcoat from Herr Becker.

As the women tended to each other, Alex joined Kete in carefully hiding the access. They seemed to know what they were doing. Karl helped by gathering dirt and dust and throwing it over the piled up rubble. While he and Alex took the first watch, Harold and Kete tried to get some sleep before it was their turn.

Six

Alex was sitting in the bus close to the broken window leading to the access opening.

He was listening to the noises coming from the street and was satisfied that Karl had found a suitable hideaway for the night. He was happy that the war was over and he liked his present assignment to watch over Karl and Harold.

If truth was to be told, though, he was more than happy about his comfortable boots. The fact that they were brand new made him feel rich beyond his imagination. He had never seen or touched such soft and luxurious leather. The Germans surely possessed greater treasures than he was told when he was drafted in Mongolia.

But, of all the things he had seen in the last day nothing compared to the wonder of indoor plumbing. He still did not understood how this worked, but come what will, he had made up his mind to rip one of the units out of the wall and take it home to his desolated desert village.

He wondered what the next day would bring in new discoveries and his fingers were busy tying and untying his lace up boots to adjust the fit of his bandages. His feet still hurt, but not as bad as yesterday and the weeks before. It had been a long day for him but he did not allow himself to drift off into sleep.

Kommissar Godunov had made it very clear that he was responsible for Harold and Karl and he had promised to give him a 'war time bonus'. (He was not sure what this was, but it sounded intriguing.)

He could hear some vehicles driving up but they continued down the street.

It was pitch black in the bus and Alex tried to see Karl who got up from his bench. He was using a small dynamo flashlight to find his way back to Herr and Frau Becker. The dynamo flashlight was another wonder Alex had never seen before. He wanted Karl to show it to him as soon as he got back to his seat.

"Tell us again how you wound up with the body guards," Frau Becker wanted to know. Karl took his time explaining the events of the day. But, he omitted the description about the exact location of the subway hide out. "We will have to get back to the Kommissar in the morning". He ended his report.

"I also took some Flieger Schokolade (chocolate), from our stash. Do you want some? Otherwise I will give it to the girl."

He reached in the front pocket of his civilian short pants and retrieved a small round tin. It was part of a rationing kit for German pilots. Herr Becker liked sweets but considering the circumstances, he refused in favor of the kid and then looked questioning to his wife.

"I told you about the resources of the boys. Where else did you think our food reserves came from?"

"I thought that they came from the school district".

"That's right" answered Frau Becker; "however, it was the boys who supplied us".

Karl went further back in the bus and pressed the lever of his dynamo light to illuminate for a moment the area where the young mother was cuddled up with her daughter. Their shaking had stopped and it looked to Karl that they were resting comfortably. Without saying anything, he placed the chocolate tin in the hands of the girl. He had also carried one of the extra blankets back and placed it over both of them.

As he turned to walk up to the front he thought that he heard a whispered "thank you" but, he might have been mistaken.

He took a place opposite of Alex who stuck out his hand towards the flashlight. Karl showed him how to operate the lever and for the next few minutes Alex kept pressing away. With one hand he pushed the lever and with the other hand he shielded the light.

When he wanted to give the flashlight back he was pleasantly surprised that Karl refused. He grunted a few syllables and stuck the hand with the flashlight in his pocket where he kept pushing the lever. From time to time he looked down to see if it was still emitting light.

Karl started in the dark to explore the contents of his jacket pockets. When he had changed into the civilian clothing he had been in a hurry. He had simply transferred all the contents from the Russian army jacket but he was not sure if he had still some HJ items on him which might be detrimental to him. He could feel the packet of cigarettes in his upper chest pockets. He never smoked. The cigarettes were from his trading goods, which he had previously left at Becker's apartment.

His other upper pocket was empty. He padded his inside pockets and all of the sudden he remembered the small present he had received about ten days ago from a submarine commander. It was the packet which Kommissar Godunov had allowed him to keep and he hoped that he had transferred it. Now would be a good time to see what it contained. He remembered the upbeat attitude of Korvettenkapitain Siegler and especially his great smile.

Alex was still playing with his flashlight as Karl found the small box in his inside pocket. It was a little longer and wider than a cigarette package, but just as flat. He hesitated for a moment before he opened the brown wrapping paper, wondering what he would find.

After he opened the box he could feel cotton wadding around a flat glass vial. It contained liquid and was closed with something like an eyedropper screw top. His first thought was that it might contain some kind of poison because he knew that the submarine commander had been involved with transferring German scientists and Nazi leaders to safety in Argentina. He also knew that all of them carried cyanide pills in case that they were caught and interrogated.

But the captain had told him that this package might save his life and that instructions were included. There was no label on the bottle but he could feel a folded piece of paper next to it.

He retrieved the flashlight from Alex and was stumped when he recognized that the instructions were not in German but in Spanish and in English. He could not read either language and it seemed to him that the instructions were either very simple or somehow condensed, because in both languages, there were less than three printed lines.

The liquid in the vial seemed to be somewhat oily. He was just about to open the bottle and smell the contents when he stopped himself in order not to make a mistake. He had waited that long and he could wait another hour or so until his friend woke up. Harold had attended an elite school when he was 12 years old and had told him that he could read some English.

In the meantime, it had gotten cold and Karl wrapped himself in a blanket. It was the first time that he was wearing shorts this year and his legs were freezing.

All during the night they could hear the singing and shouting of the drunken hordes of soldiers who roamed the intersection of the Gasteiner Strasse and the Berliner Strasse. By now, all of the neighborhood had been ransacked several times, but once in a while the mob found another hideout. The result was chillingly always the same. The screaming and pleading of the victims stopped permanently after a few gun shots echoed from the ruins.

When Kete woke up and wanted to take over the next watch, Alex was still playing with the flashlight in his pocket. Now and then the light illuminated Kete's face and Karl tried to study the expressions of the flat and Slavic features which never seemed to change. It was stoic as if incapable of showing emotions.

Karl pondered if it was just Kete or if this was also the case with all of the Mongols. He remembered that Alex's face had shown genuine pleasure and thankfulness when he had tended to his feet. But Alex seemed somehow different.

The night passed without any of the rambling soldiers coming close to the hidden bus. Kete and Alex left the vehicle when it still was dark. The streets had gotten quiet and the two guards went back to the apartment to see if anything had changed. Remarkably, it had not been looted or even touched and they all made their way back to the basement. The mother and daughter decided to stay with the Becker couple in their basement.

Karl wanted to give something to Kete who was still eying Alex's boots. He wanted to do this before they parted at Kommissar Godunov's headquarters. He thought that it might be beneficial to have two friends instead of a good one and a possible jealous one. But, he could not think of anything of value which might please the Tatar.

Then an idea struck him. He motioned to Kete to follow him to the kitchen where two nights ago he had left his HJ Fahrtenmesser (HJ issue knife). He carefully removed the sharp Sohlingen steel blade from the protective shield and handed both items to Kete.

This time he saw a change in the face of the Mongol. His eyes went wide and glittered and before he could back off the Tatar grabbed him by the ears and kissed him on both cheeks.

It became obvious to Karl that the Mongols had never received any items or presents from the Soviets except tattered uniforms, food, Vodka and weapons. Whatever else they carried on their body was the loot from the victims of the conquered territories.

It took less than a minute for Kete to attach the knife to his belt and then he started to practice a fast draw. Karl watched the unpracticed movements and hoped that the Tatar would not injure himself. They left the kitchen and joined the others at the cellar stairs.

"Are you able to read this?" Karl showed his friend the paper from the bottle. "Let's see, yes, I can read this. You should have went to school with me, then you could read it too". Harold handed the paper back to Karl.

"Cut it out, tell me what it means", Karl liked to banter with his friend, but now was not the time. Kete had already moved to the street waiting for the car to pick them up and Alex was waving Harold and him to leave the apartment.

"Oh, now you want me to translate it too? It will cost you."

"Tell me!" Karl became impatient.

"Do you want the Spanish or the English version?"

"Darn you, since when do you speak Spanish?"

"Right, if you wanted the Spanish translation I would have not been able to help you. But, now that you cursed me I am in shock, and I forgot English too".

Alex looked curiously at the boys not sure if they were really arguing and pushed them out of the door.

"And to think that I let you sleep last night and watched over you".

Karl had the paper still in his hand, ready to put it back in his pocket.

"Alright, I am sorry, let me read it again", Harold stuck out his hand.

"It will not help me when you read it. Please translate it for me".

"See? You are learning. Why did you not tell me right away what you wanted?"

Harold read out loud: "Experimental plant extract. 5 drops of ointment to 10 drops of vegetable oil to treat extremely infected wounds. Apply directly to the wound and/or to the bandage".

"So it is a medication," said Karl.

"What is?"

Karl told his friend about the vial.

"You never told me about a submarine commander".

"I am telling you now. And, honestly, I had forgotten about the present."

Kommissar Godunov's car came around the corner from the Gasteiner Strasse. It was driven by the same driver from the night before.

Before they got in, Alex showed off his new boots to the driver. Kete was right behind him and removed the shiny blade of the Fahrtenmesser from the sheath to let the first morning sunshine play on it.

The driver stared as in disbelief. Karl felt sorry for him. He reached in his pocket and handed the Tatar his pack of cigarettes, hoping to ease the envy in the driver's eyes. He was surprised to see that he had hit a jackpot. All three Tatars gathered around and admired the German factory produced cigarettes. Karl learned later that the Mongols had only known the self-rolled papyruses consisting of some ruff tobacco and newspaper.

Right now he slipped for a moment back into the apartment and retrieved another cigarette pack from his stash, which he had hidden in the bowl cover of the ceiling light. Since there was presently no electricity restored he reasoned that his stash was safe from detection.

The Mongols were waiting and smoking. They patted Karl on the shoulder and let him sit in front, next to the driver.

On the way back to the office building on the Mohren Strasse, Harold and Karl decided on a plan to get the 'luggage' from the Pompolit out of Berlin. Karl laid out several options and the boys decided to play it by ear, because it all depended not only on their own ability but also upon the Pomplit's authority and the final destination of the goods.

Harold thought that Karl's ideas were almost genius and on top of it absolute doable. But, granted, a lot depended upon the power and cooperation of the Kommissar.

"You will keep your answers very short and then immediately take the lead in the conversation. I do the thinking and adjustments as the situation unfolds. Should you get stuck I will take over. In any event, I will back you up and then throw the ball back to you." Karl decided.

Harold agreed. He had seen in the previous weeks how Karl's ideas had gained traction. He could not imagine that Karl would let him down. But just to get some additional confidence he still decided to ask one more question; "What do you really think our chances are to pull this off?"

Karl answered immediately with a question of his own:

"It is our mind and gene pool against theirs. What do you think?"

Kommissar Godunov was in the conference room waiting for them. He had used part of the last night to steal again with his police commando from the other Mongols. He had perfected his robberies to an art form. He used his carrier car to cruise the streets with his group and when they saw some worthwhile loot they got out and while the red star from the Kommissar rendered the victims helpless, his commando frisked the soldiers and relieved them of their bounty. Even in their drunken stupor the soldiers recognized a Pompolit when they saw one. The Soviet State security Kommissars were always right and the fear of them was unparalleled.

Godunov had given some thought to his actions. In the evening he had visited an assembly area of the Wehrmacht to confiscate Rucksacks from the German soldiers. He had then distributed the backpacks to his team.

He was actually satisfied with his own booty from the first night and had mainly used the second night to give the plunder to his team to assure their continued loyalty. He had also started to fill up a medium size crate where he put nothing but real worthless junk. However, when he saw an expensive watch or diamond jewelry, he confiscated it for himself. His soldiers saw no difference in the items.

A watch was a watch and anything that glittered was equally desirable and they were satisfied and happy that their commander gave them almost all of the goodies.

Their back packs started to fill up by the time they stopped their robberies at about 2:00 AM. The crate with the worthless glitter was also overflowing. Godunov kept his team on track by telling them that they would get all the Vodka they could possibly drink once they were done.

He informed his team that they would turn around to Mongolia within a few days and that they would be better off to steal and rob while they were sober and then get drunk on their way home. He had also told them that they would receive today a special war bonus. Somehow this made sense to them and as the boys with their guards arrived, the whole team was ready and eager for the new day.

It was now about 7:30 AM. After Godunov had listened to the report from Alex and admired the new boots he turned his attention to the boys.

"Have you given it any thought to how we could transport my luggage out of Berlin?"

"I have," answered Harold, "We are able to get it first to Babelsberg (a suburb of Berlin) and then to Potsdam (a town next to Berlin)."

"To Potsdam? How do you propose to get it to Potsdam? And then what?"

"Are you satisfied with the present location of your luggage?" asked Harold without answering the question.

"Of course I am happy. Otherwise I would have not have left it there overnight".

"Where you satisfied with the speed and general execution of our task"?

The Pompolit took his eyes of Harold and looked over to Karl.

"Karlchen, what gives with your friend? He has nothing but questions but did not answer me. His questions are already answered by the fact that I released you last night to your friends home."

"I guess Harold is wondering why you are questioning or doubting our abilities."

Karl took over.

"Herr Godunov, we can get your luggage out of Berlin. You know that already, otherwise you would not ask us to help you. But, we need to know why you are not doing it yourself. From what we have observed we are convinced that the whole Russian army is shaking in their boots when they are seeing a political

Kommissar. If you want us to help you, we need to know what your limits are. There must be something beyond your authority that you are fearful of. And finally we also need to know how far, meaning how far into Russia, we will need to assist you until you are able to take over."

The Kommissar got up from his chair and walked around the desk to lock eyes with Karl.

"Karl" (he did not say Karlchen) "You have some nerve to talk to me like that. I will answer some of your questions, but to ask for the limits of my authority is too much. I can assure you that it is sufficient to make you disappear for good."

He tried his best to stare down Karl.

"Look, Herr Godunov, I agree that your flame spitting tanks scare the hell out of me and also burning asphalt makes me cringe, but, in this case, we both know that you want, or even need, something that Harold and I might be able to supply. So, forget that I asked for the limits of your authority and just tell us what it is exactly what you want us to do."

Harold was stunned at the audacity of his friend. Karl, however, was not even scared. He had more than one card up his sleeve and he had never said more than he could back up. For good measure he added: "Once you tell us to what extent you need our help, we will be able to figure out how to do it."

The Kommissar unlocked his eyes from Karl and turned to Harold.

"Your friend has a big mouth. I thought that he would know how to keep it shut".

Harold tried to restrain himself, but his Berliner spirit prevailed. "Please excuse him, he just tries to help you, Herr Godunov. Karl had not had breakfast and our supper was pretty meager. Once Karl had something to eat he will remember his upbringing."

"I sure hope so" mumbled Godunov, "because by now I am ready to adopt both of you." His voice had trailed off and was barely understandable. The boys looked at each other as the Kommissar went to the door and shouted orders to bring him some food.

"What did he say?" Harold wanted to know.

Seven

The runner arrived with several onions and some black bread, coffee and black tea.

He also placed a bowl of brown hard sugar on the table. Karl looked at it and wondered what to do with it. He knew that it would not taste right in the coffee and would take forever to melt. The Germans called this kind of sugar 'Kandies' (rock candy). The commissar saw Karl's befuddlement and reached for the teapot and filled the boys' cups.

"Here, let me teach you the correct Russian way to drink tea." He reached for a piece of rock candy and placed it in his mouth and then instructed the boys to do the same.

"Now, you keep it in your mouth and drink the tea by first whirling it around the sugar in your mouth. One piece of sugar should last for several cups of tea. Depending upon how sweet you like to drink it."

"How do you eat with the candy in your mouth?" Harold wanted to know.

"You either drink or eat. We are not as rich as the Germans who do both at the same time," informed the Kommissar. "I think that even the animals do not eat and drink at the same time."

"What do you do with the onions?" Karl never had onions for breakfast.

"You eat them like an apple, try one". The Kommissar took the rock candy out of his mouth and placed it next to his cup and then reached for the biggest yellow onion on the table, peeled a few layers off, and took a hearty bite out of the vegetable.

"Why not?" Harold immediately followed the example and started to chew on an onion of his own while his eyes were tearing.

"I think that I will stick with the bread in the morning," announced Karl as he stuffed his face with the black Russian bread. It tasted kind of sweet, almost like the German Pumpernickel; just as grainy but a little softer. Karl was pleased; as long as he had bread the world was fine with him.

"Alright." The Kommissar started to slurp his tea. "Karlchen is right that you need to know some more details. My official orders are to prevent the looting of valuable artifacts in Berlin. In this capacity I confiscated various items from the plundering Mongols. Once the Belorussian army under the command of Marshall Zhukov takes over the occupation of Berlin, and this is supposed to happen by tomorrow, I have to surrender all the confiscated booty to them."

"I am sure that this plunder will undergo the scrutiny of various officers until it is returned to the rightful owners. Therefore, I decided upon a preview. My luggage consists of my personal selections. Under normal circumstances my personal luggage is not subject to inspection, however, the conquest of Berlin is far from normal and it seems that the high command does not trust me. I have been ordered to return to Moscow without luggage. This is an ominous sign and I only have limited time. I think that this is all you need to know in regard to my luggage."

The Kommissar selected another onion and shook his head looking at Karl who washed his last crumbs down with a cup of tea. Karl actually preferred coffee but drank the tea out of politeness to Godunov.

The Kommissar got up and went back to the door and shouted another order into the hallway. Karl hoped for more bread.

"Any questions?" he asked the boys as he sat down again.

"No, not at this time as I am sure that you wanted to tell us some instructions or other things". Harold took the lead again.

"No instructions but, yes, you must be wondering what the possible reward might be for you".

"Reward? We thought our reward would be that you prevent our deportation to your labor camps." Harold was done with his onion and also hoped for some bread, but, he had to admit that the onion did its trick. He was not hungry any more.

"It is now my turn to ask questions," Godunov said as he

consulted the green note book again.

"Karlchen, where are your parents?"

"My father was in the Volkssturm and I don't know if he is alive or where he might be. My mother is with my brother and sister in Westphalia."

"This about tracks with the notes I have about you. Harold, where are your parents?"

"I don't know, Herr Godunov. The last I heard was that they were evacuated by the German civil authorities".

"So your father was a civil servant?"

"Correct."

"What was his position?"

"I don't know."

"How come you don't know?"

"He never told me."

"Was he a member of the Nazi party?"

"I don't know."

"But, you attended the Napola (foremost elite Nazi boarding school) for one year?"

"Correct."

"Where did you attend the school?"

"Potsdam."

"Really, Potsdam, right here by Berlin? I know about this school. Extreme political cadet school with emphasis on leadership and languages. So, you speak English?"

"Correct."

"Russian?"

"No, only English."

"You were trained to become a political leader in the countries which were supposed to be occupied by the Germans?"

"Correct."

"Then you must also know that you could not have gained entry to the Napola if your father would not have been a highly placed Nazi official."

"I thought that you don't have much time, Herr Godunov. I don't see what these questions have to do with your luggage". Karl interrupted, because he did not like where this was going.

"Karlchen, your question is out of line. And I am still not done with you."

"Yes, Karl, stay out of this. Herr Godunov is mistaken about the entry requirements of the Napola."

The runner appeared with more bread and this time he also had a jar of milky green jam. No butter or margarine. Karl did not need an invitation to help himself to the sweet looking jelly.

When he took a bite of the bread with the green concoction he almost choked. This was the absolute worst thing he had ever swallowed. He wanted to be polite and kept his hand in front of his mouth, but the urge to get rid of the most awful taste was too overwhelming.

Spit, green jelly, bread and all, came flying through his fingers and nostrils as he bent down towards the floor to avoid exploding over the table.

"Saints in heaven, what is this stuff?" He asked, while the Kommissar could not keep from laughing. "Herring jelly" he answered.

"Herring? You mean dead fish? Good God! I had a dead fish in my mouth!" Karl shuddered and reached for the tea to wash down whatever was left in his throat.

"You mean you never ate fish?" Asked Godunov.

"No, I was hungry enough to eat raw, uncooked horse meat once and it was good and tasted kind of sweet. But dead fish? Mercy! Onions and dead fish for breakfast."

In spite of another cup of tea he could not get rid of the fishy taste.

"So, I take it that you would rather eat live fish?" The Kommissar asked still smiling.

"No, no, no, I don't eat anything that comes out of the water. Give me bread and potatoes and you can keep all the other food for yourself."

He had wiped down his face but his eyes were still wide open in disgust and tearing.

"So, Harold you were about to tell me that I knew nothing about the entry requirements of the Napola," the Kommissar started again.

"No, I only said that you are mistaken when you think that you needed a politically connected father to be admitted into the Napola."

Harold stood his ground. He trusted Karl to intervene if the subject became too hot. Besides, he knew that he was right.

"Very well, Harold, then please enlighten me about the entry requirements." The Pompolit was equally sure that he was right.

"First of all you had to be a full blooded Aryan" Harold began. "Your linage had to be dating back to 1800 and had to be absolutely clean without any trace of any impure blood. Secondly you had to show that you had above average ambition. All your grades had to be above excellent and your report cards had to state that your attention to the given subject was at all times above 100 %. You also needed to bring a letter from your teachers attesting that you studied during recess. Walking around or eating during breaks was considered to be a waste of time. Third, you had to be free of physical defects like bad hearing, bad eyesight or being left handed. Another requirement demanded that you were in top physical shape. Not overweight or underweight."

"In your entry tests there were no multiple choice answers," Harold continued. "All of your answers had to be written and contain at least 75 words. If your answer was any shorter, you failed, even if the answer was correct, because you did not provide explanations or examples. If you passed all of the above it did not matter if your father was a member of the Nazi party or a common laborer. Most of the applicants were rejected because they could not provide the documentation of their uninterrupted linage. This might also have been due to the many lost records during the First World War. That's it in a nut shell, Herr Godunov, but I'll be happy and able to elaborate."

As Harold was talking, the Kommissar's eyes went back and forth between Harold and Karl.

"No need to do that, Harold. As I am sure you can, but I believe that I heard enough, except I don't understand the requirement of studying during a break? How was this justified, but even more why would you even consider studying during a recess period?"

Harold did not have to think about his answer.

"Ambition, Herr Godunov. Ambition is probably the main characteristic which separated us from the other students. We, who applied to the Napola, never wanted to be simply the best. We wanted to be the very best. Therefore, every moment we studied, we were a step ahead of the ones who slacked off".

While Harold answered, the eyes of the Kommissar had not left Karl's face and he noted by Karl's expression that he agreed with Harold's answer.

Godunov's eyes went back to Harold. "However, I know that the father of the applicant had to be at least an ordinary member of the Nazi party."

"Excuse me, Herr Godunov. In all due respect, but, if I would be you, I would not press this point," Karl mixed in again. He finished eating his bread and was ready to take on the mind of the Kommissar.

"Karlchen, I expected you to come to the aid of your friend, but what do you mean by your remark?"

"I mean you cannot prove what you are saying," Karl warmed up. He knew what he was saying.

"Then we are at a standoff, because you cannot prove the opposite either." The Pompolit had noted the change in Karl's behavior and he sensed a challenge, but he was not ready to give in.

"Well, I most certainly can try." Karl did not want to overplay his hand, but enough was enough. "Aryans have physical attributes, especially the full blooded ones with a linage dating back to 1800. Not all of them are smart or motivated, but, all of them are blond and blue eyed. No exceptions. Hitler wanted blond, blue eyed and above average motivated, intelligent boys."

"Hitler himself, on the other hand, was dark eyed, black haired and non-Aryan," Karl continued. "Hell, he was not even a German. He was Austrian. However, he was the founder and the highest leader of the Nazi party. It follows that the Nazi movement or their officials had nothing to do with being fathers of Aryan boys applying to become cadets in the elite schools."

The Kommissar still smiled, as it seemed to be his most notable habit.

"Very good, Karlchen, you provided a convincing answer in more than 75 words. Tell me, did you also attend the Napola?"

"No, Herr Godunov, I applied like Harold, but I was rejected."

"How so?"

"They did not tell me, Herr Godunov, but since my school report cards were similar to Harold's, I think my rejections were due to my small physical body and I had no Aryan linage records going back to 1800. There might have been other reasons. I don't know."

"Enough of that. You told me what I wanted to know and I believe that if there is a way to get my luggage out of Berlin you will be able to find it. Any ideas you care to share with me?"

"Yes, but first some questions. How far do you need your luggage shipped into Russia and once they arrive will you be there or have some trusted friends to accept the shipment?" Harold was the first to ask.

"Preferably all the way to the Crimean peninsula. Yes, I have friends there who are loyal to me."

"When do you need it out of Berlin, or when would you like it to arrive?" Harold again.

"I would like it out by tonight or at least on the way by tomorrow noon."

"Alright, this takes care of the time frame," said Karl.

"You talk as if you are sending a simple package. I told you that I am under suspicion. Any package sent from me or sent from anyone, by military transport or otherwise, but addressed to me or my friends will be intercepted." Godunov was getting impatient.

"So? I don't see a problem. I agree it is somewhat of a challenge, but I can think of two possible scenarios and of one definitely doable solution. Let me ask you this: Suppose that Moscow does not find any wrong doings on your part but does not allow you to return to Berlin and retires you to the Crimea peninsula. Would you retain your rank?"

"My rank, yes. My authority might be not as far reaching as in the past. But, I will always have some limited authority."

"You told us that the surrendering Wehrmacht soldiers will be transported to the Ural Mountains and the SS to Siberia? Can we go and observe their departure for a short while?"

"Yes, we will take my full team with us. I promised them some special bonuses and they are waiting."

"Good, Herr Godunov, then consider your problem solved. I will need your transport carrier after dark tonight for about two hours, together with your driver and your most trusted Tatar. I also need Alex and if possible a car for about two hours anytime this morning or this afternoon."

"When are you sharing your plan with me, Karlchen?"

"I have three plans, Herr Godunov. The moment I know which one will work, I will share it with you. Matter of fact, I probably need you to implement the transport. There is one more thing I need to know. You don't need to tell me what it is, but I need to know if you have a sensitive past or present which some higher placed official can use to blackmail you."

59

The Kommissar was taken aback. He had endured the questions of the boys because he needed their local knowledge and when it became apparent that they were brighter than his soldiers, he wanted to take advantage of their intelligence.

But, was he subject to blackmail? Not that he knew of any dark spots on his past performances. His record was spotless clean and he wondered himself why he was being ordered back to Moscow. He felt more than he knew that he was not fully trusted, but it was a feeling mostly based upon the "without luggage or belongings" order than of anything else.

However he admired Karl's mind which was probing in all kinds of directions. Directions he had not even thought of himself.

"No, Karlchen, nothing in my past or present which might be used to blackmail me. However, come to think of it, I might have a sensitive spot. My daughter is on the way to Berlin. She is a lieutenant and my only child. She is truly the apple of my eye. I hope to see her before I have to leave for Moscow."

"Well, Herr Godunov, then we will have nothing to worry about."

The Kommissar issued the orders to summon his team to their truck. As soon as everybody was seated they took off in direction of the Potsdamer Platz.

Most of the SS assembly area on the big plaza was still extremely busy. Godunov stopped the driver to talk to the guards and then boarded the truck again.

"They already moved the first groups of prisoners to the nearest rail road stations. That's all they could tell me."

"I don't think that we have any functioning rail road stations left. The prisoners must be outside of the stations awaiting your trains. Let's drive to the Zoo bunker, they should have surrendered by now," Karl suggested.

The Kommissar ordered the driver to follow Karl's directions.

Due to the heavy congestion around the Kaiser Wilhelm Gedaechtnis Kirche, they had to stop a few hundred feet from the Flaktower of the Zoo bunker.

The doors were now open and they observed an endless stream of civilians, mostly women with their children leaving the fortress-like building. Now and then there was a uniformed soldier in between who was quickly detected by Soviets and escorted to the assembly area between the bunker and the zoo area.

Due to the heavy bombing, and also in the last four days of the heavy shelling by the Soviet artillery, most of the zoo animals had been killed.

Harold looked over to the former entrance to see if the gates where open, but there were no more gates detectable. The whole entry area was a mass of rubble and ruins.

"That's what you wanted to see, Karlchen? How do you think that this would help you to get my luggage on the way?"

The Kommissar was not impatient, but he tried to speculate what Karl had in mind.

"Too early to tell, Herr Godunov and so far I am unable to make a decision. We will have to go to one of the places where the trains leave for Russia."

"Then let's go!" The Kommissar wanted to board the truck again.

"Halt." said Karl. "Are you able to find out if the hospital had been cleared out? If not, we might need to see one of the Doctors I know."

"What hospital? And why do we need to see a Doctor?"

"There are hospital facilities on the third floor of the bunker. I know one of the Doctors. Please find out if the Doctors are still in there or where they were moved too."

"I don't understand, Karlchen, but I will find out."

Godunov waved to his team which immediately formed a cordon around him and proceeded to the guards next to the bunker exit.

Alex stayed in the truck with the boys and the driver.

The Kommissar was hardly gone when he returned again with his group. "The hospital is still functioning and they are treating German as well as Soviet casualties. It is supposed to stay operational for the next few days. However, the Belorussian Armee already entered the city and will replace the Mongols of the Ukrainian Army within the next few hours."

While Karl pondered the answer, Godunov considered his next moves.

His orders were to report to Marshall Zhukov before he was to leave for Moscow. He had not expected the Marshal to enter Berlin before the next day. The Mongols were still roving the streets plunding and he feared that it might come to a bloody conflict between them and the Belorussians, who also wanted their part of

61

the loot and the women. There was no doubt in his mind that the Mongols would beat the hell out of the Russians should they get in their way. However, Marshall Zhukov had issued a law against looting and he had several hundred tanks at his disposal to enforce it.

Eight

Karl was done deliberating with himself. Besides the assemblies of prisoners at one of the railroad stations, he also wanted to see the airfield of Tempelhof, the main airport of Berlin, and he directed the driver accordingly.

They went first to the Schlesischen Bahnhof (Schlesischen Railroad Station), which was reduced to nothing but rubble. It looked like a gigantic plow had gone through the structure. Only a portion of the entrance was still standing.

However, some of the railroad tracks were apparently still functioning and the boys observed a long line of prisoners being herded into freight cars.

Karl was studying the length of the train and he was amazed at the huge amount of used and demolished bicycles being loaded on the open platform wagons. He asked the Kommissar about it.

"There is nothing strange about it. These Mongols have never seen bicycles, and it is part of the plunder that is condoned to leave Berlin," answered the Pompolit.

"If they have never seen or used a bike, do they have suitable streets in Mongolia?" Harold wanted to know.

"Sure, but only in the cities, not in the countryside these soldiers are returning to. They will take the bikes apart and use the wheels to fashion carts. Any soldier coming home with a bicycle will be a hero in his village."

Godunov motioned the driver to pull up next to a heap of stolen bicycles waiting to be loaded. Because of the wartime shortage of rubber, most of them had small spiral wire springs screwed into the rims.

"It is time to make good on my promise to my team." He shouted a few commands to his group and they went towards the bikes cheering. "I promised them a wartime bonus, and they deserve it."

Kete was the first one to secure himself one of the few bikes that still had rubber tires. The one he selected had large red balloon tires. He pushed it on a stretch of street that was relatively rubble-free and in the next moment, he was flat on his face. He had tried to swing one leg over the saddle while he was swaying back and forth standing on one of the pedals. Then he lost his balance and crashed. While everyone in the group laughed, it soon became a serious competition.

Karl and Harold got out of the truck and tried to teach them how to ride, but there was no method that enabled the Mongols to learn within ten minutes how to ride a bike. Soon they were sitting on various pieces of rubble, tending to their minor injuries and starting to exchange the bikes with each other.

Harold decided to teach by example and showed off by riding freewheeling, his arms crossed over his chest, laughing and whistling as he passed the sorry bunch.

This turned out to be a major mistake. The whole horde got up and scrambled behind him. They all wanted the bike he was on, which apparently did not need any attention from the rider.

Their screaming alerted the guards from the railroad who came running to look at the wonder bike.

"Harold, stop this nonsense before you get killed!" Karl shouted at his friend, who was now lying on the ground with the bike between his legs and a bunch of Mongols on top of him.

One by one they got up and as they were trying to mount the bike, they were crashing again.

"How often do you want them to land on their heads?" Karl interrupted the laughing of the Kommissar, "Why don't you just tell them that in due time they will be able to ride like Harold?"

"You tell them. I can't help enjoying myself." Godunov was having the time of his life and was not about to bring order into the fiasco.

"Brain dead idiots, I'll get even with you!" Harold was cursing as he struggled to get up. He had an idea and selected a bike from the pile. He pushed it into the hands of the next Mongol and kept on selecting bikes until everyone in the group had received a bike from him with wire springs on the rims. But most importantly, he demonstrated to everyone that he could ride each selected bike freewheeling. This was pretty difficult because the springs jumped in different directions making the freewheeling effort precarious. It finally dawned on the guards that it would take some time and effort to master the art.

"Help me to convince them that the bikes with the rubber tires do not work," Harold shouted at Karl.

Karl promptly took the bike with the red balloon tires and crashed with it. In the next moment Harold also went down with a bike sporting rubber tires. The Pompolit had stopped laughing. He was no dummy and saw what the boys where trying to accomplish.

"You cannot do that boys, you are selecting the worst bikes for my soldiers and now look, the guards from the railroad have started unloading the good bikes with the nice tires."

"Wrong, Herr Godunov. The steel springs will last forever and your soldiers will have useable bikes for years to come. Where would they obtain rubber tires when they get home?"

Godunov had to agree that Karl had a valid point but nevertheless, it bothered him to see that all the better bikes were dumped in favor of the near useless ones.

There had been a few old German civilians standing close to the pile of bikes and Karl told them to take the good bikes and to disappear.

Godunov was still recovering from this change of events. "I have to hand it to you. You know how to make grown men change their minds."

"Thank you," said Karl, who kept on scrutinizing the flatbed railroad cars and their cargo as well as the guards. He did not find what he was hoping to see. All the enclosed wagons were being filled with SS prisoners. The open flatbed cars carried not only loot and plunder, but also a surprising number of guards as well as a good number of officers. He dismissed the railroad as one of his possible plans to transport the luggage.

Kommissar Godunov decided to let his team load the selected bikes on the carrier and they returned to the office building in the Mohrenstrasse.

While they were storing all the bikes in one of the rooms, a Russian officer drove up in an old German Opel. He approached the Pompolit and disappeared with him to a meeting room.

"I am summoned to meet with Marshal Zhukov and his staff. I expect to be back shortly. In the meantime, Alex and Kete will drive with you to the airport," the Kommissar told the boys when he came out of the conference room. He ordered the guards and the driver to accommodate Karl and Harold and followed the Belorussian officer to the waiting car.

"We should stop at one of the U-Bahn entrances. I would like to see the current water level," Karl told Harold as he directed the driver towards the Tempelhof Airport.

"Why do we need to know the height of the water level?" By now Harold was wondering what Karl might have in mind.

"Never mind, you will see when we get there. In the meantime, please let me think. I try to put one and one together and somehow I don't arrive at a two."

Karl watched for the nearest subway entrance and signaled the driver to stop. The inspection of the water level in the U-Bahn station took a little time. It seemed that the water had stopped receding at about two feet above the subway platform. The boys were astonished to see Soviet soldiers guarding a work detail of civilians shoveling something like lime from a truck down on the subway stairs and on top of the floating corpses in the water.

Karl was glad that he was with Alex, who was holding him on his arm as he showed his red star to the guards who immediately signaled the workers to stop shoveling.

The work detail consisted of old men, but also surprisingly of boys in civilian clothing. Karl guessed that they were between 12 and 14 years old. Harold exchanged a few words with them and found out that the older ones were under arrest while the younger ones were under temporary work orders. However, he was unable to ascertain who had issued the orders.

"Are you able to smell a distinctive odor coming from the cadavers?" Karl was asking.

"Odor? I don't know if it is distinctive. I think that is stinks to high heaven."

"Answer the question," insisted Karl, "is the smell from the corpses in the water in a unique way different from the bodies lying in the streets?"

"It seems to me that the odor is somewhat diminished once the body is covered by the chemical. You go down to the water and sniff them if you are so dammed interested in their exclusive smell."

"I am not only interested, I have to know." Karl had hoped to get a positive answer from his friend to confirm his finding. As far as he was concerned, he thought that there was a world of difference in the odor.

He beckoned Alex to follow him down to the platform. The stink rising from the inside of the station was so rank that Alex refused to get all the way down to the water. It was the combination of stale water, feces, urine and the dead bodies that was so awful and repugnant that it stopped him. He let go of Karl, who went all the way down to actually smell the bodies.

"What's the verdict?" asked Harold when Karl returned to the street level.

"I am still not sure, but I saw a rat gnawing on the remains of a body. It's not very pretty down there."

To Harold's amazement, Karl seemed to be in a very optimistic mood now that he had sniffed the subway cadavers. They got back into the transport and headed to the airport.

The orderly conditions of the Tempelhof Airport were another surprise for the boys. They knew that the airport had already been in Soviet hands for a day or two before the inner city of Berlin had surrendered.

The first thing they noted was a total absence of Mongolians. All the Soviet soldiers seemed to have much better footwear and better fitting uniforms than the Tatars.

The runways were relatively free of rubble and several German civilian work details, which also included women, were busy shoveling the remaining debris into trucks. Most of the women were dirty beyond recognition, but they seemed to be unharmed.

While the terminal itself was badly damaged and burnt, there were several three-engine planes spooling up the propellers and getting ready to take off.

Karl had seen enough. He did not want to call attention to his Mongolian guards and waved the driver on to leave the airport area.

When they returned to the office building, they stayed in the car to await the return of the Kommissar. Karl had noticed that Alex was limping more than in the morning and gestured to the Tatar to remove his boots. To his disappointment the somewhat clean feet from yesterday were still very much infected. There was pus oozing out of open cuts and when Karl removed the last layer of rags, he could hear Alex moaning. The makeshift bandages were soaked with blood and fluid and could not be used again.

"Did we bring any more rags from Frau Becker," he asked Harold, who answered by shaking his head. "We cannot bandage his feet with these contaminated rags." Karl remembered the ointment from the submarine commander and wanted to give it a try.

"I remember that Herr Becker had plenty of long-sleeved old underwear in his bedroom closet. If we could risk a fast trip to their apartment, I am sure that we can talk him out of some," Harold suggested.

"Good idea. I will use my own shirt for right now and will replace it whenever I get a chance."

Karl was ready to take off his shirt when he remembered that the instructions on the ointment called for vegetable oil. He knew that they had something like this among their stash in the subway hideout. However, to go there right now was not an option.

While the boys were debating alternatives, a Soviet staff car drove up. Godunov got out and disappeared into the building. A short time later, he sent a runner to the waiting boys and summoned them up to his office. He told them that his orders had been revised. He could stay in Berlin for another week. He did not have to report to Moscow and was ordered to report to the Soviet high command in Simferopol, a major city on the Crimean Peninsula. He hoped that he would be allowed to retire.

The Kommissar was relaxed and in an excellent mood. "I also met with Colonel-General Nikolai Berzarin, who will be the military commander of Berlin. He will also be in charge of the food supply for the civilian population. The political Kommissars as well as the military commanders are to stop all the troops from the plundering currently going on. All the Mongolian forces are to leave the city by tomorrow. There will be also lethal penalties for Mongolians getting caught in the act of rape."

"Well, this will take care of the Tatars, but what about the Belorussians? Will there be equal penalties for the Russian soldiers?" Karl wondered aloud.

"We can only respond to the current situation one thing at a time, Karlchen. Looting and raping is as much a part of war as the actual combat and I am sure that we will see some excesses by the Belorussian forces as well. Now tell me, did you see anything this morning which will assist us in getting my luggage on the way?"

"Yes, I have, as a matter of fact. Due to your change in orders, we will prepare your packages this evening." Karl announced to the surprise of Harold, who had no idea what his friend was talking about.

"But, in the meantime, could you please get me some vegetable oil? We will also need some clean bandages for Alex's feet."

Karl pointed to the filthy foot rags, which were still in the Tatar's hand. Alex had followed the boys and was now sitting on the floor, barefoot. In one hand he had his new boots and in the other hand he was holding the filthy rags.

"Karlchen, we are talking about my luggage and not about your missions of mercy."

"Your luggage is exactly what I am talking about. I need strong help to transport your stuff tonight. Unless you have someone else like Alex in your team, we will need him to be able to walk. I have some medication which might help him."

Godunov was not amused by Karl's reply. "You have not even told me your plans, Karlchen. Don't you think you should tell me something about them before you ask for bandages?"

"You just told me 'one thing at a time'. I'd like to take care of Alex while we are talking so if there is any chance of getting vegetable oil, I can get started." Karl's answer was adamant enough to cause the Kommissar to call for bandages and oil.

"What is this liquid you are mixing with the oil?" Godunov was interested enough to ask.

"I don't know. It is supposed to be a plant extract and to be applied to the infected wound," Answered Karl as he carefully dripped a few drops of the mixture directly into the oozing cuts. "This was the present from the submarine commander," he added when he discerned the questioning look from the Kommissar.

Alex seemed to relish the lotion. It must have been rendering a soothing effect, because he kept on pressing the dressing tightly against the wounds.

"How will you travel to Simferopol," asked Karl when he was done.

"What do you mean?" Godunov did not understand the question.

"Will you be traveling by car, train or air?"

"Air? No, I think that I will be in command of a railroad transport. Simferopol, since last year, is the administration scat overseeing the deportation of Tatars to central Asia. I will be one of the political commissioners."

"Good. I am glad to hear that you will remain an active Kommissar. By any chance, do you have a prominent medical facility in Simferopol?"

Again, Godunov did not understand the question. He got irritated because he thought that Karl's questions concerned Alex, who had left the office.

"Yes, Simferopol is home to the Crimean Medical University. It is the leading medical research facility in the Ukraine. But, if you think that their doctors should treat Alex, you are mistaken. Alex is a Tatar and will be deported with the other Tatars."

"I am not talking about Alex. I am talking about your luggage," Karl replied smiling.

By now, not only Godunov was lost, Harold was just as confused. He had been with Karl all morning and could not think of anything they had seen or learned regarding the safe transport of the Kommissar's boxes.

"I don't see any relationship between the passage of my belongings and the Medical Center. And make your answer short and clear before I run out of patience."

"You want it short, Herr Godunov? We will ship your luggage tomorrow, by air."

Nine

"There is no air connection from Berlin to Simferopol. Please explain." Besides being confused, the Pompolit was getting irritated.

"Of course there are no regular flights to the Ukraine, but tomorrow will be different. There will be a plane leaving Berlin for Simferopol. Your luggage will be on it and it will be guarded by four of your most trusted Tatars. Your belongings will be addressed to the university, but once on the ground in Simferopol, it will not be transferred to the medical facility. Instead it will be buried and watched by your detail until you arrive."

"Karlchen, this is sheer nonsense. Even if you found out about a flight to the Ukraine, it would go to Kiev and not to Simferopol. They would neither accept my luggage nor my four Tatars and finally, you seemed to have forgotten that I couldn't send any goods under my name out of Berlin. Nobody can ship anything unless approved by the military command. Maybe this was possible in the German Wehrmacht or in the SS, but this is the Soviet Army and we run a tight ship controlled by the military central command and by political officers. Think of something else. Shipment by air cannot be done, at least not at the present time." The Pompolit was beginning to fear that he had wasted his time with the boys.

Karl was unconcerned. He was convinced that his plan would work. But he also wanted a favor from the Kommissar and he had to play his hand accordingly. "You are most certainly right on all points, Herr Godunov. But, I did not find out about a flight to the

Ukraine. What I meant to say was that we will initiate a flight to Simferopol. In order to do so, we might need to enlist the help from one of the physicians in the Zoo Flak Tower Bunker. Which brings me to this question; are you able to arrest a specific doctor from the German medical team in the bunker?"

The Kommissar was slow in his answer. He still was not clear about Karl's plan. "If your doctor is a civilian or member of the Wehrmacht I might be able to do so. However, if he is a member or officer of the SS, I am afraid that I am unable to assist you."

"Then let's go. He is a captain in the Wehrmacht and he could be of help to us. If not, I have back up plans." Karl was getting excited. He had worked with captain Felder, who was a surgeon in the bunker, and he thought of him as a trusted friend. He could not wait to get back to the Zoo Flack Tower.

"Alright, Karlchen, but I want you to explain your whole strategy during the drive to the bunker and if I don't approve, I will not arrest anyone."

The enthusiasm from Karl was contagious and the Pompolit was more than eager to find out what Karl had planned. After all, his financial future was at stake. He had mentioned his limitations in regard to arresting an SS officer only to disguise his zeal. In reality he was ready to arrest anyone who could be of some benefit to him.

Besides Karl and Harold, he took his whole team along on the drive to the bunker. "Your turn now, Karlchen, explain; and it better be good."

"Very simple, Herr Godunov. Tonight we will get two coffins and waterproof body bags from a local funeral parlor. Then we will seek two corpses, the stinkier the better, preferably with open wounds from the flooded U-Bahn tracks. We will place your luggage in a separate part in the bottom of one of the coffins and place a waterlogged carcass on top of it. The other coffin will contain the other stiff and some body parts. We will nail and chain the coffins shut and the German doctor will write a statement full of Latin phrases and mumbo jumbo about potential contamination, extreme danger of contagious viruses, fatal epidemics, or anything else he is able to think of. He will finish the document by pleading for analysis of the corpses and then we will plaster the document with embossed seals and SS rubber stamps."

"You will show up tomorrow morning with the coffins at the

Tempelhof Airport and commandeer a plane to fly the corpses to the University Medical Center in Simferopol for examination. Four of your team members will guard the coffins in contamination suits and face masks. They will surrender the coffin without your luggage to the university and bury the other one "to prevent contamination" until you arrive. In your capacity as a political Kommissar, you will release the second coffin for examination immediately after your arrival, but only after you have removed the bottom part with your luggage. Any questions?"

The Pompolit was dazed. In his wildest imagination, he had never considered to ship his bootee under the protection of cadavers. But, it was irrational enough that it might work. "What if your German doctor refuses?"

"You give him the choice between freedom to the west or forced labor camps in the Ural Mountains. I am sure he will cooperate."

"I can arrest him, but I cannot give him freedom."

"You cannot allow that he might be interrogated at a later time by a different political team. If you cannot set him free, you can look the other way when he escapes from your confinement."

"What kind of SS rubber stamps?"

"Medical Proprietary."

"Medical Proprietary? I never heard of them, where do we get them?"

"Give Harold a potato and he will carve you one."

Harold had listened to Karl's explanations and was not overly surprised. It was typical Karl, however, he had never carved anything out of a potato, but if Karl said that he could do it, he better confirm it.

"Yes, I can carve anything out of a potato," he chimed in.

"Never mind the stupid potato. I cannot commandeer a plane without the City Commander's approval."

"Then we will obtain Colonel-General Berzarin's approval."

"And how do you propose we accomplish this?"

"It isn't we who will accomplish this. The stench will take care of it.

I have the infected bandages from Alex and after we swirl them around in the subway water, they will convince anyone. For good measure we might wrap them around some diseased body parts."

"Is there anything you have not thought of," asked the Kommissar, who was warming up to Karl's plan. While he had many questions in the back of his mind, he could not think of a serious objection.

"Yes, without your help, I don't know how to get the doctor out of the bunker." Karl knew that he had the Kommissar hooked. Even if his plot with the air transport should fail, he was determined to help the doctor to evade the looming exportation to the labor camps in the Ural.

It was getting late in the day when the group arrived close to the bunker exit, which was still congested with Russian guards scrutinizing groups of civilians who seemed to be waiting for relatives or friends.

The Pompolit was the first one out of the car with Alex right behind him. It seemed the new dressing numbed his pain. He walked a lot easier.

"What is the name of the doctor we are arresting?" the Kommissar asked over his shoulder.

"Captain Felder," answered Karl, "I can identify him. May I go with you?"

"No, I want to get in and out as fast as possible. I will find him." The Kommissar was now surrounded by his guards and started to walk to the entrance.

"The bunker facility is vast. I know my way around in there and will locate him a lot faster than you could by asking." Karl feared that the Kommissar might arrest the wrong doctor.

"Alright, but you will need to stay right next to Kete." He bellowed a command to his group, which caused them to bunch up into a tight knot.

As the group got close to the heavy steel doors they were greeted by a Russian guard detail. The officer in charge took one look at the Pompolit's uniform and stood aside. His impeccable salute was not even returned by the Kommissar, who behaved as if he was in a deadly hurry. His whole group, with Karl in the center, moved so fast through the entrance that the guard detail just stared in bewilderment at the Tatars.

One of the guards was a little too slow to get out of the way and Alex rewarded him with a blow of his fist, which was bound to damage some ribs. He had a great disdain for the Belorussian soldiers and it made him feel good to have an excuse to act brutal.

Karl directed the team to the staircase, which was filled with Russian soldiers walking up and down, but everybody got out of the way of the Tatars as they hurried up the stairs. When they passed the first floor hallway, the Kommissar noted large boxes being piled up along the walls. He had heard that a portion of the bunker served as a shelter for museum artifacts and that it reportedly also housed several antique coin collections. Apparently, the Belorussians were helping themselves to some valuable loot.

Reaching the hospital level on the third floor, Karl turned left and led the way to the surgery section. The hallway was crammed full with wounded soldiers resting on stretchers. There was obviously some kind of order in their arrangement, but it was anyone's guess if they were recuperating or waiting their turn for surgery.

The German sergeant standing guard at the door to the operating room blocked their way and Karl asked him if Dr. Felder was on duty.

The sergeant stared at Karl and the strange Mongolian faces and started to stutter, "I remember you. Yes, Dr. Felder is on duty but you can't go in. We are treating a high ranking Russian officer."

This response did not trigger any hesitation on the Kommissar's part. He just pushed the guard to the side and the first Tatar in front of the detail leaned on him while the remainder of the group entered the operating room. For a moment they were stunned, as they had never seen such bright lights. There were a number of doctors and orderlies working on several operating tables.

Dr. Felder had apparently just finished a surgery. He was applying the final stitches to a chest wound when Karl pointed him out to the Kommissar.

Godunov did not waste a second. "Are you done with this patient, Dr. Felder?"

"Yes, I am," came the answer as the doctor lifted his head to see who had addressed him.

"Good, then we are not interrupting anything. You need to come with me." The Kommissar motioned to two men of his detail who just lifted the doctor off the floor and basically carried him out the doors.

Dr. Felder did not object to being hustled out of the room and down the stairs. He had been operating for the past 18 hours with hardly anything to eat and to top it off, just two hours ago he had been informed that he was part of a prison transport destined to a labor camp in Russia. His secret hope of possibly obtaining freedom as a reward for his superb surgery skills vanished as he stumbled along between the two Tatars.

He also feared that one of the Russian officers he had performed surgery on had died and that this was the reason for his arrest. He had done his best, but he knew, given the situation, his best might not have been good enough. He did not look up and therefore did not see Karl, who was rushing towards a clerk's office, all the time being escorted by Kete.

The whole extradition did not last more than 15 minutes and it would have been even faster had it not been for Alex, who slowed down on the way out in the hope that someone would challenge the team. His feet felt better than they had in a long time and he was eager to plant them into somebody's behind.

But the GPU emblem on the Pompolit's cap and the grim faces of the Tatars intimidated everyone they met. Karl marveled again at the sheer fright the Kommissar's team caused.

He had seen fear in the faces of the Wehrmacht officers when they encountered SS commandos, but Karl thought that that was minor compared to what he witnessed now. Nobody, but nobody looked up and dared to meet the eyes of the Pompolit. It seemed that the emblem alone was a symbol of terror.

Karl and Kete caught up with the group as they were still walking down the stairs. Harold had waited with the driver in the car and Godunov motioned to him and Karl to sit in front while he took a seat across from the prisoner.

"Dr. Felder, I assume that you don't have your service book on you, but if you do, may I see it please?"

The doctor looked up, surprised by the almost accent-free, flawless German of the Kommissar. He had thought a Russian officer had arrested him, but now his body slumped even more when he recognized that he was in the hands of a political officer.

"I always carry my service book with me," he replied, and noticed to his amazement that he was not handcuffed. He was sitting between two enormous Mongols, who did not seem to look at him. Carefully, he reached into his back pocket and handed his ID's to the Pompolit, who took his time reading it.

When he was done, he handed it back to the doctor and gave

some orders to the Tatars who bunched up towards the front of the truck blocking the view to the driver's compartment.

"Please relax, Dr. Felder. I understand that the hospital staff of the bunker will leave for Russia within a few days. We will make sure that you will join them before their departure. In the meantime, we would like to avail ourselves of your medical expertise." Godunov felt sorry for the obviously undernourished physician. He estimated his age to be in the late forties and the matted gray hair indicated that he must have been working for hours without any rest.

"Then I take it that I am not under arrest," the doctor asked.

"You are a captain of the Wehrmacht and as such, you are a prisoner of war, Dr. Felder. However, at the present time, please consider yourself to be a guest of the Soviet NKVD."

"May I ask if you feed your guests, Herr Kommissar?" Due to the polite answers of Godunov, the doctor felt safe to inquire.

"You must be very hungry or a brave man, Dr. Felder. Yes, we will feed you and after a short interview you will be able to rest."

It was past 7:00 PM and the Kommissar was anxious to discuss with Karl the pertinent details of the plan. Upon the arrival at the office building he had Dr. Felder escorted to one of the rooms where he was left alone. He ordered some food, not only for the prisoner, but also for the boys and for himself. It was a fast meal and the Pompolit was ready to press on.

"Karlchen, now what? Your Dr. Felder seems to be an intelligent man and I am not too sure that that he will be as cooperative as you hope him to be."

"This should take no time at all. Please let me talk to Dr. Felder and you will see."

"Be my guest, Karlchen. I wish you luck."

"Do I have your word that you will look the other way in case the doctor disappears?" Karl wanted to be sure before he went to see the captain.

"Hold on, Karlchen. How do you suggest that he could possibly disappear? I am not known for losing prisoners."

"Alright, then he will not disappear when he is in your facility. I will need him...no; I don't need him...I want him to go with me when I get the corpses from the subway tunnel. He might just want to stay down there."

"No good, Karlchen. You told me that you need some heavy

lifting in the U-Bahn. This means that you need Alex and Kete to go with you. Believe me, nobody escapes these two guards."

"Harold is stronger than I am, he can help me do the lifting."

"Still no good, Karlchen. Harold is not even close to the manpower you need. Remember you attended to Alex's feet in order to have him go with you."

Karl looked at the eyes of the Kommissar. He wanted to determine if Godunov was backing out or if he simply wanted him to come up with a better plan. He detected an encouraging twinkle in his eyes and understood. The Pompolit just wanted an answer to a tricky situation to allow him complete deniability.

"Well, I also need caskets, which I intend to get from the 'Spich Funeral Parlor' on the Ludwigkirchplatz. There is an underground passageway from the Kirche (church) to the Duesseldorfer Strasse. The doctor might just know about it and vanish . . ."

"Better, Karlchen, much better. I doubt that the Mongols have ever seen decorative coffins. Besides, they are superstitious and would never look into a casket. Suppose your doctor friend is sleepy and just wanted to take a rest?" The Pompolit's eyes almost sparkled. "Of course, he is only entitled to a rest after he writes the documentation we need."

"Then it's settled. Let's get started." Karl took the various forms and rubber stamps he had seized when he paid the clerk's office a visit while the doctor had been detained.

He had experienced that even under the orderly German system, an official looking form with a lot of rubber stamps and unreadable signatures attached to it was never challenged. He was betting that the Soviet system was not any different.

Before he waived at Harold to join him, he picked up the stinking bandages from Alex, which were outside the door. They were still all bundled up in newspaper wrappings untouched, and he handed the wad to Harold.

So far he had been right. The awful smell deterred everybody.

While the Pompolit went to see his team and issue orders to "borrow" a truck, the boys walked to the room where Dr. Felder was detained.

Ten

"Good evening Dr. Felder." Karl greeted the surprised doctor as he entered the room.

"Karl, how did you get here? Are you all right? I hope that you are not part of our transport group to the Ural." Dr. Felder got up and hugged Karl, then looked at Harold.

"Do I know you?" he asked.

"Yes, my name is Harold. I am a friend of Karl. I am pleased to see you again." He extended his hand to the physician who gave him a firm handshake.

"Yes, I remember, you were with Karl when he needed a vehicle to requisition food from a storage facility. Well, this is most certainly a surprise. I am glad to see you both well and unharmed."

While the boys pulled up some chairs to sit down, Doctor Felder sniffed the smell coming from Harold who had dropped the paper package next to the door.

"This is some rank odor, almost indefinable, but it is close to rotten flesh." He sniffed some more, this time in the direction of Karl. "Whatever it is, it does not originate from either one of you. It seems to come from the package on the floor. Be careful. You might get infected."

"Really, Dr. Felder? This is actually the reason we are here. The political Kommissar, Godunov, has us detained to claim some body parts from the flooded U-Bahn tunnels. He wanted us to name a German medical expert and we thought of you. The Soviets have field doctors, of course, but they are not specialists of diseases. They are apparently afraid of an outbreak of some kind of a contagious epidemic. The city's fresh water system has been polluted with the broken sewer system. When we inspected the Uhlandstrasse Subway Station, we saw many floating cadavers. Some sanitary work commandos were shoveling lime, or something like it, on the corpses." Karl stopped his narrative to wait and see what the doctor had to say. The reaction was much more favorable than he had hoped for.

"Are you out of your mind carrying infectious body parts with you?" He asked in revulsion. "Do you have any idea how fast you can be contaminated? And what do you want from me? I am not an expert on epidemics, I am a surgeon, but I can tell you this much: **You are playing with fire. Get rid of that thing!**"

The doctor's face showed not exactly fear, but real serious concern. Harold started to think that Karl's plan might get out of hand. He got up and kicked the package out the door. When he wanted to close the door again, he noticed the Kommissar, who had been listening to their conversation. His face mirrored his satisfaction. Harold got back to the table and Karl started in again.

"We are just as worried as you are, maybe even more so. We really don't understand the possible consequences. But here is the strange thing, while the Russians are not exactly sure what they might have on their hands, they want a second medical opinion from a German expert. The reason I thought of you was due to the fact that they don't really want a drawn out dissertation. They already submitted a request for evaluation to a Russian Medical University, which will accompany an air shipment of corpses. What they want is a strong serious German request for cooperation."

Dr. Felder shook his head. "There is something not right with what you tell me, Karl. You don't need an air shipment of whole corpses to a university. The bundle you kicked out the door is already more than enough to analyze the body tissue."

Karl was not deterred. "With all due respect, Dr. Felder, you might be wrong. On the other hand, I might be wrong too. For all I know the Russians might only ship samples, but if you want me to, I can show you the floating cadavers and you can judge for yourself.

"No need to do this Karl. I know when I am being played. Do you expect me to believe your story?"

"No, I expect you to write a forceful appeal for assistance. You know that the situation warrants it. And in anticipation of your cooperation, I brought you the official German letterheads and various rubber stamps to authenticate your request."

Karl placed the blank documents in front of the doctor. While his voice was strong and demanding to accommodate the listening Kommissar, his eyes were pleading with Dr. Felder.

He succeeded.

"I don't know what is in it for you, Karl, but there is nothing unethical in asking for help. I will be happy to write a petition for assistance. Is there a specific university you want me to address?"

"Yes, please address it to the medical staff of the Georgievsky University in Simferopol."

"I thought that you might have an answer for that," the doctor muttered under his breath, "I will keep it simple, this way it might be more forceful." He selected the most imposing letterhead with the embossed German eagle and Swastika, and wrote in a strong handwriting:

To the attention of the medical staff of the Georgievsky University:

Due to circumstances beyond our control, we are faced with a possible outbreak of an epidemic. We request herewith your immediate cooperation in identifying the threat. Various body samples are herewith provided.

He dated the document and was ready to sign it when Harold interrupted, "Please, sign with your left hand."

The doctor complied, but looked confused at his crooked signature. "Do you care to explain, Karl?"

"It's not complicated, Dr. Felder. We, Harold and I, were given the task to recover some of the bloated corpses from the flooded subway system. Then the fear of a plague set in and we recommended you to the Kommissar to serve his need. We are also hoping to prevent you from being shipped off to a forced labor camp. While the Kommissar is busy with his other work, he entrusted me to obtain from you the recommendation. We wanted you to sign with your left hand so that your signature becomes illegible. In addition, we will plaster some rubber stamps on it. Nobody will be able to trace this document back to you."

Dr. Felder scratched his head. Now he was truly mixed up. First he was detained to be a medical expert and now he was supposed to be untraceable. He looked really uncomfortable.

"If I am undetectable, what will happen next?"

"First a question," Karl had another idea. "Do you speak English? And if you do, can you write us a likewise request, addressed to the medical team of the American High Command?"

"I can try. I took English years ago and never had any real opportunity to use it."

Harold handed the doctor another blank document and after Dr. Felder labored to construct the sentences, he used his left hand again to sign it.

"This is great!" announced Harold after he read it. Just like the doctor, he had no idea why Karl wanted the request repeated in English.

"Now what?" Felder was sure that he had not heard it all. But he never expected what Karl told him next.

"Now we drive to a Bestattungsinstitut (funeral parlor), where you will hide in a casket."

"What?" spluttered Felder.

"Well, it is not exactly my idea, but it will work. If you don't like the idea to stay in the coffin, I will give you an address to hide at and obtain civilian clothing. Within a day or so, the western allies will be entering the city. It will be your choice to turn yourself in or to try to reach your home town."

"Karl, I don't know what to say. What about the Pompolit?"

"He will be busy with other things. I will pick you up in a moment."

Harold was already hectically stamping the two documents, successfully distorting the signatures. Karl took the papers and ran behind Godunov, who had heard enough and was returning to his office. Karl entered right behind him.

"You will need a larger vehicle than our transporter, right?"

Karl nodded his answer as he spread the documents in front of the Kommissar. "Satisfied?"

"Yes, very nicely done, Karlchen. Why do we need the English request?"

"We don't need it. But it might come in helpful when you request authorization to commandeer a plane to Simferopol."

The blank gaze in the eyes of the Kommissar indicated that he was still clueless.

"Yes, well, I will explain when the time comes. We are ready to roll whenever you are." Karl wanted to get Dr. Felder out of the building.

It was not that he did not trust the word of Godunov, but experience had been a good teacher. He had learned that unless you were in absolute control, you could never be sure about anything.

Alex entered the room. He did not limp anymore. His eyes wandered thankfully to Karl as he reported to the Kommissar.

"We are in luck," announced Godunov, "Kete found a truck. And, if you can believe Alex, the driver must have had a heart attack or something similar, just when Kete arrived at the scene."

"This happens a lot when nobody is around to help," Karl felt to agree. "Are you coming with us to the funeral parlor?" he wanted to know.

"No, you have your own special mission to take care of. But I will go with you when you are ready to pick up my luggage."

"We need to pick up your luggage before we are able to go fishing," Karl reminded him, "so we will be back as soon as we obtain the coffins."

The Kommissar agreed and turned to Alex to give him instructions. Karl had the feeling that Alex would go with him anyplace he wished, instructions or not.

While the Kommissar stayed in the office and out of sight, Karl went down the hallway to pick up Harold and Dr. Felder. All the while, Alex followed him like a puppy dog. Granted, he was a huge puppy dog, but Karl felt safer than he had in a long time.

On the way down to the street, the doctor was flanked by a Tatar on each side. After they placed him in the truck, Kete took a place next to him and Karl started to give the driver instructions on how to find the funeral parlor.

The trip from the Mohrenstrasse, in the center of the city, to the Spich funeral parlor at the Ludwigkirchplatz, (St. Ludwig's church) took almost 30 minutes. It was not really that far but while the larger streets were being rapidly cleared, they were also congested. Tatars and prisoner transports were leaving the city and the Belorussians moved in. Most of the side streets were still filled with rubble and Karl, trying to find the most direct route, had to turn around numerous times.

Finally Harold had enough, "You might find your way in the U-Bahn tunnels, but above ground you are useless."

Karl did not object; he knew that Harold was right. Within

minutes of Harold taking over they pulled up at the church plaza and parked in front of the wide doors leading to the Spich Bestattungsinstitut. By some kind of a miracle the building was hardly damaged.

It was not a real institute by any means, but the sign looked impressive. Georg Spich was the name of the proprietor and the center letter in the name Spich was in the form of a candle with a little flame on the top. Karl knew the place as well as the surrounding area. A few years back, he had lived with his parents right next door. He even thought that he remembered the name of the little daughter of Georg. 'Brigitte' or something similar to it.

He cleared the memories from his mind as he tried to enter the showroom. But, like all the storefronts in Berlin, if it was not destroyed it was boarded up. Alex and Kete were ready to dismantle the entrance, but Karl knew a way through the back courtyard and within minutes they were in the storage facility of the funeral parlor. An old invalid was apparently appointed to be a caretaker and as he opened the doors for Karl, he took two steps back when he saw the two Mongols next to him.

"I need two of your most inexpensive coffins. Simple wooden boxes like the ones over there will do." Karl pointed to a small stack of wooden boxes. Only the markings of a cross on top and outlines of candles at the sides, besides some metal handles, indicated that these were not storage boxes but caskets.

The old man said nothing and just gawked at the Tatars.

"We also need something like waterproof bags to transport some water-soaked corpses."

Still no answer.

"Don't you understand me, or are you unable to talk?"

"It is a sign of the times that stores are getting looted, but stealing caskets is new to me." The graybeard finally answered.

"Yes, well, it is new to me too. I also need to borrow an additional casket. It will not be damaged. I have a friend who needs to rest for a few hours."

"Whom do you wish to hide?" The eyes of the old man started to glitter. "If it is an SS general, I'll be happy to nail the coffin shut while he is resting." Obviously the old guy was a touch unhinged. Karl could not picture an SS general walking free next to the Tatars.

"No, just show us what you have. What I really could use would

84

be a deeper coffin. The bloated bodies need a lot of room." Karl had never really seen an empty coffin and he had no idea about various depths, or if they were even available. But he was slowly running out of patience.

The electric power was out. The flickering candles shedding limited light, the coffins, and the old-timer wanting to get rid of an SS general were giving him the creeps.

"Do you have any waterproof bags or not?"

"We have some newly fangled body bags. I don't know if they are waterproof. We needed to have some on hand in case of a chemical attack." He went to a shelf and showed Karl some weighty rubberized bags. They featured large covered zippers. Karl was elated. This was exactly what he wanted and he hoped that they were watertight.

He handed three of them to Kete who took them to the truck.

When he returned, he was followed by Dr. Felder and Harold. The driver must have remained in the vehicle. While Karl inspected the few more elaborate caskets in the storage room, Harold pointed to a few dirty and old pine boxes.

"This is what we need", he declared. "All we have to do is slap some stain on them and then dunk them in the subway water. The old wood will absorb the goo and they will look awful, plus they will stink for years to come."

He dragged two of the lightweight boxes closer to the exit.

Alex and Kete took this as a signal and lifted them up to carry them out. They did not like the surroundings any more than Karl and wanted to get away from the gloomy place.

"You are welcome to the junk caskets. You don't have to pay me a penny, but a receipt would be nice." The old-timer held the door open for the group to leave and handed Karl some papers to sign.

"This reminds me," said Karl, "do you have by any chance some dark brown stain?"

The graybeard walked to the rear of the room and Karl shook hands with Dr. Felder, "Good luck, Doctor. Stay hidden until the Americans or the British are in Berlin."

The doctor was unable to say anything. He was choking on his emotions. The last few hours had been a roller coaster between despair and hope. He pressed the hands of Karl as hard as he could.

"Let's go, Karl." Harold was waiting at the door, holding a small pail in his hand. Apparently it was the stain Karl had asked for. The boys were a bit dumbfounded when they realized that neither Alex nor Kete made any attempt to enter the funeral parlor again.

Karl had anticipated that they would at least initiate a search for the doctor, but the Mongols, with their stoic Asian faces, were patiently waiting on the curb. Alex helped Karl to climb in the back of the high truck bed where he sat down on one of the caskets. Kete and Alex took a seat on the other coffin, and Harold joined the driver again in the front.

"We are ready to load your luggage. We should start as soon as possible to gain some time to prepare the cargo," Karl informed the Kommissar when he returned to the office.

"Karlchen, tell me your inner fears. What could go wrong with your plan?"

"My inner fears? I have no inner fears. Our plan is solid. As for what could go wrong? Well, for one thing, the plane could crash. For another, your guards might not be as loyal as you think and they might have a change of heart. Should the first event happen, we could easily prepare another shipment. That is if you could secure some more luggage. Should the second event take place, well, at this time I have no answer."

Karl knew that the Pompolit was not second-guessing his team. He just needed some reassurance that Karl had thought of every eventuality. For Karl however, it had come down to the simple challenge of sufficiently confusing all the participants, including the Soviet Kommander of Berlin, to allow the transport.

He had survived tougher assignments and started to enjoy the thought of a possible meeting with Colonel-General Nikolai Berzarin. He had no doubt that the general was not to be underestimated. But, he was betting on the fact that he knew exactly what he wanted, while the General had no idea what was coming his way.

Eleven

"I don't want Kete or Alex to know the layout or even to enter the hideout," Godunov was resolute in his request. "We might need to use it again." The boys did not answer. They were busy discussing the most unnoticeable manner to get the luggage into the truck.

It was shortly before midnight when the truck approached the intersection of the Uhland Strasse and the Kurfuerstendam. They passed the main entrance to the U-Bahn station and Karl noted that the sanitation detail had left a small hill of lime behind, but the guards were gone. Must be that they trusted the smell to keep any looting visitors away. Karl found it strange that the Mongolian women had no reservations when it came to cutting the throats of the wounded and then robbing the bodies of their paltry belongings. However, to go down to the subway tunnels and scavenge the water corpses seemed to have never occurred to them. It must be the stench he concluded.

"There are no soldiers or gangs in this area. I think they are all plundering up and down the Kurfuerstendam," said Harold as their wagon turned the corner on the intersection and entered the deserted courtyard of their hideout. He turned to Karl, "Let's have Alex watch from one side of the yard and Kete from the other side while the Kommissar and I hand you the boxes to load in the truck."

"After we make a dry run," Karl agreed. He did not like the idea of parking the truck on top of their sanctuary but since there was nobody in sight, the simplest way was also the fastest.

The transfer of the boxes went so fast and smooth that Karl

dared to stay a moment longer. "Give me some of the canned goods and some more cigarettes," he whispered to Harold as he heaved the last carton in the truck. The Kommissar, who had been the one down in the vent shaft, must have anticipated the request because he had gathered some of the boys' remaining food supplies in one of the blankets and handed them up to Harold.

"Go, go, go," he urged the driver as he lifted himself up on the truck bed. The Mongol understood and rumbling across the debris, he drove a circle around the courtyard to pick up the two guards.

"What next?" coughed Godunov, who must have gotten some of the cement dust in his air pipes.

"Back to the subway entrance to pick up the bodies." Karl was excited about their smooth operation and wanted to continue.

They parked the truck next to the mound of lime dust and as the Kommissar and the driver stayed in the vehicle, the rest of the team went down the main subway station entrance. Neither Kete nor Alex had any inkling of their next job and did not like the odor coming up from the platform.

When Karl pushed a few of the floating bodies aside to step into the water, the Tatars backed off. If anything, the stench had gotten worse and Kete turned to walk back up the stairs.

"Come on Harold, we need to find some corpses who have not been touched by the lime." Karl was now up over his knees in the awful smell, but he had reached the platform and his dynamo light was illuminating a cadaver dressed in a German Wehrmacht uniform. "I got a good one!" He shouted at Harold, who was still standing next to Alex, hoping that he did not need to follow his friend.

"What do you consider a good one? As long as they are not covered by the lime anyone should do."

Harold bent down to catch the floating soldier Karl was pushing in his direction. He motioned to Alex to give him a hand and it looked as if both of them were afraid to lift up the body. It seemed to Karl that they were about to drag the dead soldier over the lime-covered steps.

"Lift, you dummies. Wait, I'll give you a hand." He splashed through the goo, pulling behind him an open suitcase filled with all kinds of clothing, scaring a few rats that were feasting in the dark.

Kete, who had been standing further up the stairs, came running down again when he saw what his partner was trying to do.

While the two Tatars carried the body, Harold helped Karl with the valise. The stench coming from the trunk was worse than the smell from the bodies. Harold had some serious convulsions and Karl directed his puke to land on the clothing in the suitcase.

"Are you getting back in again to get another one?" Godunov gazed at the corpse and tried to stay clear of the mess in the truck. Karl could see that the Kommissar was exerting great effort to keep his stomach from heaving.

"No, Herr Godunov, but we need to make a small change in our plan. I underestimated the amount of your luggage. Let's drive to a hallway were we can sort everything out." Karl directed the driver to take a turn at the Lietzenburger Strasse, where he knew of old apartment buildings with large hallways, but it turned out that none of them were useable to hide the truck.

"Where to? Keep in mind that you have to cleanup and get out of your shoes." Harold was sitting in the front with the Kommissar and could not understand how Karl could stand his own smell. "Can we get any clothing for Karl from your supply wagons?" He turned to ask the Kommissar.

The Pompolit shook his head. "No, we should have thought of this before Karl entered the water. But I agree we need to get him cleaned up." Godunov could not think of a fast solution and he also feared for his bootie, which was pretty much exposed in the back of the truck.

"Direct the driver back to the St. Ludwig's Church." Karl thought of a possible solution. "We are only a few blocks away."

He remembered that Frau Becker had told him that the Catholic Church had conducted massive drives for clothing donations. However, according to her report, none of the donations had ever been distributed. She had told him that the church had been uncooperative in any of the school officials' attempts to obtain some warm winter clothing for needy school children. Karl had no way of knowing if this was the truth and he was not about to ransack the residence of the pastor, which was next to Spich's funeral parlor, but he had an idea. He wanted to search the 'Sacristy' of the church, where the altar boys changed their clothing before and after the services. If nothing else, he might be able to find some shirts to clean himself.

The truck stopped right in front of the main entrance of the church and Karl jumped out, followed by the two Tatars who were relieved to breathe some clean air. The church was only partially damaged and to Karl's disappointment, the damage had occurred where the Sacristy had been located. He was ready to turn around when saw a huge bin loaded with assorted clothing. It was standing in the small vestibule between the side entrance of the church and the large wooden doors leading to the main section. He started to rummage through the container and in no time at all he had a bundle of clean clothing for himself, including several pairs of knee socks. He even found a nice pair of leather shoes.

Alex, who had followed him into the vestibule, could not find anything in his size. Disappointed, he went out again and ran into Kete, who had used the time to investigate the ruins of the Sacristy. He had been searching for some golden vessels or other valuable accoutrements, but instead he found the decorative clothing of the altar boys. They were right next to the closet containing the ornate stoles and regalia of the pastor. Even the Kommissar looked in awe at the trappings Kete found.

In the limited light of the night sky, Kete looked like a mixture between the pope and a clown as he handed some of his plunder to Alex, who proceeded to crown himself with a tall pointed cap.

In the meantime, Karl found a container with fresh-smelling water. He took off his contaminated socks and shoes and started to wash and clean himself. Harold, who had been an altar boy when he was 10 years old, was aghast. "Are you out of your mind? You cannot wash yourself with holy water!"

"Why not? It cleans and now I smell better than ever before. Can you drink this stuff?"

Harold was nearly in shock. He wished that it were not true what he was witnessing. "No, you can do none of this. This is holy water!"

"Fine. I understand that it is holy. But if you cannot drink it or wash yourself with it, what is it good for?" Karl was done cleaning himself and did not expect an answer.

"The pastor is allowed to sprinkle some of it on your head," Harold informed him.

Karl was happy that the new shoes fit him perfectly, but nevertheless, he was washing down his old pair to take along. He smiled at his friend. "Oh, good. Now I know that I have done nothing wrong, but you have to agree that a few sprinkles would not have helped me." He looked around and was satisfied with their present location. The church plaza did not invite any roaming soldiers and was very much suited for the team to stay unnoticed for a little while.

"This will not work," said Karl when he scaled the rear of the truck and saw that the Kommissar was anxiously trying to fit his three boxes into one of the coffins.

"It would work if you had selected larger caskets," answered Godunov.

"No, you have to get rid of the square cartons. Their shapes don't fit the contour of the coffin." Karl handed one of the body bags to the Kommissar. "Here, place this in the casket and empty your boxes into it and zip it up." He skipped back out of the truck, "We won't be looking. Call us when you are done." He waited next to Harold, who was annoyed that the Tatars were in fact wearing some of the ornate church garments.

"Can't you do anything about that?" He wanted to know from Karl, who did not seem bothered at all.

Karl had nothing to say. He was thankful for the protection the two Mongols provided and their preference of clothing was not on his mind.

"I am done," the Kommissar joined the boys. He had heard Harold's question. "Don't worry about the guards, Harold. I will tell them to leave the attires behind when we leave this place."

He turned to call the Mongols to give the boys a hand with the packaging. Karl's plan was so simple that the guards understood at once.

He gestured to relieve the body of the German soldier of his heavy water-soaked uniform, which he wanted placed on the bottom of the second casket. On top of it came the body itself, which was positioned in one of the remaining body bags. He decided to leave one arm dangling out of it. This way it looked more like a rush job. Before he closed the lid, he filled the remaining open area around the arm with some of the evil-smelling clothing from the suitcase.

The body bag with the loot from the Pompolit almost filled the first coffin and he placed the third carrier bag with the remainder of the rags carefully on top to fully hide the sack below it. This time he was careful to zip the bag all the way shut.

Before he finally closed the lid, he looked around the truck bed and found the bundle of Alex's bandages. He removed the papers, which were holding it together, and scattered the putrid rags over the top.

Satisfied with the results, he helped Harold to screw the lids shut. This was the easiest part of the whole procedure. Both lids of the caskets featured bolts with a simple housing imbedded in the bottom part of the coffin.

"It would help if we had some chains to lock around the caskets. They would be more for looks than any practical purpose." Karl looked at the Kommissar, who shrugged his shoulders.

"Why don't we get some bicycle chains from the pile on the Schlesischen Bahnhof," Harold inquired, "They could serve to make the coffins look mysterious."

"How will you fasten them around the caskets?" Karl liked Harold's input, but was unsure about the implementation.

"We don't fasten them around; we just nail them across the top. We should be able to find some rusty nails in all this rubble around us."

The Kommissar agreed. "I don't know about chains, but I am sure that I can get us some nails." He ordered the driver to follow Harold's instructions to the railroad station.

The pile of old bicycles, which was quite massive the previous morning, was now reduced to some worthless pieces of scrap, but there were still some chains attached. Instead of removing the chains from the mounts, Kete threw the frames in the back of the truck. The driver barely stopped, and Kete had to run to get back in again.

By the time they reached their home base at the Mohren Strasse, it was very early in the morning. For the last two hours there had been a fine drizzle of rain, which helped significantly to reduce the battle dust still lingering around some of the smoldering ruins. Everyone was exhausted and tired, but there was no time to rest if they wanted to get the caskets on their way.

"It is now your turn to select the four Tatars to guard your luggage during the flight and when they arrive in Simferopol," Karl suggested. "We should also drive to the Zoo Bunker to 'borrow' some gas masks, contamination resistant gear and clothing to make your group look convincing for this mission."

"Let's first drive to the bunker to requisition the outfits," Godunov agreed, and summoned the remainder of his team to guard the truck with the coffins. He left Kete in charge and ordered his regular driver to drive him and the boys in his troop carrier once more to the Flack Tower. Karl seized an empty bucket. Alex was not about to leave his side and after a fast exchange of words with the Pompolit, he was allowed to join.

As soon as their vehicle approached the Belorussian guards at the bunker entrance, the Pompolit pulled rank and detained some soldiers to accompany him to the storage facility located on the sub-floor of the fortification. Harold was leading the way. He had been there before and knew where he was going. When they opened one of the doors in the far end of the hallway, Harold was relieved to see that it was packed with gas masks, yellow striped armbands, rubber boots and other paraphernalia.

The Kommissar wasted no time making specific selections. Instead, he pointed to the various cartons with the equipment and ordered the soldiers to carry the gear to his truck. Within a few minutes of their arrival, they were on the way again and Karl insisted that they stop at the subway station to fill the bucket. He wanted the foul-smelling water to pour over the caskets later.

The German sanitation detail was shoveling yet again more lime, not only over the floating bodies, but it almost looked like they were sealing the entrance. When Karl approached the stairs, the sanitation workers attempted to hold him back. If it had not been for Alex, they would have succeeded.

The Tatar grunted just once and when the Russian officer guarding the detail did not respond, Alex took the pail from Karl and pushed the Russian down the stairs and almost into the floating mess. He was eager for the Russian to dare him, but one look at the threatening figure of the Mongol made the officer reconsider. He stepped back to allow Alex to fill his bucket with the evil fluid.

It appeared that Alex was not satisfied. After he carefully transported the bucket back up the stairs, he seemed to slide and the officer was unfortunate enough to stand in the wrong place at the wrong time.

The Pompolit was almost choking to restrain himself from laughing. He got out of the car and excused Alex's clumsy behavior to the drenched Russian officer who was too shocked to say anything.

The Pompolit explained later on to the boys that he promised the Russian to level appropriate penalties against the Tatar. Alex apparently excused himself, but it seemed to the boys that he just waited for an excuse to slip once more. However, on his second attempt he was able to get the full pail into the truck.

"How do the Mongolians really get along with the Belorussians," Karl dared to ask the Kommissar.

"They don't," answered Godunov, "I am afraid that by the time the Mongolians are fully replaced by the Belorussians, we will have a few serious confrontations between them. The Mongolians fulfilled their service as the initial shock troops and are now expendable."

The Kommissar gave the signal to move on. During the drive back to their office building, the truck had to stop several times to let long, almost endless lines of POW's pass and the boys noted that even uniforms of railroad workers, street car attendants and postal workers were among them. Apparently anyone in any kind of uniform was destined to the labor camps in Russia.

"Do you maintain any records of the captives you are deporting?" Karl was pushing his luck, but he was thinking of his father, who had to be one of the countless prisoners. He was hoping for some reassuring answer.

"What for," asked the Pompolit, "None of them will return! It is payback time for the crimes your troops committed when they invaded our country."

Twelve

Karl was wrestling with an answer. Since he could not think of one, he kept his mouth shut. Harold, however, thought that this might be an opportunity to ask a question regarding his parents.

"Herr Godunov, do you know anything about the civil servants evacuated from Berlin before your forces completed the circle around the city?"

"I heard that our troops intercepted a base camp of high ranking German civilian executives and scientists by Brandenburg" (small town west of Berlin), answered the Pompolit. "As far as I know, they have been classified as war criminals and are still detained there, except for the scientists, who have already been shipped to Moscow for interrogation and evaluation." He looked first at Harold and then at Karl. "I want to talk about your parents and also about your future, but now is not the right time to do this. After we get my shipment on the way, you might wish to remind me."

They stopped next to the truck at the office building and the Kommissar ordered a runner to bring them something to eat and also to look for some nails. The breakfast came fast and consisted of dark, moist bread, tea and dried fish. While Harold risked an upset stomach and tried a fish, Karl just settled for the bread. He hoped later to get a dish full of vegetable soup, as this was the daily fare and he had gotten used to it.

The boys ate by themselves as the Kommissar was busy talking to the men of his detail. After a while, four of them separated from the group and Karl could see that they were trying to fit the gas masks over their heads. He could also see that they would never fit. The gas masks they had confiscated from the bunker were much too small for the wide Mongolian faces.

"Tell them that the masks don't need to be airtight. If the smell in the plane gets too rank, they can simply breathe through the mouthpiece and the filter. In the meantime, they can carry the masks on their belts," Harold suggested to the Pompolit when he came back for another cup of tea. He had a big piece of rock candy in his mouth, which he dropped in his hand when he answered.

"You might be right. However, I wanted them to have a deadly fear of the contaminated bodies. Right now, they think that we have two of them. One in each casket."

Karl listened and then asked, "How far can you really trust them and do they know what else is in the second coffin?"

"I can trust them here when they are with me, but no, once they are in Simferopol they will not stay around." He looked over to his group of guards and added, "I did not tell them about my luggage. Only Kete, Alex and the driver know what we did last night."

"Then one of the three will have to fly with the goods to make sure that the correct casket gets buried and not surrendered to the University. He will also have to return to tell you where the other coffin has been buried," Harold added his opinions.

"This sounded so simple when you first suggested the plane ride, Karlchen, but now it gets really complicated." Godunov voiced his concern.

"The air transport is not complicated. You are only worried because you are unable to trust your men as much as you had first told me. Can't you bribe them?" Karl sounded undisturbed, he had a backup plan, but he could also see that Harold was chomping on his bits to take the lead.

"You don't know the true nature of the Tatars, Karlchen. Once they realize that they are being bribed they want it all."

"That's it!" Harold was too excited to hold back. "You have no problem. Just give them all they want," he beamed. "Of course, you have to change your selection of men."

"What?" The Pompolit was muddled. He thought for a moment that he had understood what Harold was saying, but the last part confused him. He looked at Karl for some kind of explanation. He did not have to wait as Karl was used to Harold's ability to look at all things from opposite sides.

"Herr Godunov, what Harold is saying is to simply turn the greed of your men to your advantage."

"And?" urged the Kommissar.

"You told us that an old bicycle means a fortune to your Tatars. So, you select the least trustworthy ones and I will instill the fear of God into them by letting them take a peek and smell of the rotting body."

Harold looked at the Pompolit to see if Karl made contact. Both boys respected the intelligence officer and did not want to say the obvious. But, no contact.

"Then you promise them each, not one, but two bicycles as a reward to guard and accompany the coffins to the University. The rest will unfold by itself. Your men will surrender one coffin to the University and bury the other one and then disappear like hell to get their bikes to safety and also to get away from the corpses."

Contact. The eyes of the Pompolit lit up like a roman candle. "Kete!" He conferred with his aide for a moment and turned back to the boys, "Get the caskets finalized. I will try to reach General Berzarin."

"Ka...Ka!" Alex appeared from the building. Walking barefoot he held his boots in one hand and in the other one he had a can of nails, which he handed to Harold.

Ever since Karl had attended to Alex's feet, the Tatar had taken to calling Karl by his name. But, all he was able to say was "Ka", which was fine with Karl, who had his own challenges getting the attention of Alex. The Kommissar called Alex as if he had two separate names - Al Ex, but when Karl tried it, he always somehow missed something in the pronunciation, because the giant just ignored him.

When Karl heard the Mongol calling out to him, he decided to try something new. "Ex, Ex," he called back and then went to the front of the truck to retrieve one of the silken shirts he had seized from the Sacristy. He stood next to the driver's seat and fished from his pocket the flask with the oily medication to once more treat the feet of Alex. The Mongol climbed on the seat and extended his legs. "Ka, Ka, njiet kaput," and he pointed to his feet.

The feet were dirty but to Karl's surprise, the open cuts and wounds had closed and there was new skin forming over all of the previous infected areas. He looked in amazement at the transformation as he found it hard to believe what he was seeing.

The difference from yesterday was nothing short of a miracle.

The pain must also have gone because Alex seemed to be a changed man. His walk had changed from an aching hobbling to a light stride. His face looked happy and Karl handed him the shirt, indicating that the giant should rip it apart and bandage the feet himself. When Alex was done tying the boots firmly to his feet, he got up and out of the truck. He placed both of his hands on Karl's head and then placed a kiss on top of his own hands.

Karl did not know what to make of it and wanted to shake Alex's hand. The Tatar looked deep into Karl's eyes and repeated once more the strange ritual and then threw both of his arms around Karl's upper body. Karl anticipated getting grabbed by his ears, but it did not happen. Instead, the huge hands of Alex rested firmly on his shoulders.

"Stand still, Karlchen." He could hear the voice from Godunov behind him. "You made a friend for the rest of your life. Accept the behavior of Al Ex with gratitude."

Karl still wanted to shake hands with Alex but instead, he just pressed his own hands on top of the hands of the Tatar, which still rested on his shoulders.

"You are a very lucky boy, Karlchen. I only witnessed this ritual once before." It was obvious that the Kommissar approved of the developing friendship between Karl and the Tatar.

Kete signaled to the guard unit. He had all the confiscated bikes lined up on the wall. As he was barking orders or instructions, the men of the unit approached the lineup and started to select the bikes, which Harold had originally assigned to them.

"How do you prevent trouble when you tell them that some of them will get two bikes?" Karl asked.

"I decided against awarding two bikes. It is not necessary. One bike will be enough to light a fire under their behinds to scramble once they are done."

Karl gazed at the bikes and wondered again how these broken down bikes could possibly entice anyone to anything. In his world it just did not add up, but he took the Kommissar's word for it.

Harold jumped out of the truck. "I am done. The coffin with the goodies is solidly nailed shut. On the other one, I attached the chains to the lid. I also wiped and slapped the stain on top and around the sides. Take a look."

The coffins looked different than before. The uneven stain lent a sinister look, and the bicycle chains nailed across added to the impression.

"Very good job," Godunov nodded approvingly. Kete was also done selecting the four Tatars who were supposed to guard the transport. He leaned their bikes against the wall in the hallway and ordered the guards up to the Pompolit's office.

"Did you reach General Berzarin?" Karl was eager to get the show on the road. It was nearly 10:00 AM and he wanted to get to the airport as soon as possible. He also hoped that Godunov would dismiss him and Harold after the plane took off. He could not think of a reason why the Pompolit would have any further use for them.

The Kommissar looked up from the caskets he had studied. "No, I did not reach him personally, but yes, I was told that he is appointing German agencies to distribute food in Treptow this morning (suburb of Berlin). Then he will be inspecting an SS prisoner assembly place near the Schlesischen Railroad Station. In the afternoon, he will be in a conference with Marshal Zhukov. They will be somewhere in a useable office building near the Potsdamer Platz."

Karl did a fast calculation in his head. "Let's drive to the railroad station. And if we don't find him there, we should just drive out to the airport."

The Pompolit agreed and made room for the guard detail to board the truck. Kete had them dressed in the yellow and white striped overalls they had found in the bunker. The Tatars were happy with their new attire, which protected their uniforms. They admired each other, but experienced difficulties walking in the new heavy rubberized boots that were of a kind they had never seen before. Since they had very bad footwear in the first place, they were more than surprised that they should slip their old shoes into the new glossy boots. This made absolutely no sense at all to them. In addition to all these riches, they were also given rubber gloves and gasmasks, which they hung on their belts.

The four lucky guards were grinning and pushing each other in the sides because Kete had told them that they would be flying to the Crimean peninsula tonight and after a brief burial and delivery detail to the university, they would be dismissed from active duty. He had stamped their service ID's with numerous blue inked imprints and furthermore, he gave each of them a release letter stamped and signed by the Pompolit.

Kete had assured them that their bicycles and their portion of the general loot would be with them on the plane. None of them had ever flown before and this alone was enough reason to be excited. As far as they were concerned, their endless march to the west had ended and things could not be any better.

When they entered the back portion of the truck they were appalled by the stench, which lingered heavily under the canvas truck cover.

Harold showed them how to breathe through the mouthpiece of the mask, but Daina, one of guards, was already having convulsions. Karl had him sit next to the rear gate to expose him to the fresh air.

The only one unaffected from the stink seemed to be Alex. He followed the instructions from Karl and had the bicycles piled on top of each other towards the front end of the truck. On top of them he had placed the backpacks of the guards and some additional canvas bags with assorted loot.

The truck had reached the perimeter of the SS prisoners and as the Pompolit was walking towards several Russian cars, he was adjusting his tunic to look presentable. "Stay close to me. I want you to meet the general," he called to the boys.

He bypassed several officers who snapped to attention when they recognized his uniform. Karl marveled at the all-terrain vehicles. He could not grasp the vast difference between the regular dilapidated Russian cars and trucks he had seen and these very capable and spotless looking wagons.

"Look at these things. They look like new. Do you think they are American?" He whispered to Harold, who was likewise surprised.

"I have not seen any American troops, but these vehicles cannot be Russian," Harold agreed and looked around to see if they had missed any other indication that the Americans had arrived. There was none.

Alex, who had walked next to the boys, stopped in his stride when two Belorussian officers blocked their progress. He looked at Karl as if asking for permission to show off his abilities. He was not the least bit frightened by the guard detail of general Berzarin and the boys knew that he just waited for an excuse to flex his muscles. Karl's eyes signaled him to restrain himself.

"This guy shows no respect to anyone," Harold worriedly

commented, observing the eyes of the Tatar.

In the meantime, Godunov had found Colonel-General Berzarin and was taking him to the truck with the coffins. When Karl had heard that General Berzarin had been appointed as the military commander of Berlin, he had expected some imposing figure like the German SS commanders had been. Instead, he saw an officer of average proportions with a highly intelligent, but amiable face. He guessed the age to be in the early forties. Berzarin was visibly in a hurry and before the couple had reached the truck, he motioned one of his officers, a lieutenant, to follow him. Godunov had turned around to Karl and Harold and nodded to them to join him.

The boys could not understand the conversation between the Pompolit and the city commander, but when Godunov pointed to the back of the truck, Karl thought that they were supposed to produce the caskets.

Harold lifted up the canvas and Karl jumped in the truck only to collide with Daina, who wanted to jump out. He had puked all over himself and was holding the mouthpiece of his gas mask in front of him. His yellow striped coverall was stained with his vomit and as he wanted to jump down, he was stopped by the rough command from the lieutenant who was now standing next to Harold.

Daina backed off and emptied the mouthpiece of the mask over the top of the nearest casket. He tried to clean up his face but because he was wearing his rubber gloves, he made a complete mess of himself.

Karl took in the scene. It could not have been better suited for their purpose if he had planned it. "It's now or never," he grunted at Harold and motioned to Alex to give him a hand to move the first casket in sight of the general. With one fast motion he opened the lid of the flat German casket. The corpse was resting on top of the filthy rags and the abrupt motion caused the arm and hand to slide down from the chest and over the rim of the casket.

As the stench started to spread, it seemed that Alex understood what Karl was trying to do. He stepped to the back of the coffin and lifted it just high enough for some of the shreds to slide out.

General Berzarin, who had followed his lieutenant, was disgusted by what he saw. He had seen enough combat fatalities not to be shocked. Nevertheless, the putrid smell was unlike any other he had encountered on the battlefields.

Godunov had given him the official petition from Dr. Felder, but apparently the general could not read the German writing and handed the documents to his lieutenant.

"Enough," said Harold as he helped Karl to stuff the rags back in to the casket and closed the lid.

Karl was observing the lieutenant, who was studying the German petition and assumed that the officer could understand what he was reading.

"I wish we could have avoided nauseating the city commander. But, the subway tunnels are full of floating cadavers and we don't think that the lime will be able to stem an epidemic." Karl volunteered his opinion to the lieutenant, who looked up from the papers. He was right in his assumption. The officer understood German but was annoyed that the kid had the nerve to address him without a salute or any sign of respect.

"You could have told us about the situation without dragging the bodies in front of the commander."

"Of course, you are right, Lieutenant, but we wanted to give General Berzarin the opportunity to act before we ask the Americans for their assessment," Karl answered innocently.

"What did you say?" All of a sudden the Lieutenant was interested in what Karl had to say.

"I said that we have a likewise German medical petition addressed to the American military headquarters. But we wanted to ask you first."

The lieutenant spun on his heels and addressed General Berzarin. It looked to the boys that Karl's remark had triggered a chain reaction. Berzarin understood immediately that his decisiveness might be challenged. He asked for and received from the Kommissar, the American petition. It was unclear if he understood English, but it would not have mattered anyhow. He shredded the English petition to small pieces, said a few words to one of his other officers, and then addressed Godunov again. He patted him on the back and shook the hands of the Kommissar several times before he walked back to the SS compound.

It all went so fast that Alex and the boys hardly had time to secure the coffins and the canvas. An officer from Berzarin, with the rank of a Major, took the lead in one of the American-looking vehicles and with the Kommissar sitting beside him, took off towards the airport. They did not need the boys to guide them because the Russians had at nearly every major intersection, several signs posted. They reached the airport in record time where the whole operation really went into gear. They drove right up to the nearest three-engine plane, which was being refilled by tank trucks.

Berzarin's officer and the clout from Godunov sent everyone hopping around the plane. The major was sending for a flight crew, which was not too happy to hear about their destination. They had hoped to participate in looting the city and were complaining to each other. However, their bickering stopped the very moment they noticed the Pompolit next to the plane.

The first one to board was Daina, who became miraculously well when he was excused from handling the coffins. Instead, he was stowing away the bicycles and the personal baggage of the Tartars. Alex stumbled, kind of helplessly, in the rear of the truck. He had the bucket with the stinking fluid in his hand and was about to fall down (unfortunately, he slipped a lot) when Harold intervened just in time to prevent one of the Russian airport helpers getting soaked. The raised hand of Harold changed the direction of the pail, which landed on top of the second coffin and the dry wood absorbed most of the liquid. The soldiers pulling the dripping and stinking casket out of the truck cursed the Tatar, who was busy apologizing to the Major, who had stepped aside to avoid the tumbling bucket. Neither the officer nor the Kommissar was sure if this was an accident or, if not, who the intended target was.

Karl knew of course, but his job was done and he did the best he could to stay low. After the little incident, the actual loading of the caskets went fast and the disgusting odor started to drift throughout the plane.

As the last Tatar followed the coffins, the Major shook hands with the Pompolit, waived at the boys and boarded the aircraft through the cargo doors.

Thirteen

"I did not anticipate that the Russian officer would accompany the caskets," Karl pondered the possible consequences.

"Nothing to worry about, Karlchen. The city commander thanked me more than once that I had the foresight to prepare this shipment before the German medical staff of the bunker hospital had the time or the chance to contact the American High Command." Godunov was pleased that the general had personally commandeered the immediate air transport to the Crimean University.

"But what about the Russian officer?" Karl insisted.

"Oh, this is the best part. The general agreed with me that only one of the caskets should be given to the University. The other one will be buried until I arrive in Simferopol to take charge of the investigation."

"And...the Russian officer," Karl pressed again.

"Yes, the officer. He went along to assure that my Tatars will bury the coffin in a secluded place without alerting the local authorities. The general agreed with me that the Tatars might disappear after they are finished with their assignment. However, the officer will know where the coffin is buried."

"And, you think that the officer's knowledge of the burial place is the best part of this deal?" Karl could not figure out how this could be.

"Of course, Karlchen. Don't you see that the officer will have to report back to me to tell me about the location?"

"Yes, but then he will also report to the City Commander.

Furthermore, in time down the road, he might get curious about the contents of the second casket. I wish you would have told me this before the Russian boarded the plane."

The Kommissar listened to Karl's complaints and wondered, "What could you have done about it, Karlchen?"

"I don't know what I could have done about it. Maybe the casket would have had an accident; or the officer. In any event, the casket would not have been in the plane with the Russian," Karl was sure.

The truck was still parked on the apron, waiting for the plane to lift off. It was now accelerating down the runway. It was too late for Karl to initiate any action.

"Karlchen, Karlchen. Grow up. After the officer reports back to me he will be interviewed by Kete. Then he will disappear."

"He will disappear?" Karl started to understand, but he wanted to be sure.

"Yes, Karlchen. People interviewed by Kete disappear all the time. There is nothing unusual about it."

Karl wanted to ask if this was how the Soviets ran their troops. Officers could disappear at the whim of political Kommissars? But he restrained himself and kept his mouth shut. However, Godunov could see that Karl was disturbed by the turn of their conversation.

"Let me give you a piece of advice, Karlchen. Don't ask a question if you fear that you might not like the answer."

Karl was done worrying. He and Harold had done as they were asked to do and he thought that they had done reasonably well. But due to the Kommissar's comment, he hesitated to ask his next question. He feared that he might not like the answer. Harold had none of Karl's misgivings. He came right out with it.

"I see that the plane took off and I trust that our job is done. If you don't mind, Herr Godunov, I would like to start searching for my parents. Is it possible that you could drop us off at the place you detained us?"

"Yes, I could drop you off. You have done exceedingly well and much better than I could have hoped for. The idea with the English letter was a small masterpiece of thinking and compelled the city commander to act immediately to order the transport." Godunov stopped for a moment to regroup his thoughts. "However, if I drop you off, it would end our relationship. I have something else in mind. Besides, I have some news for you Harold.

Let's go back to my office and discuss how we can possibly assist each other in the near future and beyond."

The boys looked at each other. At this point they had nothing to lose and possibly a lot to gain by playing nice with the Kommissar. In Karl's mind at least, until the American forces entered Berlin. By now it was also late in the day and due to the fact that none of them had slept the night before, they were all pretty tired.

"Well, at least I hear no outright objections and I am still not done with my work for today. We should find something to eat and then, after you are rested, we should take this up again."

They returned to the office building and after the boys had a few deep dishes of the ever-prevailing cabbage soup, the Kommissar assigned them a small room. He had some folding beds and rough Russian blankets brought up. Before the boys fell asleep, the door opened once more and Alex walked in. He carried a blanket in one hand and in the other he had a big loaf of warm Russian bread. He broke the bread into three pieces and offered two of them to Karl and Harold.

As full as their stomachs were, the boys still found room for the freshly baked bread and paid for it by developing stomach cramps.

Alex rolled up his blanket to serve as a pillow and lay down on the floor next to Karl's cot. He mumbled something that sounded like 'spacreff', and when the boys answered with a likewise sounding word, he fell asleep within a second.

"There goes the neighborhood," Harold felt forced to remark before he drifted off.

Karl could not find sleep that easily. The one thing that worried him most was the casual remark of the Pompolit that the Russian officer would disappear. Why would he make such a self-destructive remark if he was not dead sure that the boys would not or could not betray him?

On the other hand, would the Kommissar really worry what a German boy, unable to speak Russian, could possibly say to harm him? And who would believe him?

On the third hand, (if there was such a thing as a third hand) the Kommissar had told them that he would be gone within the next week. But then again, just a short while ago, he had said something of a short-term or long-term relationship. Karl's mind was too tired to find an answer. The Kommissar himself remained a puzzle to him. In order to find sleep, Karl decided to wait with

106

his assessment until he heard what the Kommissar had to say in the morning. He looked down at Alex, who seemed to be deeply asleep, and he wondered if he had a friend and protector or if Alex was there to prevent them from leaving the building.

The next morning started with Alex bouncing around in the room. He was happy because his feet were indeed healing up. "Ka,... Ka," His face was one big grin when he shook Karl by the shoulders. He showed him the clean bandages and Karl could see that he wanted to know if he should continue to wrap his feet.

"Yes, Ex," Karl showed him, like he did yesterday, how to obtain the most comfortable fit in the large boots.

They had gone down to the field kitchen to snatch some bread and tea when a runner showed up to summon Alex. Shortly thereafter, another runner came for the boys.

"First of all I have some news for you," Godunov looked at Harold, "I had one of my agents look for your parents at the war criminal camp by Brandenburg. Your father has been transferred to our temporary political prison in Spandau (town next to Berlin) and at the present time, he is unaccounted for. Your mother was still in the Brandenburg facility and in order to protect her, I had her arrested last night." Harold had tears in his eyes as the Kommissar continued, "She should be here any moment now and I will provide transport for her and for you to take her anyplace she wishes to go in Berlin."

Karl thought about the implications of what he just had heard. He knew that Harold was, at the present time, far too emotional to arrive at any practical decision.

The Kommissar had also changed since last night. Not only was his uniform immaculate and freshly pressed, he was also far more relaxed and self-assured. He projected an unchallengeable authority this morning. His prior concern about the safety of his loot was gone and he was again in full command of his realm.

While Harold was thanking the Kommissar, he was drying his eyes and looked toward the main hallway, expecting the arrival of a car and his mother.

"Excuse me, Herr Godunov, are the western allied forces still standing down at the Elbe River?" Karl wanted to know and at the same time test the sincerity of the Kommissar. Godunov had said that Harold could take his mother anyplace in Berlin. Given the power of the Pompolit, this would not necessarily mean that

Harold's mother would be out of the Soviet's range, and therefore safe.

"What kind of a question is that?" the Kommissar glared at Karl.

"Just wanting to know," affirmed Karl. He was not intimidated by the change in the Pompolit. He had observed that powerful people, as well as physically big people, needed from time to time to assert themselves. At the very least the Pompolit was powerful. Karl knew that soon enough the Kommissar would come down to earth again.

"Alright, you did well yesterday. I will answer your question. The first, Americans as well as the British arrived last night in Berlin. Anything else?"

"Yes," answered Karl, "do you think, Herr Godunov, that they will mingle with you in the occupation of the city or will there be separate parts of Berlin under different jurisdictions?"

"Oh, now I understand, Karlchen," the Pompolit was smiling again. He was a little annoyed but, he liked the bold questions of the kid. He also admired the fast thinking. It could only serve him well in his further plans.

"I doubt it, but I do not know about different jurisdictions. We Soviets conquered Berlin and suffered heavy losses, while the western forces saved their troops." His eyes turned hard, "However, as far as mingling goes, this is definitely out of question. Our soldiers speak different languages so they could not even communicate with the French or Americans. Besides, we don't share the same values. We would have nothing but constant conflicts on our hands."

Kete showed up. He walked over to the group and spoke to the Pompolit. He looked tired as if he had not slept at all, or had gotten up very early. Karl detected that the face of the Kommissar lit up for a moment and Kete went to the kitchen to help himself to some tea.

"Did you hear from the airport if the cargo plane arrived safely in Simferopol?" Karl was connecting the dots and could not help himself from asking. He knew that one of these days he might really trigger a bad reaction, but for right now he felt safe enough to probe.

"Karlchen, I advised you not to ask these kinds of questions. But, I guess that since you were part of yesterday's action, you have a vested interest. The whole action unfolded in accordance with our plan. This is now a closed subject." His eyes told Karl more than his words.

Karl remembered that the plane had left Berlin around noon. He was not sure about the flight time to the Crimean Peninsula, but he calculated that enough time had passed for an aircraft to complete a round trip, including at least a four-hour stop at the destination. He was tempted to ask if Kete had completed his interview, but the eyes of the Pompolit told him in an unmistakable way to drop it. So he did.

He turned to Harold, who had not participated in the discussion. His eyes had not left the entrance area. "You should take your mother someplace in the west side of Berlin," he interrupted Harold's stare.

"What do mean by west side?" Harold asked.

"I am not sure, but if your mother has a relative or friend someplace in the postal district of W15 or W14, I think that would be wise."

Karl had the general map of Berlin pretty much in his head. He also knew that Harold was much better acquainted with the individual street layouts. He just wanted to give Harold a mental stimulus in the right direction.

"Where is W15 located," The Kommissar wanted to know.

"Around the general area of the Uhland Strasse. You will find it on the postal map between the Wilmersdorf and Charlottenburg districts," Karl answered.

"Good advice, you should listen to your friend, Harold. If there will be an eastern or western division in Berlin, then Wilmersdorf will be most certainly in the western section."

Godunov got up. A Russian truck had arrived and Harold raced to see if it carried his mother. He was shocked and stopped in his tracks when he saw her limping out of the vehicle. He could hardly recognize her face. She must have suffered a terrible beating as she walked deeply bent over and was helped by a Mongolian soldier.

Karl was not even sure if it really was the woman he knew as Frau Kellner, his friend's mother. He remembered her from two weeks prior when Harold's parents invited him to share a meal with them. However, the woman he saw now was aged way beyond her years.

Godunov observed the meeting of Harold and his mother then

looked away. "I am sorry," he said to Karl, "I acted as fast as I could. She was in a very bad place. Without Harold telling me where to look, I would not have found her."

He gave an order to the Mongolian guard who carried Frau Kellner up the stairs to the room where the boys had slept. Harold followed them with a vacant expression on his face. He did not look at the Kommissar or Karl. His eyes were glued to the ground.

"Do you think she needs medical care?" asked Karl.

"I think she needs rest and then we can ask her. But, unless the German medical team is still active in the Zoo Bunker, I don't think that I could vouch for her safety and even then, she might get arrested again. Tell Harold to hurry up and get her to some friends as soon as possible. Maybe your Dr. Felder is still around." The Kommissar looked sincere and Karl thanked him in the name of his friend.

"No need for big words, Karlchen. Go up to your friend and tell him that I have a car standing by. You should go along to direct the driver and also to guide him back."

"What will happen to Harold if he decides to stay with his mom and does not wish to come back?" Karl was testing again.

"I don't think that this will happen, Karlchen. I am sure that he wants to find out about his father, but don't say anything to him. He'll be back by himself."

"What about me?" Karl asked, "what if I don't come back?"

"You are not stupid, Karlchen. Given the present circumstances, you know that you won't find a safer place than with me. If you want to run away, do so after the western allies are firmly entrenched in Berlin. But at the present time, we are still combing the streets and buildings for SS refugees. You could wind up in the wrong situation. Think about it."

Karl did just that. He had heard before about the Russian method of 'sugar bread and whip', and the Pompolit seemed to be a master of it.

"May we take Alex along to help us with Frau Kellner?"

"Certainly, he would go with you anyway, unless I order him to stay with me." The Kommissar got up to go to his office and Karl went to see his friend.

"How is she," he whispered to Harold as he entered the room.

"She is in very bad shape. I can only hope that she will make it," Harold was shaking, trying to control his emotions. His mother was laying on one of the folding cots. She had her eyes closed but her breathing appeared to be normal.

"Be thankful Harold; as bad as this is, she was very lucky that you mentioned the Brandenburg camp to Godunov."

"I know," said Harold, "if I ever find the animals who did this to her...," he did not finish the sentence.

Karl understood, though this was not the time to spend on discussions about revenge. They had to think about finding a safe place and possibly medical help.

"Godunov suggested that we take her out of here. He also mentioned Dr. Felder, who might still be with the Becker family. As of right now, we have transportation available. You know how fast this can change. Let's take advantage of it."

Karl opened the door to go and to find Alex, but it looked like the friendly giant had waited for him. He was leaning on the wall in the hallway and when Karl gestured to him, he carried Frau Kellner like a baby in his big arms.

The drive to the Berliner Strasse went faster than on the previous days. The rubble from the collapsed buildings had been pushed on to the sidewalks, clearing the asphalt sufficiently to allow the military vehicles to pass each other.

Wherever the boys looked, they could see German civilian cleanup groups. They also noted various Russian details going from house to house. Apparently they were counting the dead. Every now and then they could spot a German POW in their group. But, the screaming for help and compassion, as well as the gunshots, had stopped. They also noticed that the Russians were setting up soup kitchens to feed the civilians. The efforts of Colonel General Berzarin to restore order in the city were beginning to show positive results.

Even the apartment of the Becker family was back to normal. The barricades at the entrance were gone and when Karl knocked on the battered and clumsily repaired door, he was happy to see Herr Becker responding. The old invalid beamed and pulled Karl into the kitchen.

"We are so relieved to see you, Karl. Will you be able to stay with us now?" Frau Becker entered the kitchen and threw her arms around Karl. She looked unharmed and was pleased to see him again.

Karl explained his visit and while the Beckers were eager to render assistance to Harold and his mother, they were also concerned that the boys wanted to leave again.

"Is Dr. Felder around? We would love to see him if it is possible," Karl inquired.

"No, but I know where to find him. I can go and get him right now, but it will take a while. We have to stay out of sight on our way back," Herr Becker limped to the door to leave.

"Is he alright?" Harold asked.

"Oh yes, he is actually close by and he will be happy to see you," Frau Becker assured the boys.

Alex entered the kitchen. Carrying Frau Kellner like a lightweight bundle of laundry, he looked for a place to set her down. "Over here," Frau Becker opened the door to the bedroom and pointed to her bed.

Alex set his burden down then returned to the kitchen to find something to drink. Karl could see that he admired the kitchen faucet and he walked over and showed him how to turn it on and off. Alex's face looked like a child who saw a Christmas tree for the first time. He could not understand how the water came out of the spigot. He wanted to see the other side of the kitchen wall and looked baffled at the blank wall. Karl wanted to get him out of the apartment before Alex could start to dismantle it. He barely made it.

Harold wanted to stay a little longer, but when he saw that his mother was resting comfortably, he joined Karl to leave with the car.

"How is the young mother with her child doing?" Karl inquired on the way out.

"They are bruised up but otherwise, they are fine. If it would not have been for your guards, it would have been a terrible outcome," Frau Becker answered, and assured him and Harold once more that she would look after his mother. "And thank you for sending Dr. Felder our way. He was a great help for the little girl," Frau Becker waved after the car.

Where else could I have sent him, wondered Karl to himself. The Beckers were the only people left who he knew.

Fourteen

When they reached the office building they noticed that the Mongols were leaving and that Russian soldiers lined up on the street, ready to occupy the premises.

The interrogation rooms which Karl remembered from his first encounter with the Kommissar were empty. Nobody had bothered to clean the floors and there were markings of dried blood everywhere.

"Where are they going, or should I ask why are they leaving?" Harold looked at the Tatars and he noticed that the ones he remembered as the body guards of the Pompolit seemed to be in no hurry to leave. However, the majority of the Mongols were clearing out and passed the boys as they made their way with Alex to the Kommissar's office.

"I hope that Godunov is still here to tell us," Karl was more concerned that the Pompolit might have received some urgent orders and had left for some unknown destination. Of course, they had Alex to count on but still, it was an uncomfortable thought as they could hardly communicate with him. Seeing all the Russians wandering through the hallways and knowing Alex's attitude made the boys even more apprehensive.

Karl looked at his Tatar friend, satisfied that he totally ignored the surroundings. He was carrying an almost new, shiny faucet attached to a foot long rusty pipe. It was a little gift from Herr Becker, who had found it among the ruins. When he saw the giant's fascination with their plumbing, he presented him with the spout.

The former office of the Pompolit was located on the first floor. They found the Kommissar sitting behind his work table, which was loaded with two piles of paperwork. Across from the table were five or six chairs and judging from the apparent disorder, it looked to the boys as if the office had recently served as a meeting room.

The Kommissar barked a command at Alex who took off, only to return with Kete. Both of the guards pulled up two chairs and sat next to the door. Godunov had a few more words with the Tatars, causing Kete to take his chair outside the door, obviously to sit in front of it. Alex had also gotten up and opened a window before he sat down again.

It was one of the large windows known throughout Germany as a Berliner Fenster. Its prominent feature was the huge wing-like window panes, which opened to the inside of the room.

"It is good that you came back so fast. The Belorussians are replacing the last Mongolians and by tomorrow morning every one of them will be gone. The British are already joining the Americans entering the city." The Pompolit tossed the paper piles into two separate cardboard boxes.

"Does this mean that you will leave too?" Harold asked fearfully, because he wanted the Pompolit to stay. He was hoping that the Kommissar would be able to find out the whereabouts of his father.

Godunov shook his head as he turned to face Harold, "No, did you think that I was a Mongol?" he asked with a light twinkle in his eyes. Harold did not know how to back-peddle and said nothing.

There was a hubbub outside the door but apparently Kete was taking care of it because the noise subdued and went away.

"I expect some Belorussian officer to arrive and to take over the building. However, this will not happen as long as I am in residence." The Kommissar looked pleased as he leaned forward and rested his elbows on the empty table. "You boys performed an excellent service for me and I want to repay you by offering you a once in a lifetime opportunity." He looked deeply into Harold's and then Karl's eyes before he continued, "In order for you to understand, let me tell you about myself. I grew up as an orphan in Sevastopol on the Crimean Peninsula. I have no evidence of who my parents were. I was ambitious and I guess I was a fast learner

114

because the director of the orphanage, a retired general, adopted me when I was 8 years old. He sent me to the best schools in Paris and later to the language and officer schools in Moscow. Due to the authority and influence of my step-father, I was channeled towards a political career and I am now eligible for retirement."

Again, he locked eyes with the boys and his hands formed a steeple in front of his face. "I'll make it short, I would like to adopt both of you. I can offer you the very best education and because of my connections, I can assure you a high ranking military career."

Harold was mesmerized. He had hoped for an officer's career under Hitler. And now that Germany had lost the war, he had not given his future any thought. At first he was repelled by the very idea to serve in the Russian army. However, what the Pompolit offered was worthy of consideration. Alone, the aspect of a higher education, maybe in Paris or in Moscow, was tempting.

Karl however, could not imagine a military career. Every single fiber in his body was against it. In his experience, armies were organized killing entities. While he liked the discipline of a military life, he had seen enough killing to last him for several lifetimes.

"I can read you like an open book, Karlchen. Your face has written disgust all over it. But, you might wish to consider a career in the medical or intelligence community. Look, I want to help you." The Kommissar was right on the button. Karl admired him for that. The thought of using his brain and making a career of it had definite appeal.

There was another scuffle at the door and this time a Russian officer burst into the room followed by two Russian soldiers and Kete right behind them. Before the Russian or the Kommissar could say a word, Alex had gotten up and using the forward momentum of the officer to his advantage, he jumped behind him, lifted him up and threw him out of the open window.

There were cries of agony from below. The two soldiers watched with open eyes as their officer disappeared and wanted to back off. It was too late. There was not even a real struggle. Alex and Kete herded the two hapless soldiers toward the window and they preferred to hurdle themselves out before making contact with the fists of the Mongols.

Within a minute or so, Kete was outside in the hallway again and Alex took his seat by the door as if nothing had happened. The cries from below turned into excessive moaning and cursing. Alex got up and closed the window. He did not even look down to check on his handiwork.

"Good grief," said Karl, "This is how you handle officers who disobey you?"

"Yes," answered Godunov, "do you like how efficient we are?"

"Efficient? I don't get it. What entitles you to throw officers out the window?" Harold wanted to know. He was fascinated by what happened. However, he was now more inclined to take Godunov up on the idea of a career as an intelligence officer. Obliviously they had clout in the Russian army.

The Kommissar noted that Karl still waited for an answer. "What? Didn't Hitler have the officers shot who disobeyed orders?" he decided to bait Karl.

"Yes, but only when they disobeyed major issues."

"Then we are not different. We did not execute the Russian officer. We merely threw him out of the window. It saved us time and it worked. I don't see him coming back." The Pompolit was chuckling and leaned back in his chair. "Alright, I had not expected an instant answer. Nevertheless, I need to know your decision by tomorrow." He motioned to the boys to get up. "I am moving to a different apartment facility near the Spittelmarkt and I expect my daughter to arrive tonight. My new headquarters will be near the City Commander in the Friedrichs Strasse. Kete will stay with me. My driver will take you and Alex wherever you wish to go today and pick you up tomorrow morning." He was about to dismiss the boys when he remembered something, "Karlchen, come over here," he went to the window, opened it and pointed to the top of a lamp post across the street. "I read that you had training as a sniper. Do you think that you can hit the round metal light shade?"

Karl and Harold walked to the window and Karl wondered what the real reason for Godunov's question might be. The distance to the light post and the size of the target was no challenge at all.

"If you want to see Karl's expertise why don't you arrange for a competition with one of your best shooters," Harold piped up. After witnessing the performances of Alex and Kete, he felt an urge to show off their abilities.

"Harold, shut up and let it be," implored Karl. "I guess that Herr Godunov has something different in mind than seeing me competing with his champion shooters."

"Yes, I do," agreed the Kommissar, "if you are really good at it, I want you to conduct a training course for my personal guards. They are very good at hand-to-hand combat, but their shooting is outright miserable."

"I could try to teach them but without speaking the language, it might be a futile undertaking. I also have no experience with your guns. They seem pretty heavy just to hold, let alone to hold steady enough to achieve a precise shot." Karl walked to the wall and picked up a rifle behind the table. He weighed it first in his right hand and then in his left. The gun felt kind of comfortable to him. He lifted it up and aimed across the street, lining up the unfamiliar sights. He played for a moment with the safety lever and then lowered the weapon again. "In my limited experience, this one is too heavy for a sniper rifle."

"I don't want you to train them as snipers. I just want you to show them how to shoot straight." The Kommissar pointed again at the lamp shade about 40 yards away. "Go ahead, show me what you are capable of. No trial shot and one shot only."

Karl shrugged his shoulders, "This is stupid." The gun went up, the shot went off, and the lamp shade answered with a loud ping and swayed from the impact. The Kommissar was dazed. It all happened in one single fluid motion. It appeared that Karl had not even zeroed in on the target. The gun went up and down without visibly stopping. Alex, who had joined them the moment Karl had taken the rifle in his hand, grunted his approval.

"How did you do that?" the Kommissar exclaimed.

"You told me to hit the light shade, so I did," Karl was relaxed as always.

"No, I meant how could you shoot so fast. You did not even aim the gun." The Pompolit had never witnessed faster shooting.

"Oh that, well I knew that I would hit the shade, therefore I did it as fast as I could," Karl answered evenly. "I dislike slow people," he added, because he didn't.

"How did you know that you would hit the target? You never fired this gun." The Kommissar pondered Karl's answer.

"How did I know? I don't have an answer for that. I just knew."

"Then you always know in advance whether you will hit a target or not?"

"No, not always, but sometimes I do." Karl was uneasy because he never had anyone question him about this subject. As far as he was concerned, he knew what he knew and that was it. But the next comment from the Pompolit made him think.

"With the correct training, you are able to expand on this ability Karlchen. You should take me up on my offer of a higher education."

"I know that you are right, Herr Godunov, and I would love you to teach me. I wish you would stay for a longer time in Berlin," Karl answered honestly.

The Pompolit sat down again, "I am not a teacher nor an educator. I think of myself as a facilitator."

Karl did not understand the meaning of this word. His instinct told him that it had nothing to do with actual doing. He was a practical doer; therefore, he did not like the connotation.

"We will talk more about it at another time," the Kommissar let Karl off the hook.

Harold was still at the open window and saw that the Russian officer was being carried away on a stretcher. One of the other unfortunate soldiers was still on the ground and groaning. He could not see the third one.

"Will they come back with reinforcements?" he asked.

"Not to us here in the building they won't. They know what we will do to them if they do. Though, what really keeps them away is the fear of the unknown; of what we are really capable of."

"So, you run your troops by fear," Harold concluded.

"Naturally, it works with the ones we have to keep in line."

"What if the Russian officer had orders from the City Commander to occupy this building?" Karl wanted to know the possible extent of the Kommissar's authority.

"Then the City Commander should have communicated with me first. I am sure that Kete told the officer at the door that I am unavailable and that he should leave. He took his chance by disobeying. He will not be tempted to do it again." The Pompolit got up, "I have work to do. Tell the driver where to drop you off so he can pick you up tomorrow morning."

While the boys filed out the door, Gudonov exchanged a few words with Alex, which almost turned into a little argument. Apparently Alex wanted the gun with which Karl had hit the light shade. He wanted to exchange it for his own and tried to explain to the Pompolit that he deserved the exact shooting gun. At least this was the way the Kommissar explained it to Karl when he told him to be prepared to teach a rifle training lesson some time tomorrow.

Harold objected loudly, "You should arrange for a competition shoot tomorrow. Anybody can give a lesson, but not everyone can shoot like Karl."

"If we find the time, I will be happy to see Karl's marksmenship. Spend your time wisely and discuss my offer."

"You blooming camel, you had to push it, didn't you?" Karl was not too happy as he pulled Harold down the hallway. Alex was trundling behind. He had successfully exchanged the gun, which now dangled from his huge neck right in front of his considerable frame. In his hands he still carried the faucet, but only to his backpack in the bicycle room where he stashed it way down below his other belongings.

Two of the Mongolian guards were stationed in front of the room. Karl had no doubt that if the Russians would try to enter the small cubicle, they would trigger a major confrontation. He was not sure how many Tatars were directly under the command of the Pompolit as body guards, but he guessed that they numbered in excess of twenty. The Kommissar had mentioned that by tomorrow, all of the Mongolians would be gone but Karl did not think that this would include the personal detail of the Pompolit. How else could he account for the fact that Alex was still with him and that the driver was also a Tatar?

They drove to Frau Becker's apartment in the Berliner Strasse. Herr Becker opened the door and as the boys entered, they stood face to face with the young mother and her daughter who were just leaving.

"Good afternoon, I am Karl," Karl stretched out his hand to greet the little girl who eyed him carefully and then backed off to stand next to her mother.

"You don't remember me?" asked Karl. "I am the one who left you some chocolate." Karl rummaged in his pockets and when he found nothing, he poked Harold in the side, who miraculosly produced a round tin that still had two chocolate wafers inside. "Here is some more," Karl handed her the tin, "I don't blame you for being shy, but eat the chocolate before this dummy," he pointed at Harold, "takes it away again."

"This is not fair," protested Harold, but Karl did not hear him. He was busy shaking hands with Dr. Felder, who had entered the small hallway coming out of the bedroom.

"I did not think that I would see you again, Karl. Thank you for everything."

"How is Frau Kellner?" asked Karl while Harold slipped into the bedroom to see his mother.

"She suffered life-threatening injuries. There is nothing I am able to do for her. We need to get her to a hospital."

Karl looked at the doctor's face to detect a glimmer of hope. There was none. "I do not see Alex, so I think that our car is still here." Karl ran out the door and he was right. Alex was talking to the driver and Karl motioned to him to stay and dragged Alex behind him to the bedroom. As slow as Alex was in his comprehension of mechanical things, in all other things he was a wizard.

Karl pointed to the ailing woman and gestured wildly to make Alex understand that they had to get her to a hospital. It helped that Dr. Felder still had an arm sleeve with a red cross on it. Alex picked up Frau Kellner and carried her to the car. Karl sat next to the driver and directed him to the Gertrauden Hospital. Harold, Dr. Felder and Alex were sitting next to Frau Kellner in the rear.

All of them were surprised to see American uniforms when they entered the partially destroyed hospital area. The Americans had arrived earlier than expected. Obviously there was some kind of transition going on. Dr. Felder, who had served in this hospital before he was ordered to the Zoo Bunker, knew his way around and used the tumult to his advantage. In nothing flat they were in a wing of the extension facility. Dr. Felder was immediately recognized and secured an empty gurney coming out of an operating room. Alex deposited Frau Kellner on the bed and Dr. Felder took over. He personally pushed the gurney in front of him towards the baby section. He was looking to find some privacy for his patient and he figured if there was any at all it might be in the hallway close to the newborns.

Karl noted the rising tension in the movements of Alex and he suspected it was due to the American uniforms. "I'll see you at Becker's," he shouted after Harold who followed Dr. Felder.

Alex was relieved to see that Karl was ready to leave the hospital, which was congested with Russians and Americans alike.

Karl wondered if in other areas of the city, the transition was more organized but at the Gertrauden Hospital, it was in a worrisome disorder.

Fifteen

Driving down the Hohenzollerndam, they saw troop carrier after troop carrier filled with American soldiers. Karl wondered if the Americans had any soldiers who actually walked. He could not see a single platoon marching. His first impression of the arriving Americans was that they were cleaner and much more disciplined than the Soviets, who still ran in disorganized bunches through the streets. Alex must have had similar thoughts. His eyes sparkled as he watched the clean and modern vehicles of the western allies rolling by.

While Karl wanted to direct the driver back to the building in the Mohren Strasse, Alex objected. He pointed to himself, his dirty undershirt and then made it clear that we wanted to visit Becker's apartment. As soon as they arrived, he dismissed the driver and ran ahead of Karl. Herr Becker opened the door just as before and Alex almost stumbled over him in an effort to reach the toilet.

Herr and Frau Becker were relieved to hear that Frau Kellner was now in a hospital. "As it is, there is little chance that she will survive," said Frau Becker, "I don't know her, but I hope that she will live for Harold's sake."

Karl shared her feelings. He also felt sorry for Harold and knew there was nothing he could possibly do for him. He pointed to the street and told the Beckers about the arriving Americans.

"Then we can walk the streets again," commented Frau Becker, "I had heard that the Americans are civilized soldiers. However, I understand that there are also some black soldiers among them."

"I think that the black American soldiers are not unlike their white soldiers. I heard that they have been drafted from all of the 48 states and that includes states like New Jersey and Carolina. And New Jersey is a civilized state," Herr Becker informed his audience.

"What about Carolina?" inquired Karl. "I don't remember hearing about a state called Carolina."

"I heard about Carolina. However, they are supposedly eating watermelons for dessert. It could be that this has something to do with it," Frau Becker opinioned.

Karl had never heard about watermelons and wondered if they were larger than lemons, but he thought that eating a fruit could scarcely have anything to do with being uncivilized. He hardly knew anything about the Americans. All his schooling about Germany's enemies had been about Russia, and to some extent also included England. Nobody in Germany and in his right mind would have ever thought that the Americans would come all the way to Germany.

He got up and knocked on the toilet door to check on Alex, who opened right away. He was standing in the small room barefoot and only clad in his uniform pants. All of his underwear, foot rags and his shirt were in the latrine, and Karl could see that Alex was using the big toilet bowl to wash his laundry. He had no soap, but he was happily scrubbing away. There was no wash basin or a sink in the room. Only the water spigot above a cone-shaped drain pipe.

Karl could understand why Alex used the large toilet bowl to wash his undies. However, he would have preferred the laundry bowl, which was on a shelf above the water faucet. He took it down and showed Alex how to use it.

The Tatar looked confused. Apparently using a secondary smaller bowl when the large one was available made no sense to him. He just smiled at Karl, padded him a couple of times on the shoulders, and gently pushed him out the door.

Karl joined the Beckers again and saw that Frau Becker was consulting a 'Lexicon' to read up about Carolina. "It says here that they are mostly tobacco farmers," she volunteered her new found knowledge.

"What about the watermelons?" Karl asked.

"Nothing about the melons, but if I read this correctly, the white farmers use the black people as slave laborers. I don't understand this. This is inhuman. If they would be truly civilized, this could not be. Something is wrong with this book. I think it is old." She looked at the front pages of the large reference book to determine the possible age.

"How old is America?" Karl wanted to know.

"Wait let me think, it is 1945, so America is barely 150 years old," answered Frau Becker.

"Well, then there is hardly any comparison. Given that Berlin was founded in 1237 and is now over 700 years old," Karl was sure about his calculations, but unsure what it had to do with watermelons or slavery.

A loud scream interrupted their discussion followed by a shrill screech and then it sounded as if a cow was mooing for help. Karl jumped up and lunged for the bathroom door followed by Herr Becker.

Alex stood in front of the toilet bowl imitating the sound of a cow or a calf in despair. He had flushed the toilet and with the water, his laundry had disappeared down the drain pipe. Since the German toilets had no goosenecks or grease traps, it went straight down into the major sewage line and was gone forever.

The big Tatar stared at the empty bowl. The faces of Karl and Herr Becker mirrored his disbelief. All three of them were speechless, except for Alex's howling in despair.

"Why didn't you warn him Karl?" Herr Becker asked and shuddered. "You were in here and saw what he was doing."

"What? Now it's my fault? I did not anticipate that the dummy would flush," Karl was not about to accept the blame.

Nevertheless, Alex was now without underwear and his shirt was also gone. However, he still had his foot rags, which Karl had deposited in the small wash basin when he had shown it to the Tatar.

Herr Becker decided to once more visit the apartment of the neighbor where he had found the boots for Alex. When he came back, he had two sets of large underwear and a few brown SA shirts. "Nobody would dare to wear these anymore," he remarked to Karl when he handed them to Alex, "and don't even think of asking Alex for another watch. We all owe him as it is."

Alex gratefully accepted the clothing and really admired the brown shirts, which were almost his size. Karl nodded at him when Alex proudly paraded around in Hitler's favorite shirts. "If anybody is able to pull this off and get away with it, it would be you, Ex Ex."

Alex took it as a compliment and beamed with pleasure. Karl doubted that the Mongol had ever worn an ironed shirt. One of the brown SA shirts was still brand new. The creases were as sharp as they could possibly be.

"Do you have any soap?" he remembered seeing Alex washing his laundry without soap.

"No, just a little piece left from when you were here with Alex the first time." Herr Becker could not remember when he had last seen a piece of soap for sale.

Karl thought back to when he had been in Poland a few weeks ago. At that time, the Polish people had been in a similar situation as the Berliner population was now. The Polish people had badly needed soap. Karl had been able to obtain some and exchanged it at that time for very much needed civilian clothing.

Because of this experience, he had been constantly on the lookout for soap. A little bit over a week ago, he had visited with Harold a major German military food storage facility. There had been some hubbub during their visit and he had used the opportunity to secure a few hundred bars of medicated soap, which he had stashed away at their hideout in the subway shaft. The bars were rather small, but nevertheless, he had a full box and now they would come in handy.

"Ex Ex, come over here," he talked to Alex as if he were a pet and tried to convey that he would like to go with him on a two-hour walk. He pointed at his watch, made walking movements with his fingers and then pointed again at his watch. This time he pointed to two hours ahead of the present time. As far as he could tell, Alex was game for anything and the thought of walking in the darkness seemed to appeal to him.

"We will be back before midnight. This will give us two extra hours, just in case we run into trouble," Karl told Frau Becker, who objected to Karl's leaving.

Herr Becker agreed, "If Karl can get us some soap, we have it made. I remember from the First World War that soap was better trading currency than tobacco. If you had soap, you could trade it for anything."

"The boy needs some good rest," insisted Frau Becker.

"You forget that this is Karl and he had training. Don't confuse him with soft ideas."

"I will sleep when I return," Karl agreed silently with Frau Becker. He was tired and would rather have stayed in the apartment. But due to the Mongols leaving and not knowing how long he could count on the Kommissar to protect him, he rather dared to go now. Besides, by tomorrow the Americans might discover the airshaft and then it would be too late.

The walk to the hideout went smoothly and without any interruption. Alex always walked between Karl and any passing Russian. His hulk alone deterred any of them to pay closer attention to the unlikely couple. Karl was sure that Alex had no idea where they were going and when he set a brisk pace, Alex happily sauntered along. He also saw that the friendly giant had no clue what his new brown shirt was representing. He walked with his Russian uniform jacket unbuttoned and wide open. Karl was sure that Alex did that on purpose to show off his new possession. Fortunately, it was too dark to draw attention to the offensive color.

The entrance to the airshaft was still shielded with debris and Karl wasted no time retrieving the carton of soap. It was the last one of the larger items the boys had hidden. There was still a good amount of tobacco behind the blankets and Karl stuffed his pockets with cigarette boxes. One of the small packets of ten oriental cigarettes he gave right away to Alex who lit up and scrutinized the surroundings while Karl covered the shaft with rubble and dirt. On the way back, Alex insisted on carrying the awkward but clean smelling cardboard box.

Karl remembered that a day or two before the surrender he and Harold had helped an HJ group of about 20 boys hide from the SS and also from the advancing Soviets in the bomb shelter of a nearby building. As he now passed the location, he wanted to see if the boys were still where he had left them.

He had no trouble finding the mound of debris that camouflaged the entrance to the cellar. But the boys were gone. He remembered that they had all worn uniforms and worried that they might have gone up and out to surrender to the Soviets. He searched the cellar for some messages and found a piece of cardboard with names, dates and addresses. The dates were all from today, which gave him hope that the boys might have seen the Americans and had surrendered to them.

"Ka, Ka," Alex called from the street where he had been waiting. An American troop carrier had slowed down at the nearby corner, then it picked up speed and disappeared down the street.

Karl decided that it might be best to hurry back to the apartment. He took the list of addresses along to give them to Frau Becker. Sooner or later he hoped there might be a central information entity where families could find each other again.

Herr Becker welcomed the soap with a big grin on his face and thanked Karl over and over again. It was past midnight and Frau Becker spread several blankets on the kitchen floor to provide a place to sleep.

Godunov's driver showed up early in the morning to pick up Alex and Karl. The sun was penetrating the overcast sky as he drove them to the new headquarters of the Pompolit. The structure itself was not damaged too much and Karl marveled at the ability of the Soviets to find, among all the ruins of Berlin, some functioning buildings.

Kete was already waiting for them and showed them the office of the Kommissar, which was again on the first floor. When Karl looked out the window, he saw that it was facing a huge area cleared of all debris. All the rubble had been bulldozed into the ruins of another building, where it formed a high wall of broken concrete and bricks. In the front of it were several columns of all kinds of parked motorized vehicles. While most of them looked battle worn and damaged, a surprisingly large number of trucks seemed to be almost new. Their dark grey-green paint scheme was somewhat lighter, but all of them featured the big red star of the Soviet forces.

"Where is Harold?" the Kommissar asked as he entered the room. He looked well-rested and took his place behind a desk.

"Harold stayed with his mother," Karl assumed that the driver had told the Kommissar about Dr. Felder and the trip to the Gertrauden Hospital. He looked around the room for a place to sit down. He had seen several benches in the hallway, but curiously, there was only one single chair in the small office and Godunov was sitting in it.

"Oh yes," remarked the Kommissar, who had noticed Karl's searching eyes, "I have not really moved in here." He ordered Alex to bring in some chairs and then dismissed him. "Now Karlchen, tell me how you feel about my proposal to adopt you?"

"I cannot accept it, Herr Godunov. I want to search for my father and if I can't find him, I need to see my mother in Westphalia to help her with my brother and my little sister. If I was alone in this world, I would not hesitate to accept your generous offer."

"For all you know, you might be alone in the world. You need to learn to watch out for yourself, Karlchen. You might never find your father or your mother. Even if you do, there is no future for you in Germany." The Pompolit got up and walked to the window. He turned around to face Karl, "My offer is good until I leave. Keep on thinking about it. In the meantime, I would appreciate if you could teach my guards how to hit what they are aiming at."

Karl had given this matter some thought. He had received his weapons training from the captain of a parachute assault team. It had been a rather informal but extensive training of only two weeks with the result that he became a designated sniper in the service of the HJ. He had never given his title much weight. He knew that he was a good shot, but this was about all. Besides, he did not speak a word of Russian and he even doubted that the Mongols spoke Russian. So, how was he supposed to teach if he was unable to communicate with them? The Kommissar was still looking at him as Karl had an idea.

"How many men are in your team?" he asked.

"Normally, I have over forty under my command. But as you know, most of them are gone. As of right now, I have only ten left, and they include Kete and Alex."

"Am I correct that these remaining ten are more loyal to you than the rest you dismissed?"

"Yes, they are my most trusted men and they are also matchless in hand-to-hand combat. But, they never had any instructions in firing a gun."

"Then am I also correct that they are never involved in enemy combat action?"

"Why no, they are not soldiers. They are my personal guards. But it would be nice if they would also be known to be good marksmen."

"That's what I thought," said Karl, "I take it that it is more a retirement wish of yours than a needed requirement for your team."

"Exactly," answered the Pompolit, "I am retiring in a few weeks and it would be nice to leave a legacy behind."

"Then let's get started. I will try to install some basics. However, I will need you, at least for a little while, to translate a bare minimum of the instructions." Karl had conceived a simple plan. He thought of teaching them how to line up the gun and hit a large target about thirty feet away. He thought that if he would put emphasis on speed shooting rather than on hitting something eight hundred feet out, he could conceivably pitch the Kommissar's team against a regular Russian unit. Another idea was to teach just one man, who could then instruct the others while he would correct as he would see fit.

"Karlchen," the Kommissar started, "I don't have the time it would take to translate. But, I will spend a few minutes with you. After that you will have to do with sign language."

He ordered Alex to assemble the team and then led the way to the neighboring courtyard. Instead of painting or assembling a target, the Mongols carried an assortment of plundered bed sheets next to a pile of rubble. There must have been several dozen of them and most of them were white. Not exactly clean, but excellent to serve as a target. Karl draped a large sheet over the remainder of a garden wall and stepped off thirty feet. "Tell them to fire five shots at the rags," he said the Kommissar.

It was as if he had asked to celebrate New Year's Eve. There were bullets flying everywhere and not a single one hit the target. It looked to Karl as if most of the Mongols just shot into the air. Besides shooting more than five bullets, they also screamed and hollered every time they pulled the trigger. It took the Kommissar several minutes to stop the spectacle. All of the guards looked very pleased with themselves and it seemed to Karl that they expected some kind of praise.

"Herr Godunov," Karl asked, "Did you tell them five shots?"

"Of course I did, but when they get excited they don't stop to count. You cannot apply your Prussian discipline to a horde of Tatars."

"If they don't understand what is asked of them, like counting, how do you expect me to teach them?" Karl was beside himself.

"Karlchen, all I ask of you is to teach; give it a try, please. However, I really don't expect any results."

The Pompolit padded Karl on the shoulder and turned to walk away.

Sixteen

Karl was not inclined to give up that easy. "Now I am more than confused, Herr Godunov. If you don't expect any positive results, why do you want me to teach in the first place?"

"Is this not clear, Karlchen? I wanted to see how you would approach or handle this task. Moreover, it would be nice if my guards could shoot straight. But, I don't expect miracles."

Karl pondered the words of the Kommissar, "Just one question, Herr Godunov, I know that you converse with them in Chahar, but do any of your ten guards also speak Russian?"

"Kete is fluent in Russian and Chahar. Why do you ask," the Kommissar kept on walking.

"You wanted to see how I would tackle this job, Herr Godunov. If you would issue orders to Kete to take me to a POW compound, I could possibly find a German soldier or officer who speaks Russian. This would remove the language obstacle. The rest leave up to me."

The Pompolit stopped to consider the possible consequences "I suspect that in the end this might cost me a prisoner, Karlchen. Nevertheless, I like the possibilities and we have enough prisoners to feed as it is." Godunov had a short discussion with Kete and turned to Karl again. "Kete will take you to a POW transport. He has sufficient credentials to assure that you are able to select and leave with a prisoner of your choice. He will also test the detainee's language skills. Alex and two more guards will go with you, just in case."

The Kommissar winked at Karl, who understood. He had not

expected to possibly gain the freedom of a Russia-bound German soldier. This assignment got interesting and doable. He smiled in anticipation, "Thank you, Herr Godunov, you will be surprised."

"I already am," muttered the Pompolit as he went back to his office. Within minutes, the small detail was on its way to the Potsdamer Platz, which was teeming with POWs being herded into waiting trucks.

Karl did not know where to start, but Kete took charge of the situation and approached a group of about two hundred prisoners. The guards of the group listened to Kete's request and allowed Karl to address the Germans. His appeal for a Russian-speaking soldier or officer went unanswered. Several hands went up to announce that they could speak English or French, but there was no one speaking Russian.

It took Karl almost an hour and stops at several transport units until his call was finally answered. A middle-aged sergeant stepped up to announce that he was a teacher and could converse in Russian. Kete asked him several questions until he was satisfied and motioned for Karl to proceed.

"What is your name? Where are you from? How good is your Russian?" Karl wasted no time.

"My name is Wagner. I am from Hamburg and my Russian is passable." The sergeant was equally fast to answer.

"If you are able to assist me by translating some instructions, I might be able to arrange for you to become a POW of the Americans." Karl did not believe that he could obtain total freedom for the sergeant and did not want to overload his mouth.

Wagner misunderstood, "I don't speak English," he informed Karl with a disappointed expression in his face. It was obvious that he had hoped to escape the Russian transport.

"Not necessary, let's leave while we can," Karl had noted that a Russian officer made his way to the small group. Kete intercepted him and showed his credentials. Nevertheless, the officer started an argument and pointed at Karl, who asked the sergeant what it was about.

"The officer said that he had to deliver an exact number of prisoners to the train. He has no objection to me leaving the transport, but he wants you to take my place." The expression in the sergeant's face mirrored his emotions and changed again from hopeful to hopeless.

Karl pulled him by his sleeve and placed him in the middle of the Mongols, "Don't worry, just stay close to these guys," he smiled at the sergeant.

Alex walked up next to Kete and looked down on his shiny new boots. He was impatient for a word or a signal from Kete and started to stomp his feet and opened his coat. The eyes of the officer went wide when he saw the brown SA shirt and then he emitted a high shriek. Kete had given the hulk a wink and Alex reached out and twisted one ear of the officer and almost lifted him of the ground. He simply marched the officer all the way to the car and then turned him around and kicked him with full force in the behind. The yelping of the Russian stopped when he skidded and came to an abrupt halt on the sidewalk. He had been unable to protect his forehead, which was now bleeding. Kete went over to him and sat him up against a pile of rubble. He was talking and it looked like he was asking the officer questions, but the Russian just sat there shaking his head, hardly replying to anything that Kete was saying.

Karl, who was by now used to the aggressive behavior of the Mongols, wanted to know what Kete was asking.

"He offered the officer a ride to some Pompolit's office to place a complaint," said the sergeant.

"Could you understand the response of the officer," Karl asked.

"No, not really, but I think he wanted no part of it. All I could understand was that he wanted to be left alone."

The sergeant was reluctant to enter the car. "What kind of an army is this? I have never witnessed anything like that before."

"As long as you are doing what you are told, you have nothing to worry about. You will like the Pompolit. The Mongols however, are just a little....." Karl searched in his mind to find a fitting description, "Primitive, yeah that's it, primitive."

"Primitive is alright. On the other hand, kicking an officer in the butt is an entirely different matter." Wagner kept on talking to himself while Karl urged him to board the truck. Soon afterward they reached the courtyard with the improvised shooting range.

Karl did not feel compelled to explain the whole setup to the sergeant. He just told him to translate his directives to Kete who would then, hopefully, explain the instructions to the Mongols.

"That's all," said Karl while he thought of a way to possibly bribe the Tatars to pay attention and to follow the instructions. He remembered the packs of cigarettes he had still in his pocket.

Wagner followed Karl's guidelines and told Kete that he should assemble his team. In the meantime, Karl tried to explain what he had in mind, "Keep the ammunition in a box beside you and don't issue more than five shells for each exercise," he finished his instructions.

"Can they not count to five?" exclaimed the sergeant.

"Well, maybe they can. The thing is that we need them to fire no more than five shots, and hit the target at least once."

"You are kidding, right? At this distance it is impossible to miss," the sergeant wondered what this was all about. He could not understand that there was a military unit in existence that never had instructions in shooting. Then Karl told him that they might have to bribe the Mongols to follow his directives. "This is unreal. You mean to tell me that you need to bribe soldiers to get them to shoot?" Wagner stood there with an open mouth.

"Well yes, the Russians bribed the Mongols to fight by promising them that they could plunder and rape once they took Berlin," Karl tried to explain.

"But they had no training in firing their guns? How come they defeated us and we lost the war?" The sergeant wanted to know.

"Easy now, sergeant. We lost the war because we were out produced and outnumbered," Karl felt that this conversation could go on forever and he had a job to do. "This particular unit we are supposed to instruct is a special bodyguard unit and they are apparently only trained in hand-to-hand combat." Karl looked expectantly at Wagner, hoping to touch base.

Surprisingly, from that moment on it went a lot better than Karl had expected. He did not need to bribe anyone, except maybe the sergeant, who almost went into convulsions when Karl showed him a pack of ten cigarettes. "They are yours when you get the job done," he assured the Sergeant.

It turned out that Wagner was a very good shot himself and also a good listener and patient instructor. It was either that, or he really longed for the cigarettes. He judiciously followed Karl's instructions and by sunset he had the team yelling: Eins, Zwei, Drei, Vier, and Fuenf, before each shot.

He showed them how to first raise the rifle and line up the sights on the barrel. Then he shouted "Eins", and the whole chorus joined him. While they shouted out the German numbers, they lowered the rifles and when the lineup of the barrel neared the top of the rags, they let go with five shots. When Karl felt that they started to understand the basics, he pressed for greater speed in the whole performance.

When evening came, each guard had at least three hits to his credit every time he repeated the exercise, except Kete and Alex, who scored five out of five.

Wagner's face was all smiles when Karl handed him the pack of cigarettes. Another pack went to Kete to distribute among the group as reward for their shooting.

"Please tell Kete to inform the Kommissar that we are done for today," Karl said to the sergeant, happy to now have his own personal translator.

When Godunov arrived he seemed to be preoccupied, as if he would rather be someplace else. Nevertheless, he was astonished to see that the sheets, which had served as targets, were shredded by bullet holes. His whole team was smoking German cigarettes and stood next to the remaining bed sheets, waiting for some encouraging words from the Pompolit.

The Kommissar knew what was expected from him. Words were cheap and easy to come by, so he talked to each one of them and listened to their excited comments.

"Well, Karlchen, you were right. I am surprised and impressed."

The sergeant was awestruck to hear the perfect German of the Kommissar. Karl introduced the sergeant, and praised his skill in translating his instructions.

"If you wish to show off your team, Herr Kommissar, we should be able to compete by tomorrow at noon," Karl had addressed Godunov by his title. He did not want the sergeant to know about his personal relationship with the Kommissar.

"I might be gone tomorrow morning and I probably need a few of the team to go with me. I will try to arrange something of a competition shoot with a Russian team in the afternoon. You may wish to keep on training the ones that will stay behind. I will have them stand by for you in the morning."

Karl could see the mind of the Kommissar was someplace else and that he had a problem concentrating. He hardly paid any attention.

"You are welcome to drive with Alex to the hospital and check with Harold. But I expect you to come back tonight. I will have a room ready for you." He turned back to Wagner, "You understand that you will need to stay with us tonight. You may mingle and eat with my detail. They will also show you a place to sleep." He once more addressed his group, gave an order to Alex and the driver, waved at Kete to follow him, and went back to his office.

Karl would have liked to talk some more with Wagner, but Alex and the driver gestured him to join them. They were lining up in front of a field kitchen and the smell from cooked fish was drafting in his direction. There was no way that he would eat this chowder. Actually, it was kind of a cabbage soup and he saw that there were bunches of dried fish piled up next to the soup kettles. The cooks chopped the fish into pieces; head, tails, everything, and tossed them in the boiling gumbo. Apparently this was done to heat up the fish, because he could also see that some Tatars and Russians would simply grab some of the dried fish and chew on them without bothering to cook them. Karl shuddered. He searched for the black gooey bread when Alex handed him a bowl of soup without any fish swimming in it. The goliath had noticed the discomfort of Karl and his whole face broke into a smile when he saw that Karl was happy to accept the dish.

"Did you ever hear of noodles," he asked Alex, fully aware that Alex could not understand him. The Mongol nodded at him, got up and returned with a large piece of fresh bread.

"Close enough," Karl reached into his pocket and gave Alex a cigarette. The idea struck him that he might be able to communicate with his big friend after all. He pointed at the bread and at the same time pronounced carefully the word 'noodle'.

"Noodle, Noodle, Ex, Ex", it was an instant success. Not really, but pretty close to it. "Poodel, Poodel, Ka Ka," Alex grunted back.

"Not P, my friend, N, N, Nooooodle," Karl tried again. He promptly received the same answer, "Pooodel, Ka, Ka, Poooooodel."

"Have it your way," said Karl, "if Poooodel will get me bread, then I am happy to learn."

The cabbage soup was not too bad because of the ever-present onions. Karl used the remainder of his bread to wipe out the bowl.

"Isn't the 'Klippfisch (fish jerky) soup great? I see that you finished your dish. You think that they would allow me another helping?" He heard Wagner behind him.

"If they don't, then I will have Alex here get you the whole kettle." When Karl saw the questioning expression in the sergeant's face he added, "He can do that, believe me."

"I have not had a second helping in days," said Wagner. He hesitated to approach the cooks. "These guys here have also far better food than we had in the prison camp. Look at all the wonderful fish over there."

"That does it," exclaimed Karl. He got up, took a fish from the stack and nearly slammed it in Wagner's bowl. He just caught himself in time to gently place the fish in Wagner's hand. "Here, enjoy! Since you are from Hamburg you must be a gourmet when it comes to seafood."

Alex, who had watched the scene unfold, snatched the bowl from the sergeant and refilled it.

"Thank you, very much," stuttered the sergeant and took his seat again.

"See you later," Karl was following the driver to the car. He could not bear to watch the sergeant consuming the dried fish. Alex, however, had a different mindset. He looked wistfully at the way Wagner enjoyed himself sucking the eyes out of the fish head. After a short moment, he decided to walk over to the cooks and help himself to a smaller fish, which he simply put in his pocket.

The wing of the Gertrauden hospital where Karl had left Harold in the newborn section was not as cramped as the day before. To his surprise there were many American trucks, featuring red crosses on top, lined up at the side entrance. They were busy transferring patients to other hospital facilities in the suburbs. Karl, with Alex in tow, searched the hallways, which were still filled with gurneys and patients, but it all seemed far more orderly than yesterday.

After a long effort he finally found Harold sitting on the steps of a staircase. Before he could ask a question Harold lifted his head as if he had sensed Karl's presence. His eyes told Karl what he did not want to know. He gently sat down next to him and wrapped his arm around the shoulder of his friend. For a while, neither one of them said a word.

Harold was the first one to break the silence, "Komm, lass uns gehen. (Come, Let's go). He got up and Karl was astonished at his friend's resilience. He had known Harold since they were ten years old. They had been school buddies and then subway rats and finally HJ buddies. He had been by his side when Harold's parents went missing, and rejoiced with him when they learned that they were merely evacuated. As he walked now with him down the steps and towards the exit, he could feel that his friend was willing himself to walk upright and determined.

Karl did not want to ask any questions. Harold's face did not invite any. However, he wanted to help his friend and get him talking. He had to start someplace.

"When?" he asked.

"Last night, 4:00 AM," came the terse answer.

"It is 8:30 PM now, what were you doing since last night?"

"Thinking," answered Harold, "and waiting."

"Waiting? Since 4:00 AM last night? For what?"

"For you."

"For me? Did you make yourself a time frame? How much longer would you have waited?"

"Don't worry," said Harold, "I did not set a deadline. I knew that you would show up," He looked at Karl, "I almost forgot. I think that the Russians arrested Dr. Felder."

Karl froze in his step, "What did you say? Why? When?"

"I think that it might have been an hour ago. He came to me when my mother passed away. Then he kept on working. A little while ago, I saw two Russians, an officer and a soldier passing me in the hallway. They were leading Dr. Felder into one of the offices at the end of the corridor."

"That does not mean that he was arrested," Karl thought out loud.

"His hands were tied behind his back," Harold's answers were getting faster.

Karl beckoned to Alex, who immediately fell in step with the boys as they hurried back and up to the first floor. He did not think that they had much of a chance to find and liberate the doctor. But, if there was any chance at all, then it was now before the Russians would leave the hospital with their prisoner. Harold led the way and stopped in front of a door.

"This is where they took him."

Karl tried the knob, but the door was locked. He knocked on it and could hear some sound like a chair scratching on the floor. No voices and nobody opened the door.

"Ex, Ex, Kaputt," Karl pointed at Alex and to the door. The hulk did not exert much of an effort. The door opened the very moment

Alex leaned on it. Apparently it was not much of a lock.

The room was tiny and must have served as a utility room at an earlier time. It was empty except for two men in hospital garb, bound to two chairs with the backs to each other. They had some kind of rag taped over their mouths. One of the men was Dr. Felder.

Neither Harold nor Karl had a knife to cut the men lose, but Alex pulled something like a razorblade from one of his boots and in no time at all, the five of them were out the door.

Harold was leading the way again, but before they could make the staircase, they met a Russian officer and a soldier, who were escorting another prisoner towards the room in the back.

For a moment both parties froze, but just as Harold expected that Alex would start one of his frenzies, he watched in amazement as Alex merely reached in his pocket and produced the red star emblem with the sword. The officer said something to his soldier, but kept his hand on his prisoner. Alex locked eyes with him and the officer backed down. It looked almost unreal to the boys, but after an intense stare down, the Russians let go of their new prisoner and Alex virtually herded them down the hallway and staircase using nothing but the star in his hand and his eyes. On the way down and out of the hospital they met several other Russian and American soldiers, but Alex ignored all of them and acted as if he and the two Russian teammates were the only living things around.

Seventeen

As they reached the street, Alex grunted something and the Russians stopped. Karl could see that they were deathly afraid. The soldier kept his head down and the officer almost recoiled when Alex tapped him on the back and made a dismissive motion with his hand. As if he had waved a magic wand, the two Russians took off running until they reached their car. They never looked back.

The three Germans, clad in their hospital attire, did not say a word when the boys told them to board the car. Alex shrugged his shoulders and squinted at Karl as if he wanted directions where to go. Karl knew that at this point he was not only in command of the present situation but also, that the immediate future of the three Germans depended upon his fast decision.

He directed the driver towards the Berliner Strasse and to the Becker's apartment. "I don't know where else to take you," he said to Dr. Felder, "I am sure that Herr Becker will be able to assist you and your comrades. You might also wish to consider surrendering to the Americans. I don't know if this will protect you from getting traded to the Russians. Do you know why they showed up at the hospital to arrest you?"

Dr. Felder did not answer. He had not rested since he entered the Gertrauden hospital and the last two hours had been very trying. After his arrest, he had not expected to avoid being shipped to Russia and the chain of events was taking its toll. This was the second time that Karl had gotten him away from the Russians. He did not know how to thank him, or what to think.

"The officer who arrested me spoke some German and informed me that we were supposed to accompany a POW transport. It looked to me that they were kidnapping German doctors before the British or Americans could intervene," the third man spoke up.

"Do you know each other and are all three of you doctors?" Harold wanted to know.

"Yes," the second one answered.

Dr. Felder looked at Harold, "Harold, let me tell you once more how sorry I am, but your mother was beyond any help. There was nothing I could do for her."

"I know that you did your best, Dr. Felder, and I am thankful that you were able to keep her out of pain during her last hours."

The car stopped at the Becker's apartment. "I cannot advise you on what to do," said Karl, "I would stay hidden at least until the Americans establish a presence in the city, but I have no experience. I wish you well."

He shook the hands of the other two doctors and then embraced Dr. Felder, whose emotions got the better of him. He tried to stop his tears but was unable to do so. He was holding Karl's hands as if he never intended to let them go. "Karl, Karl......," he stammered; that was all he could say.

"It is alright, Dr. Felder. You would have done the same for me," Karl had to turn away.

It was close to 10:00 PM and Herr Becker answered Harold's knocking at the door. His face was one big question mark as he stepped back to let the group enter. The other two doctors looked at each other; they could not believe that they were free to go. They had thought that they and the boys were prisoners of the Tatars and did not understand the situation. But the relief on their faces spoke more than words.

"If you want to stay here, I will cover for you," Karl said to his friend who went back to the car.

"No Karl, I need to talk with you," Harold's face was more serious than ever, "I also need to talk with the Kommissar."

During the short discussions, Alex had taken the opportunity to reacquaint himself with Becker's bathroom. He had finally mastered the use of the flush system and was excited to show off his progress.

"Ka, Ka," he bellowed at Karl and led him and Harold to the

toilet. He looked extremely satisfied as he proudly showed to the boys what he had accomplished. The walls and the toilet seat were clean and dry and the toilet bowl was empty. Karl relaxed. He had feared that Alex had another surprise encounter with the commode.

"Ex, Ex, good boy," he praised the Mongol like he would praise a puppy. He had been certain of Alex's cooperation to free Dr. Felder but he was not so sure that the Tartans would agree to leave the three Germans with the Becker family. He had observed Alex's body language as the Tatar had dismissed the Russians before, and now imitated the dismissive motion with his hand as he pointed at the three doctors.

Alex did not even bother to look. As he took his seat in the car, he remembered the fish in his pocket and started to chew on it, tail first. He nodded to Karl that everything was all right. The driver, who had never left the car, took off the moment Karl was on board. He looked enviously at the fish in Alex's hand until the giant finally offered him the head. It would have been a happy trip back if it had not been for Harold's mother's demise.

Karl tried to interrupt Harold's downhearted frame of mind, "How do you account for Alex's civilized behavior in the hospital?"

"I really don't know. It was not like Alex at all," Harold was glad that Karl had interrupted his thoughts.

"I think that we don't give Alex enough credit for his intelligence," Karl started to answer his own question, "Considering all the Russian and American soldiers at the hospital, he might have decided to 'park' his tough manners for a while. He sure got us out by doing it the easy way."

"Right," said Harold, "What amazes me even more is that you toilet-trained a grown man. I see a future for you in the Mongolian intelligence community." It seemed that he was back to his usual teasing.

It was almost midnight when they finally settled down in their appointed room. Besides two large regular beds and a couple of blankets, it also featured a table and several chairs.

"You wanted to talk?" asked Karl as he reclined on his bed.

"No, I don't really want to talk as much as I would like to discuss with you a few things. What would you say if I told you that I am more or less ready to take the Kommissar up on his offer?"

141

"You want Godunov to adopt you?"

"Well, I don't know what he meant by adopting and what it actually entails, but I kind of like the idea of a higher education and a military career," Harold answered as he stretched out and looked at the dark ceiling.

"I would say that I know you enough to picture you as an officer. But, in the Russian army? With a Soviet political Kommissar as your godfather? What are you really thinking or talking about?" Karl tried to place himself in the state of mind of his friend who had just lost his mother.

"That is what I needed to talk about," Harold tossed the blanket away and sat up on the bed. "My mother died because of the brutal injuries she received from the Soviets in the Brandenburg camp. I want to find these bastards and make them pay. No, wait, I will find these bastards. What better way is there than to join their forces. What better way is there than to take Godunov up on his offer?" Harold's voice was even, hard and determined.

Karl got up and walked to the table, "Let us consider your notion, one point at a time, Harold," for a moment he fumbled to find a chair and then sat down.

"I knew that you would help me to sort this out," Harold joined his friend at the table.

Karl thought for a while before he started, "Just to clear away some basics, Harold. We both have nearly identical values. We don't kill people. So, to join the Soviet army to find the killers of your mother might seem at first an answer to your situation, but it will be almost impossible to find them. And even if you do, I don't think that you will pull the trigger."

"You did not hear me correctly and you are not thinking big enough Karl, let me explain," Harold got up and walked back and forth in front of the window, "Please, hear me out until you answer. I am thinking in a much larger frame. We have seen enough evidence of how corrupt the leadership of the SS was, while at the same time the regular SS men were nearly fanatical in following orders, agreed?" Harold could see in the dim light that his friend nodded his head.

"No difference in the Soviet system. We have witnessed the corrupt conduct of Kommissar Godunov as well as the fanatical attitude of his team. If all goes his way, he will retire in comfort while his Tatars will be deported to central Asia. I would consider it a lifetime challenge to learn from this corrupt behavior for nothing else but my personal goals. Starting with the revenge for my mother. However, I don't intend to change my values. I did not say that I would kill anyone. I said that I would make them pay. But, on a larger scale, it will be at the very least an interesting career. A career for myself." Harold stopped his pacing and sat down again.

Karl was stunned by his friend's outpouring. At this point he was not so sure about his first statement that he thought that they had matching values. Clearly, Harold was bent on revenge, but in what he claimed to be on a larger scale was very much self-serving. Karl wondered what it would take for him to take this route himself. On the other hand, he could not blame Harold for his change in attitude. Too much had happened in the past thirty days and nothing was the same anymore.

"What about your father, Harold? Do you plan to abandon him now that your mother died?"

"I don't know if my father is still alive, if he is bound for Siberia, or if I will ever see him again. But I think that I could do more for him by joining the Pompolit than by doing nothing. Furthermore, we have not even discussed what our options are when we are dismissed by the Kommissar. I guess we could join the sanitation and clean-up brigades, and then what?" Harold's voice became more determined as he continued. "Don't forget, I can always change my mind if I don't like the course I set for myself. But at the very least, I would immediately learn to speak Russian. That would already be a great advantage."

Karl could not find too many things wrong with his friend's plot. For good measure he tried another question, "Just to make sure that I understand you correctly, you want to use Godunov's offer to serve yourself and your own interests, but not really to become an officer in the Soviet army."

"You got it, Karl. Now, please tell me what you think of it." Harold got up again. He was too excited to stay put for any length of time.

"Honestly Harold, I think that you made up your mind already. Your potential is practically unlimited and you will always have an important supporter in the Kommissar. If it were not for my family, I might even join you. But I have my mother in Westphalia, who needs me to help her with my brother and sister in case my father is dead or unaccounted for." Karl pushed his chair back and returned to his bed, "You can always count on me, Harold. We will always be friends. Tomorrow we should find out from the Kommissar how he plans to proceed. Try to get some sleep in the meantime."

"Karl?" Despite the fact it was past 1:00 AM, Harold was not quite ready to sleep.

"Yes, Harold," Karl was dead tired and his answer was slow.

"How did you do with the shooting lessons? Do we have a competition shoot tomorrow?"

Karl was falling asleep, his mind was already in dreamland and his answer was hard to understand. Harold thought that he heard something like, "Pooodel will get me bread."

"This makes no sense, Karl."

He received no answer, so he went once more over his options, which he had already contemplated when he waited for his friend in the hospital. He liked that his friend had told him that he had nearly unlimited potential. Coming from Karl it meant a lot.

By the time he fell asleep, he pictured himself as a multi-lingual mercenary gun for hire.

Eighteen

Both of the boys slept past 7:00 AM and the big surprise was that the field kitchen served bread, tea and a large variety of marmalade and jellies. The jars must have come from a plundered German warehouse because they all featured German labels.

Sergeant Wagner was sitting next to Kete and three of the Tatars belonging to the Kommissar's detail. "I wish I could stay here," said Wagner after Karl introduced him to Harold, "The food is good and I like the company of the Tatars. Do you think there is a chance for me to stay in Berlin as a translator for the Russian officer corps?" He looked expectantly to Karl.

"I don't know if this would be a good idea. They might ship you to Russia anyway to serve in the labor camps as an interpreter. In that case, you would have to work just as hard as your fellow inmates," Karl answered, "I have heard from the Kommissar that only the very sick and severely injured ones can expect to see Germany ever again."

"If this is true, then I would rather be traded to the British or the Americans," Wagner reconsidered, "maybe some of them speak German and could use my Russian language talents."

"At this time we should concentrate on preparing the Tatars for the shooting competition. If the Pompolit is pleased, you might have a chance to obtain what you wish for." Karl was done with the subject. In the meantime, Kete sent for additional sheets to serve as targets and Wagner looked at Karl for instructions.

"My strategy is simply to surprise the opponents by shooting extremely fast. Have your men repeat yesterday's exercise and then we will instruct them to count faster, much faster than before. But this time they will only count till three. We will have them shout out, 'Eins, Zwei, Drei', as fast as they can, then we will have them shooting again, but only three shells."

"I doubt that this will win any competition shooting. I would rather train them to accurately line up the barrel and squeeze the trigger when the gun rests absolutely quiet in their hand." The sergeant did not understand the underlying reasons for Karl's plan.

"Don't worry about that now. We are not training them to be snipers. We are training them to win a competition," Karl strained to explain.

"I also don't understand the counting and the shouting. It is counterproductive to holding the gun steady," the sergeant maintained.

"The Mongols scream and shout anyhow..."

Karl's answer was interrupted by Harold, "Listen, Sergeant Wagner, don't argue with Karl. You only annoy him when you cite facts to him."

"Idiots, both of you," Karl mumbled under his breath and then louder, "We will do it my way. Let's stop wasting time." He went after Kete to help set up the targets.

Alex joined the team and within a short while they were able to duplicate the previous day's outcomes. When Karl reduced the counting to three, it seemed as if the Mongols liked it even better. By about noon, everybody was excited to start the competition, but the Pompolit with his small group was still missing.

The kitchen had changed their daily fare to a thick onion soup and Kete implored Wagner to break for lunch. Karl tried to communicate to them the importance of continued training, but finally gave in.

"Ex, Ex, please bring me a pooodel," he said to the Tatar and to Harold's surprise, the giant got up and returned with several slices of fresh black bread.

"What the heck?" Harold looked at Karl.

"Yeah, it beats me too. Every time I ask for a pooodel, I receive bread," Karl grinned.

"How did you do that?" Harold asked fascinated.

Karl shrugged his shoulders, "At this time it is still unclear whether I train Alex or he trains me. All I know is that it works."

Harold looked around the table and over to the kitchen bench. There was not a single piece of bread in sight and he happily accepted a slice from Karl. He wanted to say something to Alex, but Karl stopped him with a wave of his finger, "No, no, no, you get your own supplier. Leave my guy alone."

The banter stopped with the arrival of the Kommissar and the remainder of his team. The boys had never seen Godunov look so defeated. He barely looked around as he signaled to Kete to follow him to his workplace. His guards mixed in with the others and helped themselves to the food.

"You think that something went wrong at the University in Simferopol?" Harold did not mention the shipment because Wagner had joined them, but Karl understood.

"No, there must be something else that is bothering him. He was not really himself the last time I saw him, but now it is really bad."

Kete showed up again and motioned to the boys to get up to the Kommissar's office. They found him staring out of the window. Karl had to cough several times to let him know their presence.

"Do you know your way around Potsdam?" The Pompolit turned to face the boys.

"Yes, I had some relatives in Potsdam that we visited from time to time," Harold answered, "We also had many HJ day trips to meet with other outlying units. I know the layout of the streets as well as the layout of the Palace Sanssouci."

"Good," said the Pompolit, "Do you know where the Lindenstrasse is?"

Harold had to think for a moment before he answered, "It comes off the Jaegertor and connects to the Breitestrasse, if I remember correctly. I know that it is a fairly long street; but not a thoroughfare."

The Kommissar pulled up a chair and sat down, "I received some personal disturbing news. My daughter Anna, who is a medical doctor and a lieutenant in the Belorussian army, is missing." He got up and walked again to the window before he continued, "Her division arrived in Potsdam two days ago, where she was ordered to participate in the examinations of former political detainees in a prison located in the Lindenstrasse. Nobody has seen her since, yet her unit is otherwise fully accounted for."

147

He turned around and faced the boys.

"I want to see the place and investigate myself," he turned to Harold, "How long will it take us to get there?"

"Not too long, I guess. I never went there by car. With the S train (city train) it took us about an hour."

"Then we will drive to Potsdam right after we are done with our shooting competition."

Karl wanted to ask a question in regard to the prison but was interrupted by Kete, who reported that the Russian infantry unit had arrived to compete in the shootout with the Mongolian guards.

"What are our chances, Karlchen?" Godunov wanted to know.

"You mean our chances to win? They are excellent as long as I am allowed to define the rules," Karl expressed no doubt in his face.

The Russian unit consisted of eight battle-experienced Russian soldiers under the command of a corporal. They were already taking up positions in the yard where the bodyguards of the Pompolit had trained and were waiting.

Some of the bed sheet targets were still up and the Russians fired at them from different distances. It must have been a selected elite unit because none of the shots failed. The Kommissar watched them and approached Karl, "You better start with laying down the rules. These guys are excellent shots. They will be hard to beat."

Alex grunted and barked at the Kommissar, who addressed Karl once more, "Hurry up, Karlchen. AL Ex wants to take the corporal apart. He never heard of rules and figures if he can rip the corporal a new one, it will discourage the soldiers and they will miss the target on purpose to avoid a similar beating by my guards."

Karl could see that it would only take a command from the Kommissar and the Russian detail would be cripples for life. Somehow, the corporal must have anticipated something like that. He walked to the entrance of the street and upon his command, a detail of about 50 infantry soldiers filed into the courtyard. They took their position as spectators on the side of the square.

Karl hastily conferred with Wagner, who bypassed Kete and addressed the Russian detail directly.

"Stop shooting, we will set up likewise targets for each team.

Upon my command, each team will shoot three shots. This competition will imitate combat. If you don't get your shot off in time, or miss your target, you lost because you are dead." Wagner looked at the Russian team, "Any questions? Because once you are dead you will be unable to ask."

One soldier spoke up, "What is the distance?"

"Thirty feet. Each team will shoot at its own target. We will count the hits on each sheet. The team with the most hits wins." The Russian soldiers broke into laughter. Thirty feet was no contest to them.

The Pompolit interrupted Wagner, "Wait, there are eight soldiers. They are bound to defeat us because they will score more hits than my five men," he spoke in Russian.

Wagner answered according to Karl's guidelines, "This competition is to simulate real combat. And in real combat, you are unable to match the number of opponents."

The Russian corporal stepped up to inquire about the exact sequence of the command.

"I will rapidly count to three in German, Eins, Zwei, Drei, because this is how I trained them. Any objection?" answered Wagner.

"No, not from me. Let me tell my men and then let's get on with it." He went over to his team to instruct them accordingly.

The Kommissar was still loudly protesting in regard to the uneven number of opponents when Karl piped up, "You stated your objection, Herr Godunov. Just watch what will happen."

The Pompolit wanted to protest again, but now the whole chorus from the bystanders demanded to stop the haggling and get on with the contest.

As the Kommissar was still weighing the chances of his team, Harold interrupted his deliberation, "Look, Herr Godunov, you have the whole courtyard cheering in favor of the Russians. Why not make it even more interesting for them. Make this contest worth something?"

The Pompolit was torn between trusting the boys and his own knowledge regarding the shooting incompetence of his guards. "What do you have in mind?"

"Tell them that the loser will be pronounced dead, and because he is dead, the winner is entitled to his footwear."

"I am not so sure that this is a good idea, Harold. What if we lose? Then my guys will have to walk barefoot."

Harold shook his head, "Lose? Not a chance. Besides, what have you got to lose? Have you looked at your team's shoes? They are nothing but shreds."

The Kommissar looked at Karl, who liked Harold's idea. "Excellent suggestion, Harold. The Russians are so convinced that they will win, they are ready to agree to anything."

"Alright," said Godunov, "but if my team loses, you will have to forfeit your shoes too." He walked to the center of the courtyard and announced his decision to make this a true war simulation in which the loser is actually losing something of value. He repeated his speech in the Mongolian language and the Tatars looked longingly at the boots of the Russians.

His address was answered with laughter as the Russians poked each other and pointed to the pitiful state of the Mongolian shoes. The corporal was tempted to object when his eyes fell upon Alex's brand new boots. "Yes, agreed. I'd like to own the boots from this bear."

Wagner thought that the corporal was lucky that Alex did not understand the Russian language. He was convinced that the giant would like to take a swing at the corporal.

"Enough of this shouting. You heard the rules. Get ready to act." The strong voice of Colonel General Berzarin penetrated the noise. Nobody had noticed or expected the arrival of Berlin's City Commander. He was surrounded by a group of officers and stood now next to the Pompolit.

Kete had taken his place next to Alex and the other three-team members. Karl gave a wink to Wagner, who stepped to the side and announced in Russian that none of the team members were allowed to aim before his command.

And then, it was over in an instant.

He shouted, "Eins, Zwei, Drei!" The Tatars screamed along, shots rang out and their target was shredded before the Russian team found the time to aim.

"You are dead, your whole team is dead," announced General Berzarin.

"I demand another contest," screamed the corporal, "This went far too fast. My team was not ready. We were ambushed."

"You are right," said the City Commander, "This is why you are dead. Take off your boots."

"Not my boots," lamented the corporal, "I did not shoot."

General Berzarin was unmoved, "I just told you. This is why you are dead."

There was no cheering from the crowd except from the Tatars who whooped it up. Since there were eight Russian shooters, they obtained eight pairs of boots, plus the pair from the corporal. This was just the number they needed. Everyone, including Kete received a pair of good sturdy boots, which they exchanged with each other. Except Alex, who did not need any. The Russians did not even look at the discarded dreadful footwear of the Mongols. The just hobbled barefoot to their truck.

Karl wanted to get away to the kitchen, but was stopped by Wagner who called him back. He turned around and saw that General Berzarin wanted to talk to him. The Pompolit did the translation, "I understand that you trained the Kommissar's team," the City Commander addressed him.

"No, not me. Sergeant Wagner did the actual training," Karl never accepted credit for things he did not do. Besides, he was insecure of the possible consequences.

General Berzarin studied the boy for a moment, "Explain."

"It was Sergeant Wagner who instructed the team how to line up the barrel and shoot on command. I just suggested the technique of surprise," Karl did not waver.

The General looked at Wagner, "Is this correct?"

Wagner snapped to attention, "Yes, this is correct, Herr General."

The City Commander addressed Godunov, "I don't think that you have further use for this sergeant. I need a man like him to instruct my troops, mainly, because he speaks a passable Russian. I assure you that he will stay on my staff. He is too valuable to be deported."

The Kommissar shrugged his shoulders, "If you need him, then you can have him. But if you decide otherwise, I would like to have him back."

The General took one more look at Karl, said something to the Kommissar, and then departed with his officers. Wagner saluted the Pompolit and joined them. Before he left, he shouted a short "Thank you" at the boys, who smiled and waved back at him.

Karl would liked to have known what the General had said about him, but decided that whatever it was he could do nothing about it anyway and scampered away in the direction of the kitchen. It was too early for the evening supper. He just wanted to sit down. When he turned to see if Harold was following him, he saw that his friend was being lifted on the shoulders of the Tatars. The Kommissar must have told them whom to thank for their newly gained boots.

Their cheering was interrupted by the Pompolit, who ordered all of his team to board their truck. He called at Harold to join the driver in the front and took a place next to Karl in the rear.

"You mentioned a jail with political inmates. I take it that you meant a former SS prison?" Karl asked of the Kommissar.

"Yes, what do you know about it?" Godunov was eager to hear any details.

"I never heard of it," answered Karl truthfully. It turned out that the Pompolit was better informed than the boy.

"The Lindenstrasse penal institution was a political prison of the Nazi's, which we liberated a few days before we conquered Berlin. It was the prison in which the SS doctors performed sterilization on thousands of inmates. You mean to tell me that you never heard of it?"

Karl shook his head, "No, I don't even know what you are talking about. What is sterilization?" He wanted to know.

"Not now, Karlchen. Not enough time to explain." The Kommissar leaned back against the truck awning, "Here is what I am being told. After we freed the inmates, we imprisoned the SS squads. They are presently being interrogated in a separate place and readied for transport to Siberia." Godunov shifted on his uncomfortable bench seat. "My Daughter was sent there to evaluate the remainder of the undernourished former inmates. She was last seen entering the facility with another female doctor. Her unit is fully accounted for, but the two doctors are missing."

Karl could not picture a prison with thousands of inmates. "Are you sure of the address?" he asked. "How can there be that many inmates in a building located on a regular street in the center of Potsdam?" He knew that Potsdam was originally a Garrison city under the Prussian King, Fredrick the Great, who had also built his summer palace there in Sanssouci. He wondered if the prison could have been located in the surroundings of the palace.

"No Karlchen, I have the correct address. It is Lindenstrasse Nr. 54. The building only housed a hundred or two hundred at a time.

We will see when we get there."

The truck stopped at the Jaegertor. The old monument was located on a small plaza. The Lindenstrasse started here with the number 1.

"What is the house number?" asked Harold through the window.

"54," answered Godunov, pushing the canvas to the side to get an unhindered view of the surroundings.

The truck stopped in front of a large doorway, which was closed by an iron door. Karl could see the number 54/55. A double number meant a double building.

"My team and I will search this place room by room. We might get help or encounter resistance from the Russian guards. I don't want you to get hurt. Stay with Harold and the driver until I call you."

Nineteen

There were several Russian soldiers on guard duty in front of the door. They moved right out of the way when they recognized the uniform and the rank of the Pompolit. It was already dark and Karl caught not much more than a glimpse of the interior yard during the brief time the door opened. He noted that in the rear of the yard was a tall building, about 4 or 5 stories high. It looked like it was covered with a coat of gray plaster. He didn't have enough time to discern if the rear building was connected to the side buildings and to the front, but he did see that the back building featured several rows of fairly large windows. He also noted that all of the windows were secured with steel bars.

After the Kommissar exchanged a few words with the officer in charge of the guard detail, he was invited to come in.

The very moment the Kommissar had passed through the door, the guards tried to close it again. Kete, who had stood next to the Pompolit's side, stepped forward and placed his foot between the door and the frame. He was wearing the nice pair of Russian boots he had obtained after the shooting match earlier in the afternoon. For a minute or so everyone was quiet and it seemed like a stalemate. Then the Russians slowly backed down and opened the door a little wider. Karl expected that the guards did this to obtain a little more leverage to push the heavy steel door back into the casing, thereby crushing Kete's foot. He was not alone in his assumption. As the door moved a bit more inward and then reversed its momentum, Alex reached behind the door and seized the head of one of the guards and held it with his heavy hands

right between the door and the frame. There was the sound of a
low thump, then the shrieking yell of the ill-fated soldier as the
steel door collided with his head, slamming it against the housing.
The really bad part of this situation was the fact that the Russian
guards had apparently placed a wooden or steel beam slanted
behind the door, which now hindered any backward movement to
release the pressure. The head of the soldier was a great deal wider
than Alex's hands and the giant had not even suffered so much as
a scratch. After a short scuffle and a lot of crying from the hapless
sentry, the Russians finally moved the beam out of the way and
allowed the Mongols to enter. Karl could see that one ear of the
guard was nearly severed from his head. It was hanging on by a
piece of skin and his whole head was a bloody mess.

The Pompolit came out of a side door followed by an officer and
three Russian soldiers. He looked for a moment at the Russian
guards who tended to the moaning private sitting on the ground.
When no one complained or offered an explanation, he motioned
to his team to follow the Russian officer, who led the group into
the courtyard. Godunov was already following them when he
turned back to address the boys, "The whole place is supposed to
be empty. It will take us only a short while to confirm. Stay outside
until we return."

Karl walked back and forth in front of the building and noticed
that a few civilians must have heard the lamenting of the injured
Russian. There was a small bunch of old folk gathered across the
street and next-door.

"Why don't you go across the street and ask some questions
about the activities during the last two days," he asked Harold,
before he proceeded to the crowd down the street.

He was informed that this place was indeed a former Nazi
prison, until the Russians had cleared it out.

"When was that?" he inquired.

"Two days ago. Right after that they had a big orgy," answered
an old man on crutches.

Karl thought for a moment, "What kind of an orgy?"

"I don't know," answered the cripple, "First they searched the
houses in the neighborhood for women and then they were
drinking and singing all night long. Yesterday morning they were
all gone."

"Did all the women return unharmed?" asked Karl.

"I don't know what you mean by unharmed. They were raped of course, but, ja, they were not beaten up, except…" He suddenly shut up and hobbled down the street without looking back. Karl thought that the sudden departure was odd and followed him to ask some more questions, when the old guy disappeared into a house. Apparently this was the place where he lived because he did not enter the street again. Karl made a mental note of the address and walked across the street to join Harold.

"They all confirmed that the place is empty," Harold told him. "The first troops who freed the inmates and took care of the sick and wounded left yesterday morning. Then the place was empty for a few hours. Some of the people here had the guts to go in and look around. Then, in the late afternoon, the group still occupying the place moved in."

Karl looked at the old people who wondered why these two German boys had arrived with the Mongols and when he started to ask questions, they stopped answering and disappeared as fast as they had gathered.

"There must have been very little fighting in this city," said Harold as he looked up and down the street.

Karl agreed, "It looks like the Soviets overran Potsdam on their way to Berlin, where all of our remaining defense was gathered." He pointed at the red brick walls of the former prison, "Look, it is almost untouched, except for the ornamental plaster coating next to the entrance." He shuddered because he strongly disliked brick houses. To him they looked like miniature factories, which were invariably built with red bricks. He also knew that buildings with visible bricks were always very old buildings. An initial, but sure sign of limited plumbing, and the structures were almost impossible to heat. The newer buildings, before the war, had also been built with bricks but they were more dressed up with nice beige and light gray colored facades.

"Not much evidence of bombing attacks; very little rubble in the streets when we entered the town. Hard to believe that we are barely an hour away from Berlin," Harold was still talking as the Kommissar appeared on the street.

"There is nobody here except the guard detail. Back to Berlin." His voice was as hard as his face. He did not speak to anyone on the drive back. When they arrived at their quarters, he went up to his office without any further instructions to the boys.

The next morning began with a light sprinkle and before noon it turned into a steady rain. Karl and Harold were in their room discussing how to proceed to look for their fathers. The gray-on-gray weather did nothing to lift their moods.

"There must be a way to ascertain if your father is still alive. Somewhere there must be a list of our casualties," Harold speculated to Karl, who shook his head.

"What are you talking about, Harold? Nobody knows at this time anything about the number of casualties on either side. Never mind the names."

Harold looked at his friend, "Who told you this?"

"The Kommissar. He told me yesterday that it will be a few more days until they are done counting the dead."

The rain continued to whip at the window and Alex showed up to fetch the boys for a late breakfast.

Godunov was in his office contemplating his present situation and his future actions. During the past months he had been steadily accumulating assets in various forms and in different places. He had been following the combat troops and whenever there was an opportunity to rob his fellow officers or Kommissars, he did what he could to enrich himself. He also had never hesitated to eliminate any possible witnesses.

His ingenuous technique of taking the loot from other plunderers never backfired because he regularly changed his teammates. He did this without raising any suspicion because all the Tatars were, by decree from Moscow, supposed to be deported to central Asia.

Whenever he had scored a feat with his group, he rewarded them with some plunder of lesser value and sent them on their way. His only permanent deputies had been Alex, Kete and his driver, Vadim.

The loyalty of Kete and Vadim he never questioned because they had been homeless orphans when Godunov found them. Both of them had been with him for several years. Kete had been the more intelligent one and he had sent him to school to learn the Russian language. Vadim was more like a personal servant, steadfast like a shepherd dog.

Alex was however, a wild card. He had kept him on his team because of Alex's deep-seated hatred of the Russians and also because of his brutal strength. Both of these features came in handy whenever he was facing an opponent.

On the other hand, he could not figure out what made Alex tick. He had never seen him drunk or longing to rape a woman. He knew that Alex had a wife back on the Crimean Peninsula, just like Kete. Could it be that both of them were true to their women? Highly unlikely, given that they were Mongolian warriors by nature, but unless he saw otherwise, he had no way of knowing.

The reason he pondered these thoughts was due to the fact that his daughter was missing. He had been contemplating all kinds of scenarios and until last night, he had feared that she had been killed in some kind of action, but now he was not sure.

In the course of the last few years he had made some enemies, and some of them were political officers like himself. Not as highly placed as he was, but he knew that many were yapping at his heels. He was not ignorant and he knew that this went with the territory. Besides, it was a regular price to pay whenever you reached a certain plateau in any hierarchy.

However, for anyone to reach out for his daughter was a little steep, besides extremely dangerous for the perpetrators. He was not known to deal kindly with anyone who opposed him or stood in his way. The ones who tried were already forgotten.

Also, the timing was way off. Any intelligent opponent would have waited for the Pompolit to retire, instead of attacking him at a time when he had almost unlimited power and resources at his disposal. No, moreover, if one of his enemies had kidnapped his daughter, he would have heard by now.

By the time he had entered Berlin, he already had several hoards stashed away in various locations ranging from Hungary and Poland to Danzig and Germany. He could most certainly take his time to recover them. They were very well hidden and not going anywhere without him.

Berlin had turned out to be a different challenge, because of the massive competition from the Belorussian officers and his sudden call to return to Moscow. His ploy to hide his latest booty in the subway tunnels had paid off big. Due to the German boys' actions, his plunder was already close to his home and 48 hours ago he had taken some actions to repay them. He was very good at compensating his obligations and it was always in excess of what others expected of him. After he had received positive confirmation of his actions, he had been ready to call it good and leave Berlin. But now his daughter was missing.

In the early morning, he had dispatched some of his political agents who worked for him as informers, all through the military. Until they reported back, there was nothing he could do. His thoughts had completed a full circle and he needed to step back and allow his mind some rest.

Someone was knocking on his door. It was Kete, who informed him that the boys were looking for him. He was glad for the interruption and invited them up to his office.

Karl took a chair opposite from the desk, but Harold remained standing and came right to the point.

"Good morning, Herr Godunov. I came to a decision and would like to take you up on your offer." He was wringing his hands, unsure of what to ask or add. Karl had advised him to let the discussion unfold and to keep his questions and answers to a bare minimum until he knew what was expected of him.

Godunov was surprised at Harold's announcement. He did not know exactly why, but he had hoped that Karl would have been the first to accept his proposal, but he just sat there and looked at the wet windowpanes. "What about you, Karlchen," he asked.

Karl sat up straight. "I would love to stay with you and Harold, but I have to find and help my mother."

"Well, as you wish. Nonetheless, remember that my offer is open until I leave Berlin." The Kommissar sounded a bit disappointed and then waved at Harold, "Sit down. Here is some paper and a pencil to make yourself notes. I have some questions and in order to proceed, I will need the answers at the latest by tomorrow." He pushed some of the writing material on his desk in Harold's direction. "Any particular or exact reason that influenced your decision?"

"Yes, Herr Godunov. I don't see any educational or career future for me in Germany. However..." he stopped his answer thinking of Karl's advice to keep his answers short.

"However, what?" prompted the Kommissar.

"If I have any choice, I would prefer an education and a career in the intelligence branch of the military." He glanced at Karl to detect how he was doing. Karl had not changed his expression; therefore he must be doing fine.

"Okay Harold, I saw you look at Karl. Don't worry, this is not an interrogation. We need to get some of these things sorted out to establish your interests and the most efficient timeline to proceed." He got up from his chair walked around the desk and sat on it facing the boys. "Please note that I am absolutely serious about this. Your answers will determine your future. For example, should you decide on a medical career and I sponsor you in a top medical school, then that will be it. If you wish to change your mind later on, you may do so, however, I will withdraw my support. I knew what I wanted from life when I was 14 years old and I never looked back. I expect the same from you. Another thing, I will not tolerate if you slack off in your ambition."

Harold raised his hand to ask a question. He received a push from Karl, "Don't interrupt Herr Godunov."

Harold kept quiet and the Kommissar continued, "I am offering you the education because of what I read in your service record. You always strived to be the best. I am giving you a chance to succeed, but it is only one single chance." Godunov winked at Karl, "Now is the time to ask me a question, Harold."

"Thank you, Herr Godunov. You answered what I wanted to ask."

"Right, Harold. You are opting for a career in the intelligence community, so your first priority should be languages. In order to be one of the most sought after officers, you should be fluent in *at least five languages*. You speak German and understand some English. You will need Russian. What other three languages do you wish to learn?"

Harold wanted to answer, but the Kommissar was faster, "Stop and think before you answer. Let this be the first lesson in your career."

Harold contemplated the question for a moment. "I understand. You said first at least five languages. We covered three and then you asked for another three. You are testing my ambition. I would like to add French and let you decide on the other two. It should be languages that Russia needs in the future. You know more about that then I do, Herr Godunov."

Karl's face showed that he was pleased with his friend's answer. So was the Kommissar, "Very good, Harold. Since you need to speak Russian in any event, I will enroll you in a crash program of the military. I have to see what is available. You might start as early as next week. In the meantime, you work with Kete. He will provide you with a Russian uniform and I will issue you an ID identifying you as a protégé of mine. You also have another day to decide if you still wish to pursue an intelligence career. After that your decision is final. Any more questions?"

Karl spoke up, "Yes, Herr Godunov. Did you hear anything about your daughter?"

"No, still nothing. But thank you for your concern, Karlchen."

"Can we still bunk together?" Karl wanted to know.

"Of course, Karlchen. I also have another assignment for both of you. Have you ever heard of Babelsberg Ufastadt?"

"Yes, Herr Godunov. Babelsberg is the name of a small suburb we passed on the way to Potsdam. Babelsberg Ufastadt is just the name of a city train station. It was supposed to be the German Movie production center. I was never there and don't know anything else about it."

"Yes, that is the place. I am a collector of early Nazi propaganda movies. I want you to drive over there and see if you are able to locate some copies of prewar movies. Preferably featuring some top Nazis. I am willing to trade some food for them."

Karl could not picture the Pompolit as a movie fan or collector. He must have some other reason to look for these films. "We can try," he answered, "however, I never heard of propaganda movies being made in Ufastadt. I think that you would be better off looking for copies in the Propaganda Ministerium on the Wilhelmsplatz and on the Mauerstrasse."

"We have searched the ruins on the Wilhelmsplatz. The building was already destroyed before we entered the city. There is nothing left. But I never knew of the Mauerstrasse building," he looked questioningly at the boys.

"The building does not mean anything. That was only the administration. Have you searched the basements?" Harold wondered aloud.

"What basements?" The Kommissar was all of a sudden interested.

"Does not matter," answered Harold, "either in the Wilhelmsplatz or in the Mauerstrasse. I think that I am able to get you in there."

"Even under the ruins?" The Kommissar was already summoning his team.

"Yes, exactly under the ruins." Harold's answer left no doubt.

161

Twenty

The team of the Kommissar assembled and within minutes they were rolling in the direction of the Wilhelmsplatz. Harold directed the truck to stop close to the intersection of Taubenstrasse and Friedrichstrasse. They were now right in the center of the Government and Financial area of the inner city, and Karl had no clue what Harold had in mind.

There was not a single building undamaged and most of them were reduced to huge skeletons. The rain kept coming down and due to the massive debris, the culverts were clogged up, causing considerable dirty flooding of the streets.

"All of the government buildings are connected by subterranean passages. We should be able to enter from here and then walk several blocks underground until we reach the Mauerstrasse basements," Harold informed the Kommissar.

Godunov looked up and down the street. He was not too happy with the many Russian and British soldiers searching for spoils and souvenirs in the wet rubble. "How do we find access to the basements? The entries to the buildings are buried under heaps of wreckage."

Karl had no answer. Harold had jumped from the car and disappeared among the ruins. Kete, who had been ordered to stay close to him, was also gone.

"Darn capitalists!" The Kommissar pointed to an approaching and new-looking truck. Soldiers in American uniforms squinted under the canvas at the wet Russian troops and confirmed Karl's opinion that the Americans never walked. Not even to look for war memorabilia. Perhaps they walked to the toilet, he thought, but was not really convinced of it. After all, it was the most modern-looking Army and in his mind, it was entirely possible that they had portable restrooms in their trucks.

The remark from the Pompolit did not surprise him. He knew that the Russians had a big disdain for the Americans. While they liked and enjoyed the material support from the western allies, they were far from appreciating the help. In the very words from the Pompolit at a later time: "They are like babies. They do anything to be liked. As long as they are stupid enough to give their stuff away, we take it."

Harold showed up again, "I found what I was looking for. There is an emergency exit tube in the rear of a backyard in the Taubenstrasse. Follow me."

The Kommissar ordered one of the guards to stay at the truck with Vadim and hustled with the remainder of the group after the boys. As they rushed through the ruins, they attracted the attention of some of the pillaging soldiers. Before the Kommissar reached Harold, his group was followed by a mob. Kete, who looked back for a moment, yelled at Alex and in no time at all they had several of the followers screaming and crawling on the ground. Their moaning and cursing was appalling enough to discourage any other pursuers, who scattered in all directions.

"What is this thing," Gasped Godunov, looking at a steel contraption rising about two feet above the rubble. It looked like a bent conduit that had been smashed by a falling building.

"My grandfather was a plumber and worked for the city. A few months ago he showed me his work assignments. It involved various canalization two levels underground and connected the whole government district. At a few points they installed emergency exits. This is one of them," Harold explained.

"Will this lead us to the basement of the Propaganda Administration building?" Godunov studied the approximate three-foot wide and twisted metal duct.

"This will lead to an underground structure of water and sewage pipes, supposedly connecting all the buildings except the Reichskanzlei (Hitler's Chancellery), which has its own access system." Harold was ready to crawl into the conduit.

"Wait a moment," the Kommissar reconsidered, "I don't want to risk all of us in a narrow pipe. We might encounter flooding or obstacles which could hinder our retreat." He looked at his group to select the ones he wanted to leave behind and then changed his mind again. "Harold you go in with Kete to see if you can find your way to the archives we want. Karl and Alex will stay here and wait for your return. The remainder of my team and I will explore the area around us and make sure that neither one of you is disturbed."

A few feet into the dark and twisted conduit, it started to bend down and there were several rungs installed which made it easy for Harold to descend. After several yards, the conduit ended on a small platform. Harold searched on his hands and knees for the continuance further down and found a narrow shelf with a flashlight and a flat metal case which seemed to be chained to a bracket in the wall. The flashlight batteries must have been recently replaced because the light was bright and Harold could see that the metal case was more like a protective envelope shielding a small booklet. At first glance he could not make any sense out of the many abbreviated words and what seemed to be directions. But then he noticed something like an explanation page glued to the inside of the metal cover. "We have it made," he smiled at Kete, who seemed to understand.

While Harold was still reading, Kete found a sturdy ladder leading further down. Before they continued, Harold carefully separated some pages from the booklet and stuffed them in his shirt pocket. When they reached the ground floor, he estimated that they must be at least one level below the regular basements. He was amazed at the labyrinth of passages leading in different directions. What astonished him the most was the fact that all the passageways were very well labeled. Each one had the name of the street above, with arrows pointing to the next intersection. He consulted the pages from the notebook and saw that the notes identified the various gas, water and power lines running sideways along the walls. The whole maze of pathways was surprisingly dry and there was not a sound coming from the outside.

Harold paused to tap Kete on the arm while pointing first forward and then to the ladder leading back up. Kete nodded his head to the forward direction and Harold took the lead again. He wondered why it was that there was no indication of stashed food, clothing or blankets. It looked to him like he had entered a peaceful maintenance facility untouched from the turmoil above and somehow forgotten.

It took them a good fifteen minutes of walking until they reached their destination. Harold was sure that they were below the Mauerstrasse Propaganda building. Two steel ladders in separate locations were attached to concrete walls leading up. Both of them ended below what seemed to be flat steel bulkheads.

They did not appear to be locked from the outside and Kete went up on the ladders to try to lift them upward. They did not budge. After he had exhausted his efforts he came down and Harold went up to inspect the flat surfaces, looking for some kind of locking mechanism. All he could see and feel were some grooves and indentions on one of the covers, but no locks or levers. He climbed down again and led the way back to their original entrance.

While it had been dry and warm below, he was glad to be up and above ground again. It was still raining and the fresh air felt good.

"There is no way that we can enter the building without blowing up the covers," he reported to Karl, "This should be no problem for the Kommissar, as long as his team does not overdo it and destroy the whole access shaft."

Karl listened to his friend and asked to see the pages from the notebook, "Was there any instruction page relating to the access of the various buildings?"

"No," answered Harold, "I don't know about the other buildings, but this one is definitely locked."

Kete had been talking to Alex, who took off to get the Kommissar. After listening to Harold and Kete, he decided to request a demolition expert from the City Commander, and in the meantime, withdraw his team from the area. It was late afternoon and he was anxious to see if there were any new reports or clues about his daughter's whereabouts.

"Could you leave Alex with us?" Karl asked the Kommissar. "I would like to inspect the access once more with Harold before you talk to General Berzarin."

Godunov did not hesitate at all. He wanted to get his hands on the films, if there were any, without the City Commander's knowledge. It could not hurt to have Karl take a look at the bulkheads. He might see something that Harold had overlooked, or find a third access by entering through a neighboring building.

"Alright, I will send the truck to get you in about an hour. Make sure that you are back on the street by that time."

"What do you think you might be able to see, other then what I have told you?" Harold wanted to know as the boys descended with Kete. They left Alex behind to guard the entrance.

"I am not expecting to see anything new. Just the opposite. I would like to see the ruts in the shield you told me about. Did you see any tools down here?"

Harold had to refresh his memory, "No tools, but I think that I did see some crowbars and hammers lying in various places." Harold was using the flashlight to search for other toolboxes, but he only found a hammer and several iron bars which could serve as a crowbar.

"This is the one with the grooves," Harold directed his flashlight at the cover as Karl climbed up the ladder.

"Let me have the light." Karl took the light from Harold and examined the edges of the indentations and the small furrows. He hoped to find some scratches which might indicate that the bulkhead was maybe a sliding cover. A short inspection proved him right. Not only did he find some deep marks from hammer blows, he also noted that the shield was not round but square, and the sides showed hints of grease. His eyes followed the traces and he determined the direction in which the cover could be moved. He climbed back down. "We might be in luck. Get me one of the iron bars and then we will need Kete to get up and try to push the cover not up, but to the side."

He scratched an outline of the cover and the direction of the slide in the dirt on the floor and Kete understood at once. He took the hammer from Harold and started to bang on the dish. He didn't need the crowbar because the cover started to move as soon as he hit it in the proper direction. Inch by inch the cover moved to the side until it stopped against some obstruction, but the opening was now wide enough for Karl to squeeze through.

Once he was inside, he detected several light switches, which he ignored. No use even trying. He saw that a box of some kind had stopped the slide of the cover. It was half filled with some instruction manuals and he moved it to the side to allow Harold and Kete to join him.

They found themselves in something that looked like a control room. One of the walls was covered with gauges and various instruments. On the other side there was doorway and next to it was a regular stairway leading up. Since they had only one light between them, they decided to stay together and investigate what else there was on their level.

Harold could hardly believe their good fortune when he saw that the next room must have served as a storage room for all kinds of records. There were several shelves packed with boxes of books and a rack stacked to the ceiling with wide tin film cases. The boys looked at the labels, which gave dates from 1936 to 1942. The subject titles ranged from "Olympics" in '36 to "Paris" in '42.

"Even if we don't find anything else, this should endear you with Godunov forever," Karl told his friend. They had no clue as to the order of possible importance and grabbed at random some of the reels to take back to the Kommissar.

Before they left, Harold decided to try the entry on top of the staircase. The door was unlocked and opened without trouble, but this is where the boys' luck ended. They faced a burned out hallway, blocked and filled with rubble from the collapsed building above. There was no conceivable way to penetrate the clutter.

"Here is another challenge for you, Sherlock," Harold grinned at his friend, "On this one you might have to use your hands for a change."

"Alright," answered Karl, "then this is the right one for you. But you have already what you came for, so let's forget about it and get back to Godunov. If you get lucky, he might even grab you by your ears and kiss you."

Harold did not consider this remark worthy of a reply and led the way back. When they came back to the exit of the conduit, it was dark outside and they found Alex talking with Vadim, who had parked a few feet away.

Godunov was still gloomy and depressed when the boys joined him in the truck.

"No news about your daughter, Herr Godunov?" asked Harold as he placed the reels in front of the Kommissar.

"No," answered the Pompolit, "I refuse to give up, but all the available information stops in Potsdam." He opened the cover of one of the tin boxes and inspected the reels, "These are priceless and exactly what I was hoping for." His face lit up, "Are there any more?"

"At least a hundred more," Harold guessed.

"A hundred?" marveled Godunov. If he could send a portion of them to Moscow it would be the crown of his intelligence career. All the political as well as the military officers had been tasked with the recovery of the propaganda films as they would visibly identify members of the Nazi hierarchy. The war time criminal trials were coming up and there would be no defense for a Nazi if he was featured in a propaganda reel.

But most of the reels he wanted for himself. He was not a collector as he had told the boys. Far from it. He wanted to examine the reels to extract facts and figures. Precise data used in a correct way to further his political ambitions was his stock in trade. He admired the resourcefulness of Harold. And, the best thing was that the boy had no idea about the treasure he was surrendering.

As they drove back to their quarters, the Pompolit was wondering if he should let the boys do the retrieval or if he would be better off to do it himself. There was not much time and the Americans would call in heavy equipment and churn through all the administration buildings, searching for all and any kind of documents.

"You did well, again. Go with Alex to the kitchen to eat and get some sleep. I will need you tomorrow morning early." He had decided to get the boys out of the way and to do the recovery himself.

He exchanged a few words with Alex then summoned Kete to assemble his team. While the boys were still eating, he was driving with his group to claim his newest and most valuable possession.

A few hours later, Karl woke up when he heard a truck entering the yard below him. Shortly afterwards, he thought that he heard Godunov's voice. He rose from his bed to sneak a look out of the window and saw the Pompolit's team unloading bags. They did not appear to be heavy because some of the men were carrying more than one into the building. By now Karl had gotten used to the nightly excursions of the Pompolit and thought nothing of it.

When he went back to bed he noticed that Alex, who was lying on a blanket at the door, was also awake and had watched him. "Go to sleep, Ex Ex, make ritchipooh." (Berlin slang for sleeping) Alex grunted his usual "spacreff" and turned on his other side.

The next morning was a beauty. The rain had stopped and the sun did its best to chase way the clouds. The intermittent sunshine was also cause for a celebration by Harold. He had been up early and was in the courtyard before breakfast. Shortly before, he had noticed a bird outside the window. Now he was trying to find him.

"Karl, be quiet and look around. I saw a bird this morning." He gestured excitedly at his friend and now both of them scanned the surroundings.

"There he is," whispered Karl, pointing to the brick wall, which had served as the back wall in their shooting exercise.

It looked like a small sparrow. It was one of the birds which, in previous years, lived in Berlin by the millions. However, due to the noise of the bombardments and uninterrupted fires, they had disappeared from the city. Not just a few, but all of them. This sparrow was the first bird Harold had seen since he was about twelve years old. Karl had seen his last bird in Poland. That was also a long time ago. Too long ago to exactly remember when.

"Look at the little guy," said Harold. "Can you imagine how much heart this fellow must have to search in this chaos for a home?"

"Yes," agreed Karl, "I am glad that you noticed him. This really makes my day."

The boys watched the sparrow hopp around the wall and disappear among the debris. The little birdie gave them more hope than they had had in a long time.

"You think that we will remember this bird when we are old and gray?" Harold wondered as he looked around to see if he could spot another one.

"I know that I will," answered Karl.

Twenty-One

"Good morning, Herr Godunov. Will you need us this morning to get more reels," Harold asked after the boys entered the Kommissar's office.

"No, Harold," answered the Pompolit, "You should get your new uniform this morning. Then you will meet your first language instructor, who will keep you busy for the remainder of the day." He omitted telling the boys that he was going to see Marshal Zhukov later on in the morning to present him with two of the 246 propaganda reels he had salvaged the previous night. Upon the successful retrieval of the movies, he had called the Main Directorate of State Security in Moscow and told them that he had discovered twenty Nazi documentary reels.

State Security had responded in an interesting manner. They told him that he was to give Marshal Zhukov only two of the reels and the other ones would be picked up by a special courier from the agency. Since this call, he had been deliberating how to sift through his treasure in the most time-efficient manner. There was no way that he would part with any of the films, which could serve him at a later time.

Karl interrupted his thoughts, "Excuse me, Herr Godunov, have you heard anything about the missing doctors or about your daughter?"

"No Karlchen, but I really appreciate your interest. This is now the third time that you have asked me about Anna and this is three times more than anyone else around me is inquiring."

"There is a reason for my questions, Herr Godunov," Karl

continued, "Harold accepted your generous offer and will stay with you. I would like to search for my father here in Berlin and if I am unable to find him, I would like to be excused by you and allowed to search for my mother in Westphalia." He stopped to wait for a question from the Kommissar. He was right on target.

"What does this have to do with my daughter?" the Kommissar wanted to know.

"Well, if you found your daughter, I would like to ask you right now to be excused." He ran his fingers between his shirt collar and his neck. It was not a nervous habit. His neck still hurt from time to time as a result of a scuffle he had a few weeks back with a black marketer. There was no swelling of any kind. For one reason or another, his neck simply hurt whenever he concentrated on something. "But, if your daughter is still missing, I would like to help you, Herr Godunov." Karl finished his speech. He was hoping that the Kommissar would recognize his good will and would let him go to search for his father.

He could not imagine that an intelligence officer would need his assistance in a personal matter. However, he had made a small miscalculation.

"How would you go about helping me, Karlchen?" Godunov was curious and also at the end of his rope. None of his informants had turned up a clue and he was ready to accept any help from anyone.

Karl was genuinely surprised to be asked. "That would depend upon how much and what kind of information you are willing to share with me, Herr Godunov. I would start by asking you questions and you stop me when I overstep my boundaries."

"You are really serious, Karlchen, aren't you? Alright, let's get Harold on his way to get his uniform and then we have about an hour to discuss how you could possibly help me." He called Kete, who accompanied Harold out of the office. "Fire away," he told Karl after he sat down again.

Right off the bat Karl surprised the Kommissar by the kind of questions he asked. Godunov expected the usual questions like age, hair color, height and so forth but was not prepared to answer questions, which bordered on an interrogation.

"Please tell me about your personal enemies, Herr Godunov. Who are they and where are they at the present time?"

"Karlchen, already you are out of line," exclaimed the Pompolit.

Karl thought for a moment, "Alright, then only one follow-up question in this regard. How many agents do you have on this case?"

Godunov thought before he answered. He had to admit to himself that Karl might be on the right track. But, he was not about to give him highly personal information and leave himself wide open to a young kid. After some deliberation he answered, "I don't have any agents. We don't work that way. You might call me an agent, but I don't employ any."

Karl looked at him intently. "I don't know about your titles or designations, Herr Godunov, but I want to help you. Let me ask you the same question in a different way. How many informers have you asked about your daughter?"

Again the Pompolit hesitated with his answer. The kid had guts to keep on pressing. This time he had not asked how many informers the Kommissar employed but how many he had asked for help. "I don't see how these questions will help me, or you, to find my daughter. But alright, I have asked six people to help me."

"I understand your frustration, Herr Godunov. Please, answer just one more question. From these six people how many answers have you received?"

This was easy for the Kommissar to answer, "None."

"None," repeated Karl, "Not one single lead or positive answer out of six people?"

"None, as in zero," answered the Pompolit again. These questions were stupid and led nowhere as far as he could determine.

"Great. Thank you, Herr Godunov. Then we can rule out personal enemies or revenge. Your daughter might have had an accident."

"How did you arrive at that conclusion?" Godunov was confounded.

"Easy, I just went by your answers. I cannot imagine that you have six incompetent informers. At least one of them had to come up with something, unless they are employees of someone else. Based upon your answer that your agency does not employ a chain of agents, then this is not possible either. That leaves us with the result that your people don't know a darn thing. And the reason they don't know anything is simply because none of your opponents have reached out to hurt you."

Godunov was forced again to admit to himself that Karl could be right. "Let us assume for the time being that my daughter had indeed had an accident. Let us also consider that we have not a single clue as to the where, when and how. Where does this leave us?" He had the feeling that they were finally getting somewhere, but again, he was surprised by Karl's barrage of answers.

"In all due respect, Herr Godunov. Your intelligence people sometimes surprise me. Let me answer your questions specifically in the order you asked. 'Where was the possible accident?' In Potsdam, of course. You established that it was there when she was seen the last time. 'When?' Again, you established that this was two or three days ago. 'How or what kind of accident?' Give me two days, a car and driver to Potsdam, and Alex for protection and I will have an answer for you."

"These are mighty big words for a kid, Karlchen. You should know better than to sound off like that. As you very well know, we already went to Potsdam and neither my people nor I could find any evidence of an accident. Yesterday, I had the hospitals searched in Potsdam. No reports, no victims, nothing."

Karl could not stand it any longer. He got up from his seat and stared at the Kommissar, "Once more, Herr Godunov, I mean once more in all due respect to you," his hand massaged his neck again. "I am tired of being called a kid. I was raised to be a young adult. I was trained to be a young adult. I was never trained to be a kid. I don't know about your country, but in my country, at the age of 14, we are asked by our parents to decide how we want to earn a living. Either to enter high school and become a professional or to decide upon the trade we wish to learn and start to earn a living. Either way, we are young adults and not simply dumb kids." He still stared at the speechless Kommissar. "Now, you can trust me and give me the help I asked for and I will find your daughter or, you can think of me as a child and resume your own investigation."

Karl knew his emotions were carrying him way into dangerous territory, but enough was enough. He had had it with adults who tried to belittle him. Many of them were scared and most of them incompetent beyond belief. He strongly trusted himself and still had the letters and recommendations from his commanding officers attesting to his abilities. In addition, he already knew where to look for Godunov's daughter and since he had seen the greed of the Kommissar in action, he did not have too much respect for him as an adult either. Sure, Godunov could shoot him or make him disappear, but what else was new? Besides, he was sure that Godunov wanted to know about his daughter. The odds of being tolerated were in his favor.

The Pompolit had heard enough. He admired the boy's gumption to shout out his convictions and Karl had proven to him that he should be taken serious. In addition, he could not think of a better suited German to look for his daughter in Potsdam. However, he had to keep the boy in line.

"I will let your outburst slide for today. You have been under a lot of strain in the last few weeks. Now, your actions have to prove to me that you have more than a big mouth. You want me to treat you as an adult? I can do that, but I expect results and not excuses or empty hot air."

The Pompolit called for Alex, exchanged a few words with him and then laughed. "You will not believe this, Karlchen. We just received from the Americans a small, but brand new car. They call it a Jeep. I think it is kind of open, without a roof. But for the next two days it is yours, together with a driver and Alex. I wish you well."

"Thanks, Herr Godunov, I promise you results and I hope for your sake that it will be good news."

He left the office with Alex sauntering behind him. On the way down he passed Harold, who was going up to present himself in his new uniform to the Kommissar.

"If I did not know you, I would have taken you for a Russian. However, you might have to walk while I have a Jeep at my disposal," Karl stopped in front of his friend.

"What is a Jeep?"

"I don't know," Karl answered truthfully, "other than it is American and comes with a Russian driver."

Harold's mouth was still open when Karl left the building.

The Jeep was indeed a small vehicle and Alex's large frame hardly fit next to the driver. He was one of the Pompolit's personal guards and Karl did not know his name. He was about to enter the backseat and sit sideways when an idea hit him.

"Wait," he yelled behind his friend and hurried back to the staircase to catch up with him.

"What now?" Harold wondered when Karl reached him.

"Have you met your language instructor?"

"Yes," answered Harold, "he is an older Belorussian officer with the rank of Major, I think. Why are you asking?"

"Never mind, let's go and see Godunov." Karl poked his friend in the ribs as he always did when he had a project for both of them.

Godunov was just leaving his office to meet with Marshal Zhukov when the boys turned up in the hallway. "You look sharp, Harold. Congratulations, but what about you Karlchen? I thought that you would be on your way by now," his forehead was wrinkled and he was apparently annoyed at being interrupted.

Karl tried anyway, "Yes, Herr Godunov. However, I can hardly communicate with Alex or the driver. I really would like to get into the Lindenstrasse facility today. Is it possible that Harold and his mentor could go with me? Just for today, to get me access to the prison. We will be back tonight and tomorrow I can continue on my own," he looked hopefully at the Pompolit.

"No," said the Pompolit, "I gave you exactly what you asked for. I have other plans for Harold today. Don't make me think that you shot off your mouth. Now go on your way and you Harold, wait for the Major and start your lessons." He ushered the boys out of the building and boarded his truck. Karl could see that he carried two of the film cassettes with him.

"Wow," said Harold, "you always told me to watch what I am saying. You must have really stepped into his butter dish."

"Yes, I guess I have," Karl wished that he had left well enough alone. On the way back to the Jeep, he changed his plan again. It was the third time that he had changed his plan in the last 15 minutes.

The driver had a name, 'Poti' or something like that, because he repeated it a few times while pointing at himself. 'Great' thought Karl hopefully, but when he asked him how he liked the weather, he only triggered a helpless stare; so much for communication. On the bright side, he noticed that Poti looked far more awake or even intelligent. No wonder he knew how to drive a car. Most of the men in the Kommissar's detail had always looked alike to him and he wondered why he had not noticed Poti before.

It was not even noon and he decided on a fast detour to the Becker's. He wanted to get a few bars of soap to have something to barter with when he fished for information in Potsdam.

Frau Becker was happy to see him, "What on earth you are doing to be chauffeured around like that?" she asked.

"Too long of a story, Frau Becker. Is one of the doctors still here or close by?" Karl had also hoped to see Dr. Felder again, but Frau Becker told him that she had no idea where the doctors went. She gave him several bars of soap without questioning him as to the purpose and inquired about Harold.

"As of right now, he is learning to speak Russian. Please give my regard to Herr Becker; I have to run."

His next stop was his old hide-away. He had Poti park the Jeep at the entrance to the courtyard and walked with Alex the few feet to the entrance of the ventilation shaft. It was still covered with debris and looked just like they had left it a few days ago. While Alex stood watch, Karl went down to retrieve the last few cigarettes and as he rummaged around, he also found a few more of the small round tins with the "Flieger" chocolate. He covered the entrance again. There was hardly anything left of value, except for some blankets and maybe some cans of food, but he figured that the place itself might still come in handy.

As the Jeep turned into the Kurfuerstendam, Karl could see that the Russians were setting up a soup kitchen. General Berzarin turned out to be an efficient City Commander. He seemed to care for the civilian population.

The drive to Potsdam was slow. They had to yield to the massive troop transports coming and going in opposite directions. Karl did not see any more Mongolians. He could not distinguish between the Belorussians and the Ukrainian forces. Except for some badges on their uniforms, they all looked alike to him. But the fact was that the initial fighting forces were now being replaced by temporary occupation troops and on the main thoroughfares, there were now also Polish transports as well as British, French and American movements. Karl could not help but marvel at the diffcrence a week made.

While just a few days ago all these forces were bombing and beating the hell out of the defenders of Berlin, they were now converging on the city in a peaceful manner. Not exactly orderly, but nevertheless peaceful.

As the Jeep passed Babelsberg/Ufastadt, Karl was thinking of Godunov's interest in the Propaganda film reels. He recalled the unloading of bags last night and was sure that Godunov had emptied the basement in the Mauerstrasse. Whatever the true motivation was, he was sure that the Kommissar did not have some weird collector habit.

They had reached Potsdam, which was relatively undisturbed by troop movements. Karl asked Poti to park for a moment behind the Jaegertor Monument. He had to rethink his strategy. At first he had wanted to observe the Lindenstrasse prison for a while. However, when they had cruised down the street, he had been surprised by the beehive of activity at the entrance of Nr. 54/55, and decided not to stop.

True to his training, he was now adding up what he knew. When they were here before, the Kommissar had told him that the prison was empty and that there was just a small unit of new guards moving in. Now, there was a convoy of trucks, apparently loaded with SS prisoners, lined up at the entrance. On his short drive by, he had only seen Russian trucks. Not a single British or American vehicle. There were some other details he remembered, but he required additional information before he could put it all together. What bothered him the most was that the Kommissar had told him that another woman doctor was missing; not just his daughter Anna. However, in all the other discussions later on, the other woman doctor had never again been mentioned. It was understandable that the Kommissar worried first and foremost for his daughter, but did no one care or even ask for the other woman?

One thing was for sure. There was a limit to what he could do by himself. His two Tatars were very good for protection, but useless for gathering information. He needed help.

Twenty-Two

Karl looked at Alex and Poti, who sat back in their seats with one leg on top of the hood and the other dangling over the side. He had given them a package of cigarettes to share, and both were happily smoking away.

He noticed that another Russian truck loaded with prisoners rounded the plaza and rolled down the Lindenstrasse. The prison was too far down the street to see from his present observation point, but he assumed that this truck would also line up behind the others. This also meant prolonged activity around the entrance.

For a moment he considered driving back to Berlin and asking Herr Becker to come with him. He pictured him walking down the street, asking questions of the locals. But as fast as the thought had surfaced, he was already dismissing it. Herr Becker was a stranger in Potsdam and on this street. No one, either in Berlin, or for that matter in Potsdam, was talking to strangers anymore. The informants of the SS had made sure of that.

Except, yes, there was an exception, as he continued his line of thought. The exception was right in front of him as he looked across the plaza.

Two boys, maybe eleven or twelve years old, were coming out of a side street. They were entering the plaza kicking a can to each other, like playing soccer without a ball. Karl motioned to his companions to stay put and approached the boys from the direction of the Lindenstrasse behind him.

"Hello boys," he stepped between them and kicked the can to the oldest looking one.

"Who are you?" The oldest one was not kicking the can back to him.

"I am Karl. Who are you?"

The boy squinted at him, "You are not from this neighborhood. What are you doing here?"

Karl smiled at him, "Looking around," he pulled a piece of dry black bread from his pocket and started to chew on it.

The younger one stepped up to Karl and extended his hand, "I am Gunther. If you have some food to share with us, we will let you play with us." Karl shook the dirty little hand.

"Sorry, I have no food and no time to play. But, I have some chocolate to share; if you want some." He opened one of his tins and let the boys take a look at the chocolate wafers. He took a single wafer out, broke it apart, and gave each of the boys one half without eating any of the chocolate himself.

"Mensch, Gunther, Flieger Schokolade!" the older one exclaimed, and then stretched out his equally dirty hand to shake hands with Karl. "My name is Heinz. It would be fun if you had the time to play with us," he pointed across the square. "We own this plaza," he announced.

"How can you own this Plaza?"

"We are the oldest in this neighborhood. Others can play here too, but only if we allow it."

"Well, thank you for your invitation," said Karl, "but I have not much time. I need to keep looking around."

"What are you looking for? Maybe we can help." Gunther had seen that there were more chocolate wafers in the tin and hoped to get another half or even a whole one.

"I am looking for my older sister. She disappeared on this street," Karl pointed to the Lindenstrasse behind him.

"Ouch, my Mamma said that no one comes back from one of the houses down the street. We are not allowed to go very far down this street." Heinz mumbled more to himself than answering Karl.

"Not true," exclaimed Gunther. "My sister went to a party in one of the houses down there and came back; but she is now sick and in bed."

Karl hoped that he had hit pay dirt. He remembered the old civilian who had told him that the Russians had rounded up women for a party. The invalid had also told him that the women had been released after a night of drinking and carousing.

"Listen Gunther, do you think that I could talk to your sister? She might know about my sister."

"I don't know if she is well enough to talk with you. Yesterday she was crying all day and today she is sleeping," Gunther answered sadly.

"Do you think that I could ask your mother some questions?" Karl tried again.

"If you had some chocolate or food for my mother, she might talk to you." Gunther was excited to have found a possible way to get some more chocolate.

Heinz was not to be left out. "Yes, if you have some chocolate for my mother, I would let you talk to her, too. She knows plenty about the Lindenstrasse."

Karl was weighing his options. If he wanted to push his luck, he could go right now with the boys. The mothers would surely have some answers for him. The alternative was to ask the boys if they had any friends who lived further down the street. This would also give him the opportunity to waive at Alex to stay where he was. He was sure that the Tatars would follow him with the car as soon as he disappeared down the street. He decided to ask the boys about their friends.

"I have some chocolate for your mothers," he announced to the joy of the boys, "but first let me ask you, do you have any friends living directly on the Lindenstrasse?"

"No friends, just little Otto," answered Heinz.

"Ja, little Otto, he lives down the street. He is younger than we are. He is also very stupid because he is left-handed," Gunther chimed in.

"My Mamma says that you should not call children stupid because they are left-handed," Heinz defended little Otto.

"Maybe he is not stupid," allowed Gunther, "but he is surely left-handed."

Karl had seen many teachers beating the left hand of boys when they attempted to write with it. The left-handed children had always been ridiculed and laughed at, but now was not the time to debate it.

He had used the verbal exchange between the boys to wave once more to Alex to stay where he was. The boys went back to their street and Karl followed to talk with their mothers.

Gunther dragged Karl into a small apartment and told his

mother that he had found a new friend with chocolate. His mother looked kind of old to Karl to have such a small boy and she was not about to let Karl into the bedroom to see her daughter. "What do you want to know?" She looked at Karl suspiciously. Karl decided upon direct questions. He had nothing to lose. He had read the last name of the family on the nameplate on the front door and wanted to be polite and show his good upbringing.

"Frau Krause, my name is Karl, and I would be very pleased if you could help me. My sister and I live in Berlin and she came here a few days ago to search for our uncle. She was last seen in the area of Lindenstrasse 54 and is now missing. I understand that your daughter attended a party at this address and I wonder if she met her or saw her."

Karl returned the searching look from the woman with a steady look of his own and was relieved when he saw her lighten up. "I can ask my daughter. How old is your sister and what is her name?"

Karl had to think for a moment because he had not asked the Kommissar about the age of his daughter. Godunov looked like he was close to 50 years old and his daughter was a doctor... "She is 28 years old and her name is Anna."

"Wait here," said Frau Krause. She liked the polite boy and left him in the kitchen.

"May I have the chocolate now?" asked Gunther. Karl opened the tin again and gave him a wafer to split with Heinz. He could see that Heinz was trying to see if there were any more wafers in the tin. "What about the chocolate for my mother?"

"Your mother might prefer a bar of soap," answered Karl.

"Wwwhat?" stuttered Gunther. Before Karl could answer, Frau Krause entered the kitchen again. "My daughter might know something about your sister, but she seemed to be confused. She would like to see you," Frau Krause showed him to a room, "but no longer than five minutes," she added.

Karl entered the small room with a single bed in it. His eyes had to adjust for a moment to the darkness, which was caused by the heavy curtains in front of the window. He could not estimate the age of the girl or young woman resting below a heavy feather bed.

"Guten Tag," (Good Day) he greeted the woman.

"Guten Tag," came a remarkably strong answer. Frau Krause stepped next to the bed and placed a huge pillow under the head of her daughter. "You are looking for your sister with the name of Anna?" The girl made an effort to sit up and her Mother helped her by placing another big pillow behind her shoulders.

"Yes, I am," said Karl.

"Anna, Anna; yes I think I met a woman with that name. Does your sister speak Russian?"

Karl could see now that it was a young woman, maybe in her late teens. She had a hard time focusing her eyes but her voice was steady. "Yes, yes, that's my sister. She is a doctor and is fluent in several languages," Karl got excited.

"I don't know about that," came the answer, "her German left a lot to be desired."

Karl could hardly contain himself, "That's my sister, for sure. She probably spoke in a broken German to confuse the Russians into thinking that she was really a Russian."

"She did not do a good job at it. While we were forced to sing and dance, she was several times raped by a Soviet official who did not believe her."

"I was afraid that this is what happened to her. Did she leave with you," Karl was afraid of the answer.

"No, she was barely able to move." The voice got weaker. "When they let us go, two of the other women helped her to walk out and took her along. She was lucky."

Karl thought for a moment, "Do you know where the women might live who took her along? And why was she lucky? You just said that she got raped."

The young woman seemed to get tired and slumped back on the pillows. Her mother was anxious to get Karl to stop his questions, "You may come back tomorrow and ask her again. Please leave the room."

Karl had no choice and started to walk out when he thought that he heard something like, "Because the .... other........ woman got........" Karl stopped and looked at Frau Krause. "What did she say?" He asked her.

Frau Krause pushed him into the kitchen. "I did not really understand her either. I think she said the other woman who pretended to be Russian got killed."

Karl started to quiver in his excitement. He was so close and still so far away from knowing the full story. When he was back in the kitchen he had to sit down.

TRUST TO A DEGREE

Frau Krause studied him intently, "I understand why you are shaking. However, now you know that your sister is alive. Come back tomorrow morning and you may ask my daughter again." She liked Karl and was considering inviting him to stay the night with her son, when Karl seemed to get control of his emotions.

"I will be happy to return tomorrow morning, Frau Krause. Thank you for helping me. May I offer you a bar of soap for your kindness?" He reached into his pocket and showed her the soap.

"You don't need to do that, Karl, but I really could use it." She reached eagerly for the bar.

"You could have gotten Schokolade from him," advised Gunther, but when he saw the happy expression on his mother's face, he was satisfied.

"Let's go to my mother. She knows a lot more about the Lindenstrasse. You can ask her all kind of questions." They stepped back on the street and Heinz was hoping that his new friend would still be interested.

Karl, however, had a different idea. He knew that the boys could probably find out what he needed to know. "I need to get home to tell my mother the good news. But, if you want some food or even a tin of chocolate, I will let you earn it."

"Really," said Heinz, "what do you want us to do?"

Karl gave each of the boys another wafer before he continued, "You heard what I heard. I still don't know where these other women took my sister. I could maybe go from house to house and eventually find her. But you could do this much faster by asking all your friends about her." He looked expectantly at the boys to see if he had them hooked.

Gunther started to dance around, "Come on, Heinz. This will be fun." He looked up to Karl, "What time will you be back?"

Karl guessed that he could be back early in the morning, but wanted to give himself some leeway, "I will meet you here shortly before noon. How is that?"

Heinz did not care about the time. He was more concerned about the reward, "Promise that you will bring us chocolate again?"

Karl had only three unopened tins left. "Yes, I promise, but I might have something even better."

The eyes of the boys rested on him. "There is nothing better than chocolate," said Gunther.

"Yes, there is. It is called rock sugar," replied Karl.

"How can it be better than chocolate?" Gunther wanted to know.

"It is sweeter and it takes a long time to melt in your mouth. You can suck on it for almost an hour."

Both boys stared at Karl. They had never heard of rock sugar. They hardly remembered regular sugar.

"We will wait for you right here at the plaza, Karl, and we will ask all our friends about your sister."

Karl was satisfied with what he had accomplished. He was a lot closer on the trail than the Kommissar. He waived the boys good-bye as they ran into the next street to call on their friends.

The Jeep was still standing where Karl had left it. Poti was sleeping in the driver's seat and Alex had been observing and following Karl on foot. He was not worried about Karl, but he was clearly happy when they were back on the road to Berlin.

When they reached their quarters, it was already dark. Karl found Harold where he suspected to find him, in the kitchen facility.

"How was your day? Did you learn anything," he asked Harold as he helped himself to a dish of cabbage soup.

"Mensch, Karl, the Russian language is hard to learn. I can only hope that the major doesn't run out of patience." Then his face lit up, "But, I know now what Alex says to us before we go to sleep."

Karl was interested enough to ask, "What?"

"Hundeblut," (Dogs blood) answered Harold.

Karl thought that he misunderstood, "Hundeblut? That does not make any sense."

"No, it doesn't, and to top it off, it is not even Russian. It is a Polish curse word. I think that Alex must have picked it up when some Pollack cursed him before he fell asleep."

"Dogs blood is a Polish curse?" Karl wanted to be sure.

"No, no, Karl, 'spacreff' is a Polish curse word. Dogs blood is just the translation," Harold was obviously proud of what he had learned.

"Hallelujah, the saints are drunk! Here I am going on a mission to find the missing daughter of the Kommissar and you entertain yourself with curse words." Karl got up to get himself some tea. "On second thought, I might reconsider and join the intelligence community too."

The door opened and Alex stuck his head in the kitchen. He motioned to the boys to follow him up to the Kommissar's office.

"Alex told me that you were talking to some children in Potsdam. Do you have any news for me?" Godunov was encouraged by Karl's smile.

"I think that I will find her tomorrow. But I need a pound of your rock sugar."

The Kommissar stared from one boy to the other and then to the bowl of hard candies on his desk. "You will find her tomorrow with rock sugar?" he asked incredulously.

Karl decided to tell Godunov what he had found out and ended by saying, "I am out of chocolate, but I need something to reward the boys and their friends."

"You are wasting time. If my daughter is injured, then she might be dying while we are discussing awarding children." He yelled something at Alex, who hurried to assemble the team.

Karl was afraid that the Kommissar wanted to start a house to house search in the Lindenstrasse, "What do you intend to do?"

Godunov was almost shouting at him, "I speak German and can ask for my daughter a lot better and faster than you can."

"Herr Godunov, you forget that whoever did anything to your daughter might have also shot the other Russian female doctor. He or they might think that your daughter is dead. If they find out that you are conducting a search, they might get to her before you do."

The Kommissar was not listening. Instead he was giving orders to Kete.

"Herr Godunov, you cannot afford to take the chance. Besides, don't you want to find out who the official is who did this to your daughter?" Karl was almost pleading.

The Kommissar turned to face Karl, "We do not have the time to discuss this. You did well by finding out that she is alive. If you have a solid plan, I will listen to you on the way." He stormed out of the office without turning to see if the boys followed him.

His team was already in the truck. He must have given some detailed instructions because the Jeep was ready to roll with Poti at the wheel.

Twenty-Three

The Kommissar boarded the jeep and nodded to the boys to sit behind him. The traffic was just as heavy and congested in the late evening as it had been during the day, and it took a while until they hit the thoroughfare to Potsdam.

"If you have a plan, now is the time to tell me," the Kommissar prompted Karl.

"My plan was to obtain solid leads from the boys and then go with Alex to possibly find her. She could be any place in Potsdam."

Instead of an answer, the Pompolit just grunted to Karl to keep on talking.

"Once I had her secured, I wanted to see if I could obtain some information as to who the originator of the festivities was. It could have been the departing guard detail, or if Gunther's sister was correct, it could have been a high-ranking officer who wanted to use the facilities of the prison. We don't even know if your daughter really treated or saw any remaining political prisoners."

"What are you saying, Karlchen?" Godunov had somewhat settled down, but the last remark from Karl alerted him again.

"I am thinking that for one motive or another, your daughter might have been ordered, under some kind of pretense, to the prison for the sole reason to be raped." Karl was answering while he was already wondering what their next step could be, once they reached the Lindenstrasse.

"I can't imagine a reason for such actions," said the Kommissar.

Karl was undaunted, "You never answered my questions in regard to your political enemies. Therefore, I believe you that you cannot imagine who would do a thing like this to your daughter, or to you. But, you need to consider the possibility."

Godunov was getting hot under the collar. Karl was right. He had to consider all of the contenders who were snapping at his heels. "Karlchen, how on earth can you even conceive of these fantasies?"

"If you would have seen what the SS commanders and the Wehrmacht officers did to each other, then you would know that these fantasies are based upon reality," he wanted to add that he did not know in what kind of fantasy world the Kommissar was living in, but he left well enough alone.

"Then," Godunov began, "what do you suggest, Karl?"

Karl wanted to answer, but all of a sudden he realized that Godunov had called him by his correct name; without the ending which defined him as a child. The ending usually reserved for mothers and grandmothers calling their small children. Could it be that Godunov finally accepted him as a young man?

"By the time we reach the Jaegertor, it will be past midnight. Too late to wake up Frau Krause and too early to expect any results from Gunther or Heinz," Karl's hand went up to massage his neck again, "I think that it would be more productive to wait until we have additional information. And thank you Herr Godunov, for calling me Karl."

The Kommissar smiled to himself. There was not much that the boy missed. He would have loved to keep him as a protégé. The real reason for wanting a German apprentice was the fact that he wanted to start an innovative network of agents and informants who worked for no one else but him, and who had no allegiance to any officer's family in Russia. Harold was a perfect fit and so was Karl. Both of them thought independently, had a disciplined upbringing, and were sufficiently intelligent to learn and to be taught. The thought of having a native German in Berlin and in Germany to serve his interests was overwhelming. He could see himself as a retired Pompolit, living in comfort on the Crimean Peninsula, pulling strings without fear of being detected. What more could he ask for? He had been blessed with a bright daughter, but everyone in the political hierarchy knew that she was his daughter and he could not conceive of using her to serve his ambitions. Moreover, the fact that she was missing showed him how vulnerable he was to blackmail.

187

"You might be right, Karl. We need information about Anna's whereabouts. Here is what we will do; once we reach the Lindenstrasse, we will split up. You will work with Harold and your group of children. Alex and Poti with the Jeep will support you. I will drive to the prison and find out about the troops who were in charge during the time of the festivities." The Kommissar reassessed his strategy. "You can rest in the car until you think it would be an appropriate time to contact Frau Krause. I, however, will start as soon as we arrive."

Karl had no problem resting immediately. He could sleep on command, practically anywhere and at any time. "Wake me when we reach the Lindenstrasse," he said to Harold, hoping to get at least an hour while they were still driving.

It was far longer than an hour because the cars of the Pompolit had been stuck in a convoy of Russian and American trucks, with no one knowing where they were going. Harold had finally directed them over secondary streets to their destination. By the time they arrived, it was already past four o'clock in the morning.

"We should meet here at ten to exchange information," said Godunov as he left the Jeep to board the truck. Both cars were standing at the Jaegertor.

"I almost forgot," Godunov came back to the jeep and handed Karl a paper bag with rock sugar.

"I'll be darned," said Karl, "He must have ordered Kete to get this bag."

Harold grinned his boyish innocent smile, "We will have plenty, Karl. I took his bowl as we were leaving." He pointed to the stoneware bowl filled with candies, which he had been hiding under the back seat.

Alex came to claim his seat next to Poti and looked longingly at the sugar bowl. Karl handed him a handful and received in return a thankful smile. He offered some sugar to Poti who declined. *He probably would rather eat a dead fish*, thought Karl. The truck with the team entered the Lindenstrasse and Karl waited for half an hour until he gestured to Poti to follow. The street in front of Nr. 54/55 was empty. The prisoner transports from the day before were gone and so was the Pompolit with his team. The guards must have allowed him to enter the yard. Karl had Poti park the Jeep across the street, but a few houses further down. He wanted to observe for a while.

"Your turn to sleep," he told Harold as he got out and motioned to Alex to come along. He walked with him several houses up the street and then returned to the car. None of the houses they passed had any lights on, which was in stark contrast to the jail, whose rear buildings were brightly illuminated.

Karl had enjoyed the quiet walk. All of the houses they passed were undamaged. The street was void of any rubble and looked like a small-town street in peacetime. He was settling back in his seat and started to daydream. He must have been sitting like that for over an hour when he noticed some movement. Alex must have noticed it too. His big bulk had shifted and he was observing the other side of the street. Someone was entering one of the houses because they could hear a door shutting. Alex seemed to think nothing of it because he resumed his old position again. Karl thought that it was kind of odd. Why would people walk this early in the morning? As far as he knew, there were no regular jobs to come home from. It was still dark and he looked at his watch. It showed close to 6:00 AM and he wanted to wait another hour before he called on Frau Krause.

He was about to continue his daydreaming when he heard the door again, but no one was entering the street. It must have been someone else coming home or visiting somebody. He decided to keep his eyes open. A little while later, Poti woke up and Karl signaled to him to stay quiet.

Nothing happened for a while until he saw that a door across the street opened. An older man entered the street. He was severely limping as he hobbled along and Karl discerned a white arm sleeve with a red cross on it. He waited until the fellow was pretty far down the street and then quickly caught up with him.

"Good morning," he startled the old man, "My name is Karl. I live further down," he pointed in the direction they had just come from. "How is Anna doing?" He skipped like a little kid and scratched his knee.

The old guy kept shuffling along as if in a trance. He did not even look up. "They should have called me sooner ..., wait a minute. You are who?" he stopped and peered at Karl.

"I am Karl. I am a friend of little Otto. Sometimes we play together. I don't mind that he is left-handed." He acted like he was a touch irrational and hoped that the old guy knew little Otto or had at least heard of him.

"Oh, ja, little Otto. He is a nice kid. But how do you know about Anna?" his voice was now a lot friendlier.

Karl was still skipping, alternating on his legs and smiling at him. "Oh, you know, all the kids on the street know about her. They even say that she is a Russian. Did you treat her? How is she doing?" he talked hastily with a high-pitched voice like a frantic child would.

The old timer scrutinized him more closely. He looked at Karl's knee socks and short pants, "I wish that you kids would not chat about things which do not concern you. Anna will be all right. That is all I will tell you. Auf Wiedersehen." (Good-bye) He resumed his waddle.

Karl answered with an "Auf Wiedersehen" of his own and skipped back to the car.

Harold woke up as Karl approached, "Stop this nonsense. You behave like a little child." Poti was amused by Karl's antics.

"Harold, listen up, we have to decide what to do next," Karl told his friend what he had found out.

"We should plant ourselves in front of the house across the street and wait for Godunov to come out of the prison," Harold suggested.

"Which house?"

"Well, you just told me that you saw where the old man came from," answered Harold.

Karl shook his head. "That does not mean that Anna is there. The Red Cross guy could have treated one of the other German women. All we know is that Anna is somewhat well and in this general area."

Harold shrugged his shoulders, "It would be at least a start. You could pretend again that you are her brother." He looked at Karl, "I mean, you don't have to skip and pretend that you are demented. Anybody can figure that out by themselves."

"Right," said Karl. He had a comeback, but decided against it. Instead he voiced his idea, "You stay here and watch who is coming and going. Hide behind these two fellows," he pointed at Alex and Poti, "I'll take off to see Gunther and Frau Krause. It is only a ten-minute walk. Should Godunov leave the prison before I return, bring him up to date, but implore him to wait until I get back. I promise that I will hurry." He wanted to leave alone, but Alex insisted on going with him. Karl argued and gestured until he finally gave up.

Alex won, however he did not walk on Karl's side, but followed him on the opposite side of the street. Karl wondered how he could explain to Frau Krause that he was back so early and decided to tell her that he had been sleeping in Potsdam.

"Karl, come in, we have good news for you," Frau Krause was an early riser. "How come you are back so early?"

Before he could answer, Gunther showed up, "Good morning, Karl. I hope that you have my chocolate or the rock sugar you promised."

"Not so fast," answered Karl. "Did you earn it?"

Gunther grinned from ear to ear, "Yes, we know where your sister is."

Karl pulled the sugar bag from his pocket, "Where is she?"

"She is someplace in the Lindenstrasse," answered Gunther.

"Where exactly?" Karl was wondering if Gunther really knew the address. He was holding on to the sugar.

"Karl, I have something to tell you," Frau Krause started to explain, "I am sure that you know that some of the girls and the women who attended the party in the Lindenstrasse got hurt."

Karl nodded his understanding.

"So, the neighbors got together and started some kind of a first-aid group," continued Frau Krause. "There are two houses in the Lindenstrasse and one house in the Breitestrasse in which the women are hiding and being cared for."

Karl interrupted her speech, "Did you know this yesterday Frau Krause?"

She shook her head, "No Karl, this is what the boys found out. They all talk to each other. Some of their mothers are missing and some of their mothers are hurt. Gunther and Heinz talked to their friends yesterday evening and then told me about it."

She offered a cup of a hot beverage to Karl, which he had never tasted before. She called it 'Brown Tea'. It was not too bad, but kind of bitter and Karl suspected that the residents of Potsdam had more access to food then the people of Berlin.

There was a knock on the door. It was Heinz who was in a hurry to shut it again.

"Good Morning, Karl. Do you know that you are being followed," he asked all excited. "I saw you crossing the plaza and there was a Russian soldier following you. He is now standing across the street and watching this house. I did not know what to do but I felt that I had to warn you." He went to the front window to look out.

"Thank you Heinz. I think I saw him before. He looks to me like a harmless drunk who is lost. I did not know that he followed me all the way to this house."

Frau Krause became agitated, "Karl, you have to leave. Here are the addresses of the safe-houses. I wrote them down for you. Please, go now."

Karl looked at boys and the woman. He understood that she was concerned about the safety of her daughter. He stuck the paper with the addresses in his pocket. "Thank you very much for all your help. If this soldier is really following me, then I will lead him away from here." He gave the paper bag with the rock sugar to the boys. "This is for you to share with your friends who told you where to find my sister."

He shook hands with all of them and walked out. Heinz wanted to follow him, but Frau Krause told him to stay with Gunther until the Russian soldier was gone. She was relieved to see that the husky soldier was indeed following Karl and finally disappeared.

Karl was walking at a fast pace to get back to the jeep. He was comparing the house numbers on the street with the numbers on his piece of paper and noted that one of the numbers was the house he remembered from his first trip to the prison. It was the house the old invalid had disappeared into after he had asked him some questions about the jail. The other number was the house the Red Cross man had visited. Karl wanted to report to Harold and send him to investigate the other house in the Breitestrasse, when the gate of the prison opened and the familiar truck of the Pompolit pulled out and left in direction of the plaza.

"We will search all three houses at the same time," Godunov declared after Karl had finished his report.

Harold was not happy about this decision. "Herr Godunov, why don't you let Karl and me visit the houses one at a time. This way, we don't upset the caregivers and alert the families that their safe-houses have been discovered," he suggested.

"No, Harold. I don't want to waste any more time. I don't know how severely injured my daughter is. You can stay behind if you want and assure the families that there will be no repercussions."

"Repercussions," echoed Karl. "What about some food or

medical supplies for the people who helped your daughter?"

Godunov turned to face him, "That's enough." His eyes glared at the boys, "We are not running this by committee." He ordered his team to split up but before they understood what was asked of them, he was interrupted by the actions of Harold.

He had crossed the street dragging Karl along and was knocking on the door where the Red Cross man had come from. "Open up, I want to see Anna." He kept on beating on the door until it opened. Harold stood to the side because of his Russian uniform. He did not need to worry because Karl was now in front of the door and was being waved in.

The Kommissar barked a command at his team and then was right behind him. "Anna!" he yelled at the top of his lungs as he stormed through the entrance. There was a moment of silence and then Karl could hear a mixture of German and Russian shouting, which was almost instantly followed by cries of joy. Karl could discern the deep voice of Godunov and a much higher female voice.

"We found her," Karl announced as he came out of the house and motioned to Harold and Kete to enter.

When Karl went back into the hallway, he saw an old couple standing next to a door leading into a bedroom. The woman was trembling and both of them looked utterly confused at the Kommissar, who was holding his daughter in his arms. Karl and Harold tried their best to explain to the couple that they had nothing to fear and that they would be rewarded for their kind actions.

"We really did not know that she was a Russian soldier," the old man said over and over again. "We only knew that she needed help." He looked at his wife who was eager to assure. "We would have notified the proper authorities. Really, we would have."

Twenty-Four

"How did you know that Anna was in this particular house," Karl asked Harold when they were in the jeep again, leading the way back to Berlin.

"I did not know," answered Harold. "I just thought that if Godunov sent his teams to the three addresses at the same time, it would destroy the little safety net of the families. So, I took a chance." He was feeling good about his actions and hoped that Godunov would reimburse the old couple for the bedding and blankets his team had requisitioned to provide a somewhat comfortable spot for Anna in the truck.

They had almost reached the inner city of Berlin when the truck flashed its lights to signal the jeep to pull over and stop. Kete, who had been riding with the boys, went to see what the unscheduled halt was about and shortly thereafter summoned the boys to the Kommissar.

"Can you find Dr. Felder for me," he asked Karl.

"We can drive by the Becker's apartment and ask if they know of his whereabouts. Otherwise, we might try the Gertrauden Hospital, but I doubt that he went there." Karl wondered why Godunov wanted to see the German doctor instead of taking his daughter to the nearest field hospital of the Russian army.

"Lead the way, Harold," the Kommissar was eager to keep on going, but he motioned to Karl to join him in the truck.

This was the first time that Karl had the chance to get a look at the Kommissar's daughter. She was resting quietly between piled up bedding and blankets and seemed to be sleeping. All he could really see was her ebony black hair.

"How is she doing?"

"The German families must have treated her well. I think that she will be alright, but I want her examined by a physician." The Kommissar spoke calmer than he had in a long time. He seemed to be relieved. His face was relaxed and the deep wrinkles on his forehead were gone. Karl was glad to hear the good news.

He dared to ask, "Why do we need to search for Dr. Felder? Can't your military doctors check her out much faster?"

"I have not talked much with my daughter but at this time, I don't want anyone to know that she is alive and that I found her." The Kommissar turned away from his daughter and faced Karl, "I have my reasons," he continued. "If we don't find Dr. Felder at the Becker's, I want you to get me a German doctor from your Gertrauden Hospital."

The truck came to a stop in front of Berliner Strasse 26, the Becker's apartment. Harold was the first one out and knocked at the door.

"Open up, please, this is Harold. Don't let my uniform fool you."

Karl got up to follow him when the Kommissar held him back, "Oh, before I forget it Karl, I want to thank you for finding my daughter. You accomplished something I was unable to do."

It seemed to Karl that the Pompolit was uncomfortable, almost kind of guilty in expressing his appreciation. He thought at first that this was normal for a high-ranking official. They were probably not used to thanking anyone. But then he remembered that Godunov had thanked him before when he had taken care of his loot. This time it was definitely different. He silently cursed his own sensitivity. However, something in the manner of the Kommissar was not normal. He was sure about that.

Karl smiled at the Pompolit, "You are welcome, Herr Godunov. I am glad that I was able to help you." He searched the face of the Kommissar, but he could not make eye contact with Godunov.

Harold interrupted the awkward moment by announcing that he had scared Frau Becker with his Russian uniform, but that she waited for them to enter. The Kommissar surprised the Becker couple with his fluent German when he asked for Dr. Felder. Herr Becker told him that one of the other doctors from the Gertrauden Hospital was in the neighborhood and offered to go find him.

"Yes, please ask him to come right away. Tell him that Karl is here too, and that he has nothing to fear from me." Godunov was impatient to get his daughter out of the truck and into the apartment.

Frau Becker offered their bedroom to serve as an examination room, and shortly thereafter, Herr Becker showed up again with the doctor right behind him. As the Kommissar waited eagerly for the results of the checkup, Karl conferred with Harold about how and where he could possibly start to search for both of their fathers. He hoped that Godunov would finally dismiss him while Harold would stay with the Tatars or at least with his language instructor.

"Godunov had told us that my father was being detained in Spandau (A suburb of Berlin). This should serve as a beginning. Maybe Godunov is able to point you towards a starting point to search for your father," Harold speculated.

"I wish that he could. However, he told me some time ago that they don't maintain any records of the deported soldiers. So I doubt that he is able to help." Karl's hand went up to massage his neck, "I will ask him if we could search together for a day."

Godunov did not hear the boys' conversation. He was walking back and forth in the small kitchen sipping a cup of Frau Becker's tea. Harold walked out to get him some rock candies from the jeep when the door to the bedroom opened and the doctor came out.

"No reason to worry, Herr Kommissar," he announced for all to hear. "Whoever treated her first, took good care of her cuts and bruises. She suffered a nasty cut below her abdomen, but this will heal in time. Otherwise, I don't think that this young lady suffered any internal injuries. Of course, it would help if we could take some x-rays." He tried the light switches in the kitchen and shrugged his shoulders. "The power is still out and I doubt that the hospital has repaired the generators."

The Kommissar was obviously pleased by the news. He thanked the doctor for his service; and the doctor left in a hurry, happy to be released. When he went out the door, he winked at the boys.

Godunov helped his daughter back into the truck and then turned to Karl, "If you wish, you both may stay here. I will leave Alex with you." The Kommissar looked questioningly at the boys who nodded their agreement. "Good, then it's settled. I will send you the jeep tomorrow with some food supplies for the Beckers and the doctor, and also to take back to Potsdam to the people who had helped my daughter." He looked at Karl who had, like always, a question. "Yes, Karl, make good use of the day and the jeep. I expect you and Harold back tomorrow night at my quarters. That's what you wanted to know, isn't it?"

Karl shook his head, "No, not exactly, but thank you Herr Godunov for your kindness. I wanted to ask if you want my ointment for treating the wounds on your daughter. You might wish to try it on the minor cuts first. It completely healed Alex's feet." He looked in anticipation at the Kommissar.

"I will think about, Karl. I will let you know tomorrow night."

Godunov looked away as he answered and then had a few words with Alex before he took off with his convoy. Karl was certain that the Kommissar had avoided looking him in the eye. He knew that Godunov felt uncomfortable when he talked to him, but he had no inkling as to why that was. He wanted to share his feelings with Harold but on second thought, he decided against it. He knew in advance that Harold would call him a sentimental neat freak who wanted everything in a certain order. But he could not help himself. He knew instinctively that something was wrong, and he worried about it.

The Beckers wanted to know all about the Pompolit and his daughter. Harold gave most of the answers and told them about Potsdam. He also told them that he had accepted an offer from the Kommissar, which required that he had to wear the Russian uniform. He gave no further details. Herr Becker grew a little frustrated because most of his questions went unanswered.

"Really, now, Karl. What is this arrangement between Harold and the Kommissar?"

Karl was sitting half asleep on the kitchen chair. It was still early in the evening, but besides the few hours of sleep last night in the car, he had hardly had any rest, "I think that the Kommissar has arranged for Harold to learn the Russian language. Otherwise, I don't know much about it. I had my own assignment in Potsdam."

Frau Becker could see that he was tired. "Let the boys sleep it off," she told her husband and looked over to Alex, who was already sleeping on the floor next to the kitchen stove. There was not enough bedding to go around but the boys were happy to be allowed to use the small living room, where they slept on a carpet.

The next morning came fast. Karl and Harold were up early and discussed how they could make the most of the day. The Beckers were late risers, and the boys had privacy to discuss their plans.

"Where do you think we could get some information about the data of the dead soldiers," Harold asked his friend.

Karl wanted to be sure that he had heard correctly, "You want to know about the dead ones?"

"Yes, think about it," answered Harold. "The Kommissar said that there are no records of the prisoners who are being deported to Russia. So why not search the records of the dead soldiers? If our fathers are dead, we don't have to search any further. If they are not listed as dead, then they might be prisoners and we can ask Godunov if there is any way he can help us to obtain information."

Karl thought that there was some merit to this line of thinking, but then he remembered that the Allied authorities were still counting the dead.

"Maybe next year there might be some data available but today, we would get nowhere. Let us think of a more productive way to spend our day."

Harold looked kind of disappointed, "So where do we start?"

Karl did not have to think very long, "You said yesterday that the Spandau facility might be a starting point. I suggest we take off as soon as the car gets here. First to Spandau, then to the Schlesischen Bahnhof (Railroad station) and then to Potsdam."

Harold agreed that any action was better than none. "Why do you want to visit this particular railroad station?"

"We passed the railroad plaza yesterday and I think that I saw a large group of small children. It might be an assembly point for the homeless children. I want to see if they have enough to eat. If not, we might be able to appeal to Godunov for help." Karl was also hoping that some of the children might have been on a transport from Kottbus and maybe he could find out about his friend Peter, who had disappeared with a group of about 40 boys on a train from Poland to Kottbus.

There was a knock on the door. It was Poti carrying a box filled with tins of margarine, pig's lard and a small bag of flour. He exchanged a few words with Alex, who went out and returned with a small box of various bandages and some vials of pills. There was a plain piece of paper attached to the vials which read, '*Pain pills*'.

"Thank you," smiled Herr Becker, who had heard the knock on

the door and came out of the bedroom. He admired the canned goods and called his wife to brew some imitation coffee. Poti had also brought a big, almost two pound loaf of the black Russian bread.

Herr Becker opened a can of the pig's lard and Karl gorged himself by eating two slices of bread with his favorite Aufstrich (Topping).

The last time he had eaten pig's lard was several weeks ago and he could not understand why Alex preferred the dried fish he had received from Poti.

When Frau Becker heard that the boys planned a visit to the railroad station, she wrote her name and address on several pieces of paper and gave them to the boys.

"Here, hand them out to some of the homeless children. When they show up here, I will try to find a place for them."

Karl was itching to get going to Spandau, which was almost an hour away, depending on the traffic they might encounter. As the boys were going to the car, Herr Becker was again questioning Harold about his Russian uniform.

Harold, who was still unwilling to give any more details about his deal with Godunov replied, "I accepted Godunov's invitation to become his protégé, that's all, Herr Becker. I will let you know when I am told more about it." He sat in front next to Poti and Karl took his usual seat in the back of the Jeep.

A short while later they turned into the Heerstrasse, which was the major thoroughfare leading to Spandau. It was there that they saw for the first time, American trucks with black-skinned soldiers. Even Poti was surprised. More than once he stopped the Jeep for no other reason than to get a better look at the colored Americans.

It seemed to Karl that Alex could care less. He was searching behind the back seat to find another fish. When they reached the center of Spandau, Harold had an idea of where to start their quest to find the prison. He had noted that there were now British as well as French vehicles around them and they all seemed to go to or come from the Bergstrasse. He motioned Poti to follow the next American truck that stopped at a gate guarded by Russian and American soldiers. It looked to Karl as if the gate was at the entrance to a huge schoolyard of some kind.

Poti parked the jeep next to the gate. Karl got out and joined a group of elderly civilians gathered close to a four-story building. Within minutes he found out that they were in front of a military compound. Apparently, it served to house a specific group of prisoners. He heard the term 'Nazi War Criminals' mentioned and did not understand what that meant. He had heard of criminals, but never *war criminals*, Nazis, or any other kind. He speculated that this was just another label for SS prisoners, but then he heard that many civilians were also detained. He wondered if it was here that Harold's father was being held.

He had gotten back to the Jeep when Harold approached him. He had tried his school English to converse first with a British soldier, and then with an American driver.

"We can't get in here," he informed Karl. "The place is equally guarded by the four allied troops." He shrugged his shoulders and tried to get a peek beyond the gate. Besides the many allied vehicles, there was nothing special to see.

He went again to the American driver he had talked with previously. Karl saw that is was a colored soldier.

"The Americans are a lot friendlier than the British," he told Karl when he returned.

"How so?" Karl asked.

"Well, this fellow here told me that this is just a temporary facility to sort out suspected criminals from the real criminals. The real criminals will be transported to a more secure place, while they await trial. The British soldier told me nothing. He was just as stiff as a German prison guard might be."

The boys decided to ask the Kommissar about this place and went back to the Jeep. Both of the Tatars seemed to be happy to leave. Poti had tried to converse with a Russian driver, but neither one of them could understand the other one.

"Right here is where your future language skills would come in handy," remarked Karl as Harold guided them back to Berlin and to the railroad station where Karl had seen the homeless children.

They found the place without any problem; however, the station itself was gone. There was nothing but a huge mountain of ruins and rubble.

There were several crowds of children milling around. Boys as well as girls and they seemed to vary from 8 to 12 years old.

Karl wondered why they were in different groups. "Let's talk with all of them," he told Harold, and got out of the car and walked up to the nearest one.

The children told him that they were from different 'KLV Lagers' (Children Evacuation Camps) and that they were waiting for relatives to pick them up.

"How long have you been waiting," Karl asked one of the older children.

"I don't know," came the answer. "Maybe three or four days, or a week." The little boy looked like he was about 10 years old. His face looked dirty and his eyes were sad. However, as he looked at Karl, his eyes seemed to show a flicker of hope.

"Where are you spending the nights," asked Karl, "and what do you do for food?"

The boy pointed to the ruins of the station, "There is plenty of dry shelter among the ruins and the Russians come and feed us every morning and evening," he again eyed Karl expectantly.

"Who told you to stay here and wait for your families?"

"Oh, there was a pastor here when we arrived. He told us to stay in this area, but he never came back."

As Karl talked to the boy, more and more of the children gathered around to hear what the big boy who arrived in a car had to say.

Karl was glad that the situation was not worse. At least the children were not hungry. He would not have known how to get food for them. He tried to count how many there were, but gave up when he got to about 80. One thing was clear; they all needed a home, or at least some adult guidance.

Twenty-Five

Harold came across the plaza to join Karl, "This is pretty bad. Some of them have been here close to two weeks. Any idea what we can do?"

Karl did not answer right away. He was thinking of explaining the tragedy to the Kommissar and asking him for advice and help, but then dismissed the idea. Godunov had his hands full with his daughter and was scheduled to leave Berlin.

"Here is what we'll do," he told Harold, "you will take the Jeep back to Frau Becker and ask her to come right back with you. See if she can bring a friend with her. Tell her that we will pick her up and take her home when we come back from Potsdam."

"What do you expect Frau Becker to do? She cannot handle this many children either," Harold objected.

"No," Karl agreed, "but she is the only one I can think of. She had a similar situation on her hands when I came back from Poland. I agree that this many children are overwhelming, but she has experience and might know of a place, maybe a church or something, where she will be able to organize some kind of a central Auffangslager (catch all camp)."

"I don't know," said Harold scratching his head. "This is too much for any one person to handle."

Karl almost shouted at his friend, "Harold, get going! You think of reasons why this is hopeless. Let's instead think about how we can get started. These kids most certainly can't do anything by themselves. Once we get started, things will fall into place. Tonight I will ask the Kommissar to be released by him. I want to help Frau

Becker and I also want to look for other children. I don't think that this is the only place in Berlin where children have been abandoned."

Karl was adamant and shoved his friend in the direction of the car and then had a second thought, "Ex, Ex," he shouted at Alex, who understood and joined him.

"I expect you back in less than an hour!" Karl yelled after Harold as the Jeep took off. He padded Alex on the shoulder, "Stay with me my friend," fully aware that the Tatar could not understand him. Alex just grinned and motioned to Karl to continue with whatever he was doing. It was still before noon, but the sky clouded up. Karl feared that it might rain, causing the children to scatter and seek shelter.

He turned to the boy he had spoken to before, "What is your name?"

"Franz," came the answer.

"Alright Franz. My name is Karl. You are now in charge. Ask your friends to help you. I need a count of how many children are here in this area."

Karl could see that these children had spent some time in a KLV camp. Their discipline kicked in and within minutes they were lining up in a double row, as if in front of a kitchen. He counted 84 children, mostly boys, but there was a group of about 15 girls, who must have been in a girl's camp.

"Listen up," Karl shouted, and the din from the children subsided. "In a short while you will have some women here who will take your names and addresses. They will try to help you find your parents or relatives. In the meantime, I would like to know if any of you were in a camp by Kottbus." Nobody raised a hand or answered. "What about Stettin?" (City on the Baltic Sea). This time, nearly all the hands went up. "Great, now I want you to tell me the name of your school here in Berlin."

It turned out that all of the children were from the Moabit School District. Good, thought Karl, this would speed up the search for the parents. He told the children to stay close together and asked them if they still had their registration cards from the KLV camp.

Most of them were wearing them on a string around their necks and by the time the Jeep arrived, Karl had a great deal of information about the group.

Frau Becker had another woman with her and could hardly believe her eyes when she saw the many children on the square. She was thankful for the information that Karl had gathered.

"I wonder how these children got here. Berlin had been closed off from the outside for quite some time. These children must have arrived before the Russians came in."

Karl had forgotten to ask this obvious question. He turned to Franz who was still standing nearby, "Where were you before you arrived at this station?"

"We had been waiting for our parents in the Carl Bolle School," answered Franz. "Then the Russians came. I think they wanted the school for themselves. They drove us here and they had a German priest with them who told us to wait here for our parents." Ever since Karl had told him that he was in charge, Franz was eager to answer questions.

"Were the girls with you when you were in the Carl Bolle School," Frau Becker wanted to know.

"Yes, they were there before my camp bus arrived."

Karl wanted to get on his way to Potsdam, "I will pick you up and take you home on my way back," he smiled at Frau Becker. "Thank you for coming so quickly."

She returned his smile with a handshake. "We should thank you for calling us. Right now, Frau Reinert and I will gather additional data and tonight, we will visit the Evangelic church on the Hohenzollerndam. It should be large enough to serve as a central shelter."

Just as Karl started to board the Jeep, he had an idea. "Franz, come here," he called at the boy who was mingling with the other children. "You want to come with me for a ride?" He wanted to do the boy a favor and cheer him up.

"No, thank you," answered Franz, "I don't want to leave this place. My mom might be coming any minute and I don't want to miss her." His sad eyes looked longingly at the Jeep. He had never experienced a ride in a car and Karl could see that he really wanted to come along.

"Give your name to Frau Becker and she will look out for your mom. We will be back in two hours."

Franz shook his head again, "No, I would rather wait."

Karl felt sorry that he had triggered an emotional response. He could see that Franz had tears in his eyes. He reached in his pocket and handed Franz one of his last three remaining tins of chocolate. "Here, share this with your friends."

When Franz recognized the chocolate, his eyes dried up, "Thank you Karl!" He took the tin and waved to another boy as he walked away.

The road to Potsdam was clear of transports and the jeep reached the Lindenstrasse in record time. Poti recognized the street and drove right up to the house where Godunov had found his daughter. Karl reached for the blankets and bedding and Harold grabbed the carton with food tins and medical supplies.

The boys had to knock a few times until the door opened. The old man recognized Karl, but was weary of Harold's uniform. Karl explained that the food was a reward from the Kommissar. He did not want to disturb the couple any more than their visit had already. "Thanks, for what you did for Anna," he told them as he boarded the car.

He directed Poti to the address of Frau Krause, who did not open the door when she saw the Russian uniforms of Poti and Alex from her window. However, she did recognize Karl, who tapped on the glass and asked to be let in. But the door still remained shut.

"Harold, get Poti to move the car on the other side and a little ways down the street and wait for me," Karl called to his friend, and waited to resume his tapping until the Jeep had moved.

"Frau Krause, Gunther, open up please. I just need a minute of your time." He knocked on the door again. He lifted his hand to knock a final time when the door opened. Gunther stuck his head out.

"You can't come in Karl. My mother said that you lied to her when you asked about your sister." His serious face lit up when Karl handed him the last two tins of chocolate.

"Here Gunther, share this with Heinz. I just wanted to say thank you for your detective work."

"Was it really your sister?" Gunther stepped out on the street and closed the door behind him.

"No, Gunther. I am sorry that I lied to you and your mom. I have no time to explain, but it was a lady I had to find and I want to thank you.

He shook the boy's hand and turned to leave when Gunther asked him, "Have you seen any American soldiers?"

Karl stopped and faced the boy, "Yes, I have. Why do you ask?"

Gunther came closer and whispered, "Are they really black? Frau Wegberg told me that the black soldiers will eat us."

Karl took a step backward; he was shocked by Gunther's question, "What did you say? Who is Frau Wegberg?"

"Frau Wegberg is my teacher. When we still had school, she was telling us that black people are cannibals. She explained that this means they eat their enemies."

Karl was stunned and searched for an answer. "See those yellow Mongols in the car down there," he pointed to the Jeep. Gunther nodded his head. "Now these are normal people when they are sober, like you and me," Karl tried to explain. "But when they are drunk, they are bad people; really, really bad people. Now, the American people are not that way. America is a big country; much, much bigger than Germany. They have people of all kinds of colors, but they are not cannibals." He tried his best to dispel the obvious fear in Gunther's face.

"I don't know if I should trust you, Karl. You lied to me before." Gunther was still in doubt.

Karl thought of something else. "This teacher, Frau Wegberg, was she wearing a 'Party Bonbon'?" (Slang for Nazi emblem)

Gunther tried to remember. "Yes, I think she did."

"Well," said Karl, "this might explain why she told you this nonsense. A regular Prussian teacher would have explained to you the difference between a civilized country and cannibals." Karl smiled and poked Gunther in his side. "Relax, Gunther, I don't know much about the Americans, but I do not think that they eat their enemies." He wished that he had more time to talk. "Maybe we will meet again, Gunther. Please tell your mother that I am sorry that I lied to her. Auf Wiedersehen." (Good bye) He shook Gunther's hand.

"Auf Wiederschen, Karl." Gunther seemed unhappy to see that his older friend had to leave.

"You will not believe what I just heard," Karl started to tell Harold about Gunther's question.

Harold was aghast. "The few conversations I had with the colored American soldiers were a lot friendlier than what we witnessed between the Russians and the Mongols. Do you think that this teacher told the children this garbage on purpose?"

Karl shrugged his shoulders. "I don't want to speculate on what her motive was. Maybe she was stupid and did not know what she was talking about." Karl wanted to be charitable.

The trip back was again very fast. The Russians had set up their soup kitchen at the plaza, where they were feeding the children as well as many civilians. Frau Becker was already waiting and asked to be dropped off by the church on the Hohenzollerndam, which was a short walk away from her apartment. Her friend, Fau Reinert, wanted to stay with the children.

Harold looked at the sky. It had really clouded up. "This might develop into a real cloud burst any moment. Are you sure that you want to stay here?" he asked Frau Reinert.

She affirmed her decision. "The children have waited for a long time for their loved ones to come and pick them up. They are pretty much at the end of their hope. They need to know that someone cares for them. A little rain will not kill me."

Poti had also observed the sky and was busy putting up the canvas cover on the Jeep. Alex was trying to help him and Karl could see that they were getting nowhere. Instead of just draping the canvas over the top, they were removing the whole assembly.

"Numb nuts, both of you." Karl called them a variety of names, which they smilingly accepted as he helped them to close the cover.

During the drive to the Hohenzollerndam, Frau Becker told the boys that she intended to establish a search team to find the relatives of the children. "Don't worry about them anymore. As long as the Russians are feeding them, we will do everything possible to find their relatives."

"I will try to help you if the Kommissar dismisses me tomorrow," Karl told her as the Jeep pulled up at the church.

The sky had finally opened up and Frau Becker ran towards the church, which seemed to have suffered some damage.

A short time, later they were at the Pompolit's quarters and went up to the first floor to see him. Godunov was pacing the room as the boys knocked on his door. His daughter rested comfortably in his bedroom, which was located on the floor above. In the early morning hours he had been able to ascertain from her what had happened.

She had told him that she had been ordered, together with the other female doctor, to examine the political prisoners who had been detained by the SS. The Russians wanted to be sure that the female detainees were healthy enough to be released. Her military unit had left the two doctors behind when it advanced into Berlin.

While the doctors were still examining the last prisoners, the original Russian combat troops were replaced with a new unit, which was to guard the incoming German prisoners. There was some confusion as to who was in charge of this transfer until a high ranking Ukrainian Zampolit (Political Deputy Commander) took over to assure an orderly transfer. Nothing was even close to an orderly transfer. The Zampolit was totally drunk and so were the troops with him. While they were storming through the cell blocks of the prison, they stripped Anna and the other female doctor of their uniforms and locked them up together with some of the other remaining prisoners.

The Zampolit had promised a few of his political friends a victory celebration and his soldiers were combing the neighborhood to search for females. The women were then forced to drink vodka until they danced and cheered. Afterwards, they were raped by the soldiers.

Because of their protests in fluent Russian, Anna and the other female doctor had been dragged in front of the Zampolit and his political friends. There was no hearing, or anything near it. The Zampolit enjoyed himself by having Anna for himself, by torturing and raping her before he collapsed in his stupor. She passed out when another officer cut her with a knife. When she regained conciseness, she saw that the other doctor had been shot. The party was over and the Zampolit and his friends, as well as the Russian soldiers, were gone. The prison was empty. She remembered that some of the German girls helped her out of the building and took her to a German family. She had no memory or idea as to the name of the Zampolit or of his unit.

When Godunov had heard what had happened, he had sprung into action. His agents and his informers had been coming and going all day long and by the late afternoon, he knew who the culprit was. It was a Ukrainian political officer named Sodbileg Kozlov. He had the equivalent military rank of a Lieutenant General.

He was known as a drunk and a constantly sloshed incompetent individual. The only reason that he was in a high-ranking political position was the fact that he had extremely powerful friends in Moscow. They were powerful enough that just the idea of revenge was unthinkable. Even more distressing was the known fact in the Russian political hierarchy that Godunov was a rival of Kozlov.

Godunov had no fear of Sodbileg himself and due to his imminent retirement, he did not worry about him. But he dreaded the investigations and repercussions that would follow if something would happen to the Zampolit.

Godunov had wrestled with different scenarios, but all of them could connect him in one way or another. He could not shoot Kozlov, ambush him or poison him. His personal servants and bodyguards could handle Sodbileg and his squad. But they were known as his private detail and would invariably implicate him as the possible perpetrator.

Godunov had always been exceptionally careful and therefore, had a spotless and unblemished record. He could eliminate nearly anyone, but Kozlov was not one of them. His thoughts were interrupted when he heard the knock on his door.

As the boys entered he had a sudden idea, "Sit down, and tell me what you did today." He hardly paid any attention to the report of the boys. Instead, he used Kete to communicate some orders.

"Alright, I am glad to hear that you used the day constructively. Now Harold, I want you to wait outside the door with Kete. I want to have some words with Karl."

He went to the rain-streaked window and looked out before he turned to face Karl. Within a few minutes, he told Karl about Anna's ordeal and his decision to eliminate Kozlov. He also told him that his hands were tied and he could not do it himself.

"Karl, I trust you. You are a trained sniper. I want you to kill Kozlov. I will send Alex, Kete and Poti along for your protection." For the first time since yesterday, he locked eyes with Karl. The eyes of Godunov were hard as steel as he continued, "I will even reward you beyond your expectations."

Karl's eyes had not blinked. They were as straight as an arrow as he replied, "You have the wrong man, Herr Godunov. I don't kill."

"Well now, Karl, you were a sniper. You mean to tell me that you never killed anyone?"

"Yes, Herr Godunov. I was trained as a sniper. But no, I survived the war without killing anyone; and I am not about to do it now." Karl's voice was hard as he continued, "Matter of fact, even if I would agree to shoot Kozlov, I am as good as dead. The

209

three bodyguards you send along would be material witnesses against me. I would not survive." He locked eyes with the Kommissar, who started again.

"What is it with you Karl, don't you trust me?"

Karl was not intimidated, "I trusted Hitler, the SS and our teachers. I trust everyone, including Harold and you ... to a certain degree.

It looked for a moment as if Godunov lost his self-control. He felt like slapping the boy around, but knew it would not serve his purpose and Karl knew it. He was as steady as a rock. Godunov was quiet for a moment, which seemed like an eternity. The Kommissar decided on a different approach.

"Don't you see what this bastard did to me and my daughter? What would it take to change your mind?"

"There is simply nothing that would change my mind, Herr Godunov. A wise man told me once that when the chips are down, your decision depends upon how much you value your values. I don't intend to change my values, Herr Godunov."

"Right," said the Kommissar, weighing his options of how to play his final card. He went back to the window and stared out into the streaming rain.

Karl got up and turned to leave, "Auf Wiedersehen, Herr Godunov." He was certain that the Kommissar had no further use for him.

"Auf Wiedersehen," replied Godunov. "Good luck with your values."

Now, that was a cheap shot, thought Karl, and opened the door.

He was almost outside when he heard the Kommissar, "Karl,"

He turned around and saw the Kommissar still staring out of the window, "Yes, Herr Godunov?"

The Kommissar did not turn to face him, "I know where your father is."

Karl felt as if the walls were closing in on him. He raced to the window and looked out.

Down in the courtyard stood his father in an old German army coat, wet and drenched from the rain. He wore glasses and was small; only five foot, four inches tall. Next to him stood Kete. He lifted his father's head to look up to him.

"You win!" Karl shouted at the Kommissar, as he stormed out of the door.

TRUST TO A DEGREE

AUTHOR'S NOTE

Thank you for reading **Trust To A Degree**. I hope you enjoyed it as much as the first book in the series, **Loyal To A Degree**. I have had one or two people ask me if the books are really based on a true story and I assure you they are. I realize for some, it may be difficult to imagine that the stories are about a 14 year old boy rather than a grown man, but times were different then. Very different than they are today.

When I published Loyal To A Degree, I had not anticipated the response I would receive from readers. Many wanted to know more about Karl and his life in the years before the story took place. The questions they asked sparked an idea for another book so as I work on the next installment in the series, **Partners To A Degree**, I am also working on a prequel that will give readers the opportunity to get to know more about Karl, and his friend, Harold. To those readers who had questions and wanted to know more, Thank You!

I enjoy keeping in touch and interacting with my readers, so I post as often as I can on my blog at **www.horstchristian.com**. If you have questions or just want to leave a comment about my books, please feel free to stop by at any time. You are always welcome!

Best regards,

Horst Christian